CHASING SHADOWS

A DCI REECE THRILLER

LIAM HANSON

CRIME PRINTS

Copyright © 2022 by Liam Hanson

All rights reserved.

No part of this publication may be reproduced, distributed, or transmitted in any form or by any means, including photocopying, recording, or other electronic or mechanical methods, without the prior written permission of the publisher, except as permitted by U.K. copyright law. For permission requests, contact author.

The story, all names, characters, and incidents portrayed in this production are fictitious. No identification with actual persons, living or deceased, is intended or should be inferred.

Published by CRIME PRINTS

An Imprint of Liam Hanson Media

ISBN-13 : 979-8841466024

For my wife and children

Current books in the series:

───────────────────────

DEADLY MOTIVE
COLD GROUND
KILLING TIME
CHASING SHADOWS
DEVIL'S BREAD

CHASING SHADOWS

Chapter 1

PRESENT DAY: CITY ROAD, CARDIFF.

On any other Monday morning, Archie Ives would have had a little over three minutes to live. One hundred and eighty-nine seconds, give or take. Not that he had any inkling of the impending threat arriving on the road outside; busy as he was, arguing the toss with the arsehole sat in what had always been *Archie's* seat.

There was nothing special about the one in question. No extraordinary functions making it particularly sought after. It looked like all the other seats on the bus. Its fabric was worn thin in places. Stained with God only knew what. The floor and seat undersides played host to a buffet of used chewing gum, soft sweets, and smokers' phlegm.

But it was still Archie's seat. The inner one of two positioned in the first row on the right after climbing the step painted with a single yellow safety line. And Archie wanted it back. Like a petulant child entering the school playroom only a few minutes too late; his favourite toy found in the possession of another.

'I sit there,' he said, fighting to keep his voice on an even keel. 'I always sit there.' He took a sideways step, making ample room for Arsehole to get up and move somewhere else. The stranger didn't budge and continued to stare out of the window, his attention held by something of a greater interest. Maybe he hadn't heard Archie's whining request. Perhaps the man was deaf. Stupid. Or pure, bloody-minded, even. It really was impossible to tell when he refused to give anything away. Archie tried again, and this time, put a finger to his chest to emphasise his point. '*Mine.* Do you hear me?' Even that got him nowhere.

Archie wasn't a violent person and had never been much of a fighter. Even as a boy at school, he'd left that sort of thing to others. He was, nevertheless, getting very close to saying or doing something he knew he might later regret. Calming himself, he huffed loudly.

Arsehole and Archie were of a similar age and build. Both wore fitted white shirts with grey trousers that finished short of their ankles. Archie's navy blue baseball cap was the better quality of the two. A memento of the 2017 British Grand Prix that he and his friend Coombsie had gone to watch after winning a competition at work.

Arsehole's cap—in Archie's opinion—looked to be the cheap rubbish bought from an online auction site. Regardless, the similarities in the young men's physical build and facial appearance were there to be seen by anyone who cared to look.

'Are you going to move or not?' Archie asked through gritted teeth. 'Well. Are you?'

Arsehole's head didn't turn away from whatever was on the other side of the window. He spoke, but was only just audible above the background noise. 'I don't think I am.'

He wasn't deaf, then. Thick as pig shit, as first thought. Archie rose on tip-toes but couldn't get sight of whatever was out there. He heard the dying revs of a powerful motorcycle. Then little more than the normal hustle and bustle of any busy cosmopolitan street. 'Look mate, I've been taking this bus for . . .' He counted, but the altercation was making it difficult for him to concentrate. 'For ages,' was the best he could manage.

Arsehole's gaze broke away from the street and fixed on Archie. His eyes were red, giving him the appearance of someone who was sleep deprived. Or on drugs. 'A change of scenery might do you good. Make you less needy.'

A challenge.

Archie gripped the floor-to-ceiling handrail so tightly the skin over his knuckles blanched of all colour. He squinted along the narrow aisle of the bus and considered his next move. Being polite hadn't worked. Huffing, neither. What if he swung a punch at the smug git's gob and got it over with?

What then?

People were already staring. Each of them a potential witness to what would undoubtedly be interpreted as an act of physical assault on his part. A few shook their heads in disbelief that someone could make so much fuss over a bus seat.

A rosy-cheeked woman pointed, staccato fashion, at a choice of empties. There were several untaken seats available.

That didn't matter one bit to Archie Ives. *His* seat was the one by the window. Next to the step with the yellow stripe.

There were raised voices coming from the front of the bus. Doug, the driver, was in an argument of his own. It was going to be one of those deeply annoying days of late summer madness. Extreme heat and humidity could provoke such a thing in susceptible people, just as a full moon often challenged the sanity of others.

A biker wearing a visored helmet and black leathers was marching up the aisle; Doug shouting at him to come back and pay his fare. The biker ignored the instruction and continued on his way.

No one was listening to what they were told.

Realising he was on a hiding to nothing, Archie cut his losses and trudged to the back of the bus in a monumental sulk. By the time he got there, the biker was only a few paces short of the yellow-edged step. He looked like a Star Wars villain, minus the light-sabre and flowing cape.

Doug was out of his cabin, shouting louder, and following up the aisle. Albeit, at a slowing pace. The biker came to a halt on the step, lowered the zipper of his leathers, and reached deep inside.

Archie craned his neck to get a better look. He felt a pull in the pit of his stomach that couldn't be blamed entirely on the previous night's pizza.

Arsehole shifted position. Turned to face the biker. His earlier show of devilment deserting him when a pistol was levelled at his head. His right hand came up in a defensive reflex; flesh and bone useless against a bullet that tore a route through to the centre of his head. When it punched a neat hole in the bone between his eyes, he recoiled against the window, blood, brain, and all manner of yucky stuff showering the glass only milliseconds before it shattered and rained down on top of him.

That was when the screaming started. High-pitched and deeply annoying. Doug did an impressively swift about-turn for a man of his portly stature and hurried away with several passengers following close behind.

There were two more shots fired in quick succession. Both muffled like the first. Each hitting the dead man in the centre of his chest. The biker put the gun away and raised the zipper of his leathers tight to his neck. He patted Arsehole's clothing—it seemed wrong to refer to the deceased in such a derogatory way—and took his shoulder bag before leaving.

Archie's heart thumped an erratic beat in his chest. He couldn't swallow and struggled to bring his rate of breathing under control. Was this what it was like to have a heart attack? He hoped not.

LIAM HANSON

The motorcycle started up with a heavy revving heard through the open door at the front of the bus. It sped away into the morning traffic, screaming louder than any of the passengers it left behind.

Archie pressed his face against the window, but got little more than a glimpse of the rider as he pulled away from the kerb. The bike might have been lime green. He was looking into a rising sun that made him squint, and couldn't be sure. He put his head in his hands and retched while the dead man leaked body fluids only a few rows away.

That was his seat.

It was always his seat.

The one by the window. Next to the step with the yellow stripe.

Chapter 2

Detective Chief Inspector Brân Reece was drinking sweet coffee and reading the sports pages of the newspaper, when DS Elan Jenkins knocked on the wood surround of the office door. 'It's open,' Reece said, stating the obvious.

Jenkins stayed where she was. 'There's been a mu-*rrr*-der.' She rolled the 'r' and very much exaggerated it. If she'd expected Reece to pass comment on the fake Scottish accent, he didn't. Instead, he folded the newspaper and gave her his full attention.

'Where?'

Blushing, Jenkins said, 'Top end of City Road. This side of Mackintosh Place. A shooting on one of the Cardiff-bound Edwins buses.'

That got Reece's attention quicker than most things. He tossed the newspaper into a bin next to a filing cabinet. It hit its intended target, but the bin wobbled and toppled over, depositing an empty coffee cup and a crisp packet on the carpet. 'Tell me it wasn't a school bus?' he said, launching himself onto his feet and forcing an arm through the sleeve of his suit jacket as he rounded his desk. 'Is the gunman in custody?'

'No kids involved.' Jenkins moved away from the door and followed once Reece had crossed in front of her. 'It's just the one victim, as far as we know. A Peter Larson, according to his bus pass.' She extended the length of her stride, already struggling to keep up. 'Gunman's still at large and made off on a motorcycle.'

When Reece slowed, the two of them almost collided. He twisted to look over his shoulder and fiddled with a crease in his shirt collar. 'Make sure we get all available CCTV for that area.'

Jenkins nodded. 'Ginge is already on it.' They were on the move again. Marching along the landing outside the incident room. 'Uniform are taking names and contact details of everyone present. Statements too.'

Reece hopped over the wayward hose of a vacuum cleaner and thanked a woman who was holding the door open for them. 'No one leaves until we're on scene,' he told Jenkins.

The rusting Peugeot 205 refused to start on the first attempt. Came nowhere close to starting on the second, third, or fourth. Reece got out and loomed over the ageing engine bay, pulling randomly at leads and any number of electrical connections. 'Pass me that aerosol can from the glovebox,' he shouted through the grubby windscreen.

'This one?' Jenkins held it through the open side window. 'It says *damp start* on the can. I don't think that's your problem. Not in this heat.'

'When did *you* become an auto-mechanic?'

Jenkins folded her arms and went into full pout mode. 'I'm just saying it's too hot for damp to be the issue.'

Reece gave everything in the engine bay a good spray down. 'Turn it over. Quick. Before it evaporates.'

'Now you want my help?'

'Just bloody do it!'

'I am. I am,' Jenkins said, sliding across the seats. She turned the key and pumped the pedal. The car coughed and promptly died.

Reece appeared from behind the raised bonnet with the spray can in hand. 'Not like that. You're flooding the engine.' He rested the can on the wing of the car and motioned for her to get out.

'It's had it.' Jenkins took the keys from the ignition. 'Just scrap the thing and be done with it.'

'Give,' Reece said, holding out his hand. 'Keys.'

Jenkins stepped onto the concrete pad and handed them to him. 'What a waste of time this is. We could have been halfway there by now.'

Reluctantly surrendering to the fact his junior might well be right, Reece called his mate Yanto in Brecon and spoke into the handset with a fair amount of aggressive hand gesturing.

'Sell it for scrap,' said Yanto. 'That's the best advice I can give you.'

'Not you as well.' Reece spun away from the vehicle, his suit jacket flapping like a matador's cape. 'Just tell me how to get the sodding thing going.' He paced along the empty parking bay next to his, listening to all the reasons why trying to start the Peugeot was a lost cause. 'A big help you've been,' he said, hanging up without warning. He raised his head to a clear sky and screwed his eyes shut. He opened them slowly. 'I hate Mondays.'

'I can book us out a pool car.' Jenkins nodded at a row of parked vehicles opposite and added: 'Any of those take your fancy?'

'You make it sound like I'm ordering from a dessert trolley.' Reece removed his suit jacket and tossed it onto the front passenger seat before getting in on the driver's side. The forecasters had been right. It was going to be another scorcher and there was no end to it in sight. He turned the key and pumped his right foot against the accelerator pedal, swearing for all he was worth.

There was a scraping noise from somewhere deep beyond the dashboard. Then a pathetic cough from the engine bay itself. More scraping. More coughing. The Peugeot came alive, belching thick clouds of noxious blue smoke from its rattling rear end. 'Who's the Daddy?' Reece shouted over the din. He stuck his head out of the window and called to Jenkins. 'What are you doing out there? Are you coming, or not?'

Chapter 3

THEY WENT ALONG LLOYD George Avenue and Hemingway Road. On the approach to the first roundabout, the Peugeot started coughing the same blue smoke it had back at the car park. Jenkins turned to look when the motorist behind them sounded their horn. 'Here we go again. Same old.'

Reece lowered the clutch and gave the engine what for. They got across the roundabout, though pretty, it wasn't. From there, they travelled north towards the city centre, skirting it, before turning left up City Road. 'Do you know what they used to call this place?' Reece wagged a finger at both pavements. 'The area just here.'

Jenkins pushed back in her seat, its ageing springs making a twanging sound every time she moved. She couldn't get comfortable and resorted to resting her full weight on a single buttock. 'Nope, but I've a nagging suspicion I'm about to find out.'

Reece tapped the steering wheel. 'Death Junction.'

There was no denying how busy it was out there. Numerous white delivery vans waited in front of an eclectic mix of both traditional and foreign food shops. There were people loading and unloading. Some carrying boxes. Others laden with garments weighing heavily on an extended arm. Shoppers sampled perishable goods displayed outside some of the shop fronts. There was music and chatter. The air infused with the smells of freshly ground coffee and Eastern spices.

Jenkins had witnessed it many times previously, but couldn't help being totally engrossed. 'Really?' She sounded surprised. 'The traffic isn't that bad.'

'The name Death Junction has nothing to do with the traffic flow.' Reece pulled to a stop at a crossing, his right foot giving the accelerator pedal little peace. 'They used to call it Heol-y-Plwcca.' He nodded deeply as he spoke. 'That's Welsh for *road to the pleck*. Pleck,' he repeated, as though Jenkins should have known what it meant. He rolled his eyes when he realised she didn't. 'A pleck is a plot of land.' He pointed at the road outside, not loosening his grip on the worn and cracked steering wheel. 'And on this particular stretch of land, they carried out all the public hangings. The condemned man, woman, or child, in some cases, was made to walk all the way from the jail to the gallows in one final humiliation before having their necks snapped in front of a baying crowd.'

Jenkins stared at him with her jaw partly lowered. 'Why would you tell me something like that?' She put a hand to her face and hid behind it. 'Why?'

Reece did a double take. 'What have I done now?'

Jenkins lowered her hand and raised her voice. 'You don't know?'

'I'm telling you how it was back then.' Reece looked away. 'I won't bloody bother next time.'

'You do that.'

He pulled the car to a stop behind the crime scene bus and applied the handbrake without pressing its button. 'This poor sod's been shot through the head. You want me to ask the pathologist to paint a happy smile on his face before you go in and take a peek?'

Jenkins stretched and thumped his arm before he was out of range. 'I hate you.'

Chapter 4

THERE WAS A POLICE helicopter hovering overhead. Yellow and black. Hanging there as though suspended at the end of an invisible line. The slap-slap of its rotor blades echoed off the shop walls and hot tarmac, driving away the resident crows and gulls.

Bystanders gawped at it. Pointing. Offering opinions. Alternating their attention between the sky and the happenings in and around the stationary bus.

Uniformed officers were busy erecting screens next to the vehicle. None of them tall enough to fully obstruct the macabre show from view.

One such uniform approached the Peugeot, making wide circles with a finger extended from a limp wrist. He looked like he was instructing them to turn round and leave the area.

Reece got out and produced his ID. 'Who's in charge?' he asked, fully taking in the scene before slamming the car door. It took him three attempts before the catch engaged in the closed position.

The officer quit gesturing and looked nervous in the DCI's company. 'That'll be him over there, sir.'

There were two Authorised Firearms Officers—AFOs—deep in conversation next to the front wheel of the bus. Both wore helmets with chin-straps and black tactical gear. They had Heckler and Koch MP5 carbines slung across their chests.

Reece ducked beneath a sagging length of blue and white police tape and held it up for Jenkins to follow.

The pavement had been cleared of shoppers for twenty metres or more in either direction. The same was true for the area across the road.

The passengers had been rounded up and corralled into a nearby café emptied of its existing customers. A moustachioed man of Italian descent was pestering anyone wearing a uniform, insisting on knowing who was paying for the coffee and pastries he'd been made to supply.

One of three ambulances in attendance pulled away from the kerb with a loud whoop-whoop of its siren. Its occupant was an elderly gentleman with worsening chest pain. The crowd reluctantly moved to let it pass, some of them rising on their toes, hoping to get a glimpse of what was going on inside. Then it was off, speeding into the distance, singing a much louder and more insistent song.

'Morning, Detective Chief Inspector.' A gritty-sounding voice delivered the greeting. Maggie Kavanagh, senior crime reporter with the South Wales Herald, called to Reece from the other side of the road. She waved an arm overhead in an attempt to catch his full attention. Flakes of silvered ash from a half-smoked cigarette snowed onto her beehive hairdo. Kavanagh wore a Columbo-style coat during the cooler seasons of the year. On this occasion, she'd chosen a summer dress with a fair amount of makeup. 'Any truth in the rumour this might be terrorist related?'

Reece cast an eye over his multicultural audience. 'I'm ruling nothing out at this point, Maggie. Nothing at all.'

The reporter inhaled on the cigarette until she turned a shade nearer blue. Squinting through copious amounts of smoke, she used both hands to switch off her voice recorder. 'I get first dibs on whatever you know on the way out.'

Reece made no promises. As yet, there was no story to tell. He approached the senior firearms officer and waited for the man to finish what he was saying. Producing his ID again, he said, 'Morning. I'm Reece. SIO for this case. What can you tell me?'

'The victim is a white male in his mid-twenties,' the AFO said, coming away. 'One head shot. Two rounds closely grouped to the centre of the chest.'

'A professional hit?' Reece hadn't known what to expect on the way over. Shootings in the city were thankfully rare and mostly drug-related whenever they happened. Weapons drawn in the heat of the moment. Discharged in anger, or in fear of attack. This sounded different. There was more than a suspicion of it being a cold and calculated murder of some unsuspecting individual. That didn't necessarily make it any less difficult to solve.

The AFO lifted his goggles and rubbed the corner of his eye. 'I'd say the killer knew what they were doing?'

'Ex-military?' Reece asked.

'Comfortable with a weapon, certainly. And very calm and clinical if what the passengers are saying is anything to go by.'

'Are we good to get on?' Reece asked, catching hold of the bus's handrail.

'The scene has been cleared,' the AFO told him. 'Doctor Death's already aboard, waiting for you.'

'Who?' Jenkins asked with a deep frown.

'Frost, I think she said her name was. Not much of a talker, that one.'

Jenkins folded her arms. 'Well, if you took the time to—'

Reece gave her a gentle shove towards the pavement before she could say something she shouldn't. 'Go fetch us some coveralls.'

She leaned into him and whispered: 'He's got a big gob, that one.'

Chapter 5

Once appropriately dressed, they logged their names and ranks with the scene guard and got on the bus.

The main doors being open did little to lower the stifling temperature inside. It was unpleasantly humid. The engine was shut down and the air conditioning system with it. The sweet smell of spilled blood was obvious to anyone with a trained nose. Vomit baking on the back seat only added to the heady mix.

There was a huddle of people dressed in matching coveralls towards the rear of the bus. One of them was taking photographs – a rapid-fire *click-click* following wherever the man went. Someone else was busy with blood splatter analysis. Another CSI used a small brush, black powder, and clear tape to lift prints off the hard surfaces. There was no sign of Sioned Williams, Crime Scene Manager. She'd be waiting back at base, making herself available for members of her team to seek her experienced input whenever they required it.

Dr Cara Frost—Home Office Forensic Pathologist—turned to face the new arrivals. 'I hope you two skipped breakfast.'

Reece thought it odd that she wouldn't have known Jenkins's routine that morning. It was of no real concern to him and he let it be, refocusing his attention on the gruesome scene. 'Tell us what you know so far,' he said, trying not to inhale the stench.

Peter Larson was slumped against what would earlier have been an intact window. His head and upper torso hovered precariously above the road. His bottom half was pressed against the metal side of the bus, preventing him from fully tumbling out. His mouth was wide open. Chest and groin soaked with bright red blood.

On the window of the row behind was what Reece could only assume to be bits of brain tissue cooking in the hot sun. The whitish-grey flecks reminded him of scrambled eggs done without their yolks. Not a pleasant thought. He studied the holes in the front of Larson's previously white shirt. 'Someone wanted this man dead.' Reece sidestepped, giving Frost enough room to drag her examination case off the adjacent seat. 'Anything for ballistics to be getting on with?'

'A couple of casings from the floor.' Frost stood side-on to the detectives and pointed along the street outside. 'The bullet from the headshot is somewhere out there. The two from the chest will be all yours as soon as I get him opened up.'

Reece bent at the knee and traced the likely trajectory of the missing bullet, concluding it might well be lost forever. He knew such finds were often claimed as macabre souvenirs by warped members of the public. It not hitting a child or other undeserving person was a small mercy he was willing to take. He followed Cara Frost down the aisle of the bus to the front exit.

Jenkins went with them. 'Shall we go and hear what the passengers have to say?'

Reece spoke over his shoulder: 'Have Ginge find everything he can on our victim. I want to know who this Larson fella is, and who he's pissed off recently.'

'I'm already onto it,' Jenkins told him.

'And don't forget the CCTV footage,' Reece continued. 'The stuff from the bus, as well as from the street outside.'

'I know. I know.'

The sun's glare caught Reece square in the eyes as he stepped off the bus. He raised a hand to shield them, grateful for the short-sleeved shirt and lack of tie worn beneath the claustrophobic coveralls. Jenkins had earlier commented on his choice of smart navy suit and light blue shirt, saying she couldn't remember the last time she'd seen him wear anything but black at work. His answer had surprised him as much as it had her. He was making the first tentative steps of moving his life on. That didn't mean forgetting about Anwen. Far from it. He pressed a hand to the café door and read the green lettering on the glass. *Giovanni's*. 'Brace yourself,' he said, preparing to enter.

Chapter 6

ARCHIE IVES HADN'T WAITED on the pavement with the rest of the passengers. There was no sit-down coffee and pastries at Giovanni's for him. No standing in a dwindling queue while the next available plod scratched their arse before calling him forward to give a statement. Instead, Archie skirted past the screaming throng and legged it up the nearest side street before anyone in uniform clapped eyes on him.

Collapsing in the temporary shade of a shop doorway, he bent at the waist, gasping for breath, his thighs aching from the build-up of lactic acid. His mouth was so dry his tongue stuck to the roof of it. His lips were split and bleeding onto his teeth. What little spit he possessed stank of vomit.

A concerned passer-by slowed to ask if he was okay and refused to let him be when he asked her to. The woman caught hold of his arm and attempted to usher him inside a busy charity shop against his will. He freed himself from her unwelcome grip and got going again.

His heart was galloping in his heaving chest and had there been anything left in his stomach, he'd have emptied it onto the hot flagstone pavement. As it was, the pizza crusts were drying nicely on the back seat of the bus. He swallowed a mouthful of bile that burned his throat like the cheapest of supermarket spirits. When he left the area, he did so listening for the return of a speeding motorcycle.

Their journey back to the Cardiff Bay police station was no less eventful.

No one had dared go anywhere near the smoking Peugeot while Reece attempted to start it. It took him almost ten minutes of struggling before the vehicle coughed itself to life; Jenkins giving him no peace the whole time. They pulled away from the kerbside in a wide U-turn that had uniformed officers frantically shooing everyone out of the way. Reece honked his horn to speed them along.

They didn't get far before the Peugeot encountered another serious mechanical issue. Reece jumped out and threatened to abandon 'the bastard' on the side of the road and walk the rest of the journey to the bay.

Jenkins somehow started it. Revving until the vehicle almost shook itself apart. Reece refused to swap places with her after that;

unwilling to risk having the car enter what might well amount to a terminal stall.

Only fifteen minutes after their arrival at the police station, Reece was to be found sitting at the head-end of the long briefing table, eager to get things going. He'd already given his usual 'phones off' instruction.

Chief Superintendent Cable was in attendance and waiting patiently. A shooting on a Cardiff bus would result in a heap of scrutiny from top brass and the politicians who twanged their strings. Cable would be expected to make an announcement anytime soon.

'Okay,' Reece said, clapping the air above his head. 'Let's get started.' The room went quiet without having to be asked a second time. He took a couple of minutes to outline what he and Jenkins knew so far.

The witness statements corroborated one another. Mostly. An old gent had claimed to have seen the devil himself walk up the aisle of the bus. Horns, fire, and all. That got a chuckle from most in the briefing room. No one was surprised. There were always reports of aliens, Elvis, or the mother-in-law, at any crime scene.

The use of a noise suppressor attached to the barrel of the handgun, together with the head and chest shots, pointed towards a seasoned professional and not some disgruntled wannabe settling a long-term score.

Reece leaned forward in his seat, seeking out Ginge, one of his newer detective constables. 'What can you tell us about our victim?'

The lanky DC opened his pocketbook and read without looking up. 'Peter Michael Larson. Born fifth of June, nineteen ninety-five. Recently released from HMP Whatton in Nottinghamshire – that's the biggest male sex-offender prison in Europe.'

Reece knew the type of perverted criminal that particular prison specialised in, but wanted more specifics on what Larson had been sent down for.

Ginge closed his pocketbook with a slap. 'He did just short of four years for sexual assault on a nine-year-old boy. Larson was a coach at the kid's football club.'

Detective Constable Ffion Morgan tapped the table with the pad of her index finger. 'That's your motive right there. The vic's a paedo. Is the child's father known to us?'

Ginge shook his head. 'There's nothing on record.'

Morgan checked with Reece. 'We still speak to him, right? If only to rule him out.'

'You bet we do. Does Larson have any known associates or haunts he likes to frequent?' Reece asked. Ginge said he hadn't come across any as yet. 'What about an address for the boy's parents?' Ginge read it out, again referring to his pocketbook. Reece told Jenkins and Morgan that he wanted them to pay the family a visit just as soon as the briefing was over.

Jenkins confirmed the address with Ginge. 'Are we to bring the father in for questioning?'

'Speak to him at home first,' Reece said. 'See what your gut feeling is. We need to rule him in or out – and sharpish. Does Larson have any surviving family?'

This time Ginge spoke without the help of his notes. 'A mother living in upper Llanrumney. Father unknown.'

'We'll need to inform her,' Reece said. 'Before she finds out from the press or anyone else wanting to turn the screw for a story.'

'Ffion and I can do that as well,' Jenkins offered. 'It'll save someone else a trip out there.'

Reece checked his watch. It was after midday already, but well before dark. 'You don't need me telling you to be careful over there.'

'We're big girls now,' Jenkins joked. She stretched on tip-toes, but couldn't match Morgan for height.

Reece wagged a finger in warning. 'Tell me you're listening.'

Jenkins settled on her heels. 'Loud and clear, boss.'

'What's the latest on the CCTV from the bus and nearby streets?'

'Still waiting for most of it to come in,' Ginge said. 'I have asked.'

'Chase them. We don't know Larson's the only intended target. And I want as much info as you can give me on that bike. It's bright green, so it shouldn't be too difficult to spot in a crowd.' Reece leaned to his left to get a better view of Sioned Williams. 'Anything on that stray bullet?' He knew he was being hopeful.

'Uniform are searching.' She shrugged. 'You know what it's like with these things.'

Reece did. It wouldn't have surprised him if the bullet was already hanging from a cheap chain around some numpty's neck. 'Questions, anyone? Okay, let's get back to work.'

Chief Superintendent Cable rose from the seat next to Reece's. 'I'll brief ACC Harris. He'll be keen for us to release a press statement as soon as. We can't have the public worrying that this has anything to do with a local terrorist cell.'

Reece followed her as far as the door with a look of deep concern on his face. 'How do you know it doesn't?'

Chapter 7

JENKINS BOOKED OUT A pool car for their trip to Llanrumney. A Ford Focus with the usual battle scars. The bodywork was scuffed in places and the wheels were badly kerbed. But it was still a damn sight better than Reece's Peugeot on any day of the week.

There was nothing to be gained by getting her Fiat 500 trashed once the locals found out who it belonged to. And find out they would. She'd made that rookie mistake only once in the past; returning to the vehicle not ten minutes later to find a crude drawing of a pig's face and *oink, oink*, scratched into the bonnet's paintwork. To make matters worse, her claim for the repair was turned down on the basis that she should have used a Force car for undertaking official business.

Never again had she been so naïve.

The Focus started on the first attempt and pulled away from the Cardiff Bay station without drawing unwanted attention to itself.

The Larson residence was easy enough to find. A front door daubed with **Peedo Barstud** misspelled in bright red paint made it stand out in a street of what some might charitably describe as *tired-looking* properties.

Most of the houses had at least one window broken or boarded over. All came complete with cracked external render and any number of wonky or missing roof tiles. There were car wheels and stained sofas stored in the front gardens, where a few of the locals were making themselves comfortable in the hot summer sunshine.

Jenkins picked her way between topless teenagers riding bicycles in the middle of the road. 'It's like a scene from *Zombie Apocalypse*.'

Morgan wound her window fully closed and clicked the door locks. 'I don't think any self-respecting zombie would dare show their face around here. There's not a normal-looking person among them.'

Jenkins pulled to a full stop, clipping the kerb with her front wheel, adding another injury to the soft aluminium. 'Don't leave anything of value in the car.'

A tall, skinny man crawled off a sofa in the nearest garden and swayed his way down the weed-strewn path towards them. He held a crushed cider can in his hand and wore a dirty pair of grey marl joggers with a white vest-top and thick neck-chain. He was heavily bruised, with evidence of past self-harming to his forearms and wrists. 'What the fuck we got here, then?' he asked once he'd made it as far as the crumbling pavement. He had an unhealthy interest in Ffion Morgan and was already getting way too close. 'Hey, Sweetie.' He pronounced it 'shweetie.' Possession of only three or four teeth having a lot to do with it. 'How'sh about you and me go for a little lie down?'

'How'sh about you piss off before I zap you with my Taser?' Jenkins tapped her right hip and gave the man the briefest of smiles. 'It'll play hell with your fillings,' she said, studying his dental work from a safe distance.

The man stared, but didn't speak. Swaying like a tree in the breeze, he took an unsteady step and just about managed to remain on his feet. Accompanied by the loud cheering of onlookers, he returned to his sofa with the seat of his joggers sagging like a wet nappy.

'You spoilsport,' Morgan said, feigning disappointment. 'I was *in*, then.'

Jenkins put a hand on the small of her colleague's back and directed her along the pavement. 'He wasn't your type. Not nearly enough bling.'

Mrs Larson opened the front door wearing a drab dressing gown and nightie. Her eyes were bloodshot. Her face as wrinkled as a mongrel's scrotum. In her right hand were the smouldering remains of a filtered cigarette. In her left was the battered packet and lighter.

Jenkins found it impossible to tell if the woman had only just got up from bed, or was on the verge of going back. She introduced them both and showed her ID.

What little they saw of the house was clean and tidy, but stank of smoke and the lack of a good and sustained airing. There were faded photographs on the wall, mantelpiece, and coffee table. One was of a young boy building sandcastles on the beach. Jenkins recognised the area as Three Cliffs Bay in the Gower Peninsula in Swansea and came over with a sudden pang of childhood nostalgia. The boy looked innocent and happy. She understood why, having spent many a childhood summer at the campsite there. The memory reminded her to ring her mother that evening.

Another photograph showed the boy—now a few years older—skateboarding in a park. There was a garden scene in a third photo, where the same child was having fun with a hosepipe and water. There were none to be seen of Peter Larson as an adult.

It was never easy informing a parent of the death of their child. Not even when the deceased was a warped sexual predator.

Jenkins delivered the news sympathetically. She sat and held Mrs Larson's hand while the dry-eyed woman stared blankly out of a window. She'd obviously cried herself empty of tears some time ago.

Morgan went to the tiny kitchen to make tea, opening and closing cupboards in search of biscuits she never found. There wasn't much else for her to do.

'We saw what was written on the walls and the door outside,' Jenkins said. 'That can't be easy for you to live with. Would you like me to ring someone and get it cleaned off?'

Mrs Larson lit another cigarette from the nip of the one she was smoking. If she shook her head in response, then it was barely noticeable. 'They'll only do it again,' she whispered.

'Did anyone threaten Peter?' Jenkins asked. 'Threaten his life, I mean.' The old woman's hands were shaking so badly that when she put the cigarette to her mouth, it fouled against her lips. 'If there's anything you can tell us. Anything at all.'

Mrs Larson got up and went to a cabinet next to a portable television set. She pressed on a push-to-open door and reached inside. Jenkins's eyes connected with Morgan's. They might just get an early lead to work with. Mrs Larson returned with what looked to be a dozen or more folded sheets of paper.

Jenkins opened the first and read it to herself. She passed it to Morgan and read the next, repeating the read-and-pass manoeuvre until there were none left.

'I don't blame them for any of it,' Mrs Larson said, sounding like an automaton. 'How can I?'

Jenkins gathered the letters and held them at an arm's length. 'Most of these are death threats against your son.' She took an evidence bag from her pocket and put the letters safely inside. 'We'll need your fingerprints at some point. For administrative purposes.'

When Mrs Larson agreed to formally identify her son at the city morgue the next day, it was with nothing more than a silent nod.

Chapter 8

They returned to the pool car to find a large turd drying on the hot bonnet. Jenkins wasn't convinced that it belonged to one of the neighbourhood dogs. 'Pass us a hanky.'

Morgan went through her bag and offered a handful. 'You're not really going to grab hold of it, are you?'

'Have you got an alternative?' Jenkins said, getting ready to give it a go. 'It's either that or drive about the *shitty* with it sitting there.'

It took Morgan a while, but she got it eventually. 'That's funny.'

Jenkins glanced over her shoulder. 'What's that saying about all looks and no brains?'

'Cheeky sod. How many GCSEs did you get?'

'You can be academically clever but still have no common sense,' Jenkins said, hunting for somewhere to deposit the tissues and excrement. There wasn't anywhere. 'Evidence bag.' She waited for Morgan to open one and dropped the parcel inside.

'Are you saying I've got no common sense?'

Jenkins went to the rear of the vehicle and opened the boot. 'Get in.'

Morgan gawped. 'In *there?*'

'No!' Jenkins's chin fell onto her chest. 'I rest my case. You get in the front. The shit goes in the boot.'

Morgan caught hold of the door handle. 'Why the hell are we taking it with us?'

'What else do you want me to do with it?'

'But it'll go rank within minutes.'

'It's in a sealed bag. It's airtight.'

Morgan put her window down. 'I hope you're right. You know me and stinky things. We're not a good mix.'

Jenkins checked the rear-view mirror and pulled away to loud cheers from the residents. Mrs Larson stood motionless in her downstairs window. 'I won't regret the day I stop having to do that. The poor woman is just about destroyed.'

'She's probably glad to see the back of him,' Morgan said, bending to fit her bag between her feet. 'I know I would be.'

'Isn't a mother's love supposed to be unconditional?' Jenkins asked, doing her best to ignore the noisy onslaught outside.

'Could you forgive him if he was your son?'

Jenkins braked to avoid a cyclist doing a wheelie along the centre lines of the road. She waited before taking the next left turn out of the street. 'I doubt I'm ever going to know the honest answer to that.'

Morgan took a nail file from her bag and started on her thumb. 'You and Cara could always adopt. Plenty of same-sex couples do.'

'Slow down. We're not out of the honeymoon period yet.' They went steadily across the next junction and joined the main traffic a bit further on. 'Are you and Josh properly back together now?'

'It's like it never happened. I was so freaked out by the whole breast cancer thing, I overreacted. The poor sod had no clue how to deal with me.'

Jenkins wasn't sure how to phrase her next question. 'You chose not to have the preventative mastectomies.'

Morgan slowed with the nail file and stared straight ahead. 'It wasn't malignant, thankfully. I went with what the surgeon advised in the end.' Her attention moved to the side window and a group of kids who were drawing on the pavement with coloured chalks. 'I still have the threat of that dreaded gene hanging over me. That ugly bugger hasn't gone away. But hey-ho. Lady Luck's been on my side so far.'

Jenkins felt her stomach turn over. 'You two deserve a break. You've been through the mill these past twelve months.'

'You're not wrong there.' Morgan unscrewed the lid from a bottle of water and took a swig. 'Want some?' she asked, offering it.

'I'm good, thanks.'

She took another drink before putting the bottle and nail file away in her bag. 'Hey, I nearly forgot to ask. How come they let you loose with a Taser? They said no when I asked.'

Jenkins laughed. 'It was my phone. Igor was never going to work it out for himself.'

Chapter 9

IT TOOK THEM ONLY minutes to get to the other side of Llanrumney. Jenkins hadn't called ahead to announce their visit. If the family was somehow involved in Peter Larson's death, then there was no sense in giving them a heads up.

The front door was ajar when they got there. Jenkins tapped on it and rung the bell simultaneously. 'Hello. Police.' There was a radio playing music somewhere inside and the yappy barking of a small dog. She pressed the bell a second time, summoning a man who looked to be in his mid-forties. 'Mr Oughton?'

'If you're God Squad—'

'Murder Squad,' Jenkins corrected and produced her warrant card to prove it. 'Are you Lee Oughton?' The man grunted something that might have been a yes. 'Can we come in?'

Oughton was drying his hands on a tea towel. 'Why? What's the problem?'

There was a neighbour loitering in the garden of the property next door. Pretending to water his hanging baskets and dead-head any petal with a droop. 'It's best if we do,' Jenkins insisted.

Oughton turned his back on them and went in. 'Shut the door behind you. I don't want the dog getting out onto the road.' He caught hold of the animal and carried it under an arm.

In the privacy of the living room, Jenkins repeated introductions. Morgan produced her ID for what it was worth. The homeowner didn't look the slightest bit impressed. 'Do you know why we're here?' Jenkins asked, casting an eye over the contents of the room.

Oughton dropped into an armchair and fanned a hand at the sofa opposite. The dog sat on his lap, yapping and baring its teeth at the detectives. 'Nope.'

'Really?'

Oughton stopped stroking the dog and called a woman's name. To Jenkins, he said: 'The crystal ball's on the blink. You'll have to explain.'

'Why the hostility towards us?'

A door opened to reveal a painfully slim woman wearing white shorts with a yellow vest top. Oughton held the dog at arm's length. 'Have him, will you? He doesn't like them.'

The woman took the animal but didn't leave the room. It kept yapping. 'Who are these people?' she asked.

Morgan smiled. 'We're police officers. And *you* are?'

'Sally. Lee's wife.'

'Jack's mum?' Morgan asked.

The woman looked suddenly concerned. 'What's happened to him? Where is he?' She went to a door at the foot of the stairs and called the boy's name repeatedly.

Oughton flew to his feet. 'How can *anything* happen to him? He doesn't go out. Ever! Not since that perv . . .' Oughton cocked a fist as he twisted and turned. 'Not since that pervert touched him up.'

'That's why we're here,' Jenkins said. 'This is about Peter Larson.'

'Four years. Four *fucking* years is all he got. We should have hanged him from that lamppost at the end of the street when we had the chance.'

'You said something similar in court. You're lucky the judge didn't hold you in contempt for that.'

'I'd have made the world a safer place for women and kids. That's way more than your lot do.'

'Is that what this is about?' Jenkins asked. 'In your opinion, the legal system failed you. Now everyone who's part of it deserves short shrift.'

'I'll say it again. Four years for kiddie fiddling. I rest my case.'

'Can we move on?' Jenkins asked.

'Move wherever you want. You know where the door is.'

Jenkins was getting fed up with the man's attitude. 'Where were you between the hours of eight and nine this morning?'

Oughton's eyes narrowed. His lips came together and, for a short while, formed an almost perfect O-shape. 'What do you mean?' It was almost a whisper.

'This morning,' Jenkins repeated. 'Between eight and nine. Where were you?'

'Here.'

'Can Mrs Oughton vouch for that?'

Sally turned to point through what must have been the kitchen wall. Her sudden movement set the dog off again. 'We had breakfast outside,' she said, fighting to keep hold of the struggling animal. 'Lee likes to get a few jobs done in the garden and goes to bed late-morning.'

'It's well past your bedtime,' Jenkins said, checking her watch. 'What makes today different?'

Oughton thrust his hands into the front pockets of his jeans. 'Apart from the pair of you keeping me up?'

'If what your wife says is true, you should be well asleep by now. I was curious why you weren't.'

Oughton smacked his lips. 'I managed to get some kip during the night. Between fares.'

'It was a quiet one,' Sally said.

Jenkins looked from wife to husband. 'Tell me more.'

'There's nothing more to say. After chucking-out time at the clubs, I made my way home.'

'Lee drops the car off here,' Sally said. 'Then he walks the dog to the newsagents. Saves me doing it later in the day.' The animal must have known they were talking about it and stopped barking to lick the woman's face.

Morgan balanced her pocketbook on one knee and used her teeth to take the top off her pen. 'What time were you there?' she asked from the corner of her mouth.

Oughton put a hand to his brow and shook his head at his wife. 'Just before eight.' He slowly looked away.

'And what time did you get back?'

'Half an hour later. Give or take a couple of minutes.'

'We'll check,' Jenkins said. 'Are you sure?'

'I'm positive.'

'Do you have anything in the house with your handwriting on? A shopping list stuck to the fridge door? A note for the milkman, maybe?'

Oughton frowned. 'What do you want with my handwriting?'

Jenkins took the bag of death threats from her pocket and donned a pair of gloves. 'We'll need a sample from both of you.'

Chapter 10

Reece was busy rearranging photographs on the evidence board. Some, he took down or slid to one side. Others, he annotated with black or red marker pens, depending on their level of relevance to the ongoing case. He was suddenly aware of someone approaching from behind. 'You both made it back in one piece,' he said, twisting to look over his shoulder. 'Any trouble?'

'It wasn't so bad,' Jenkins said, dropping her belongings onto an empty chair. 'And Ffion's found herself a date for the Policeman's Ball.'

Morgan followed her colleague over to the evidence board via her desk. 'Shut up, will you? He was bloody gormless.'

'But he does have a place of his own,' Jenkins said, trying hard not to laugh. 'How best to describe it?' She looked to the ceiling, seeking creative inspiration from the dirty polystyrene tiles. 'A sofa with a view,' was all she could come up with.

Morgan put her hands to her ears and turned away. 'That's enough now. No more. *Please.*'

Reece put the top back on the marker pen and tossed it onto the table with a pile of others. 'How was the mother when you told her about the shooting?'

Jenkins took a half-empty bottle of water off her desk and took a noisy swig. She grimaced and wiped her mouth with the back of her hand. 'It's warm.'

Morgan took it from her. 'You should have put it in the fridge before we left.'

'That advice is of no use to me now, Ffion.'

'I meant next time we go out.'

'The mother?' Reece repeated, trying to get a word in edgeways.

Jenkins went to her things and collected the evidence bag from her jacket pocket. 'Mrs Larson didn't look at all surprised by what happened to her son.' Jenkins handed the death threats to Reece. 'These aren't all of them. The others were thrown away before she had a change of mind.'

Reece thumbed the plastic bag and read what little he could see through it. 'Did she recognise the handwriting on any of them?'

'Not that she admitted to.' Jenkins held the water bottle against her chest and rested her chin on the screw-top lid. 'I've told her we'll need her fingerprints for elimination.'

'Is she willing to ID her son's body?'

'She wasn't happy when I asked her, but yep, we got there in the end.'

'Good. Get these over to Sioned's team as soon as you can. See if she can't get a wriggle on with them.' Reece handed back the evidence bag. 'Not that I'm expecting our shooter to have telegraphed his intentions. Most of these will have come from the neighbours.'

'Probably.'

'What about the parents of Larson's victim?' Reece asked. 'What did they have to say for themselves?'

'The dad's downstairs,' Jenkins said. 'He's got some proper explaining to do.'

Chapter 11

Reece watched the interview unfold from behind a one-way glass screen in the observation room. His first impression of Lee Oughton was the man looked perfectly capable of holding his own in a scrap.

Oughton was hunched over the table, supporting his stubbled chin on a clenched fist. He wore a copper bracelet on the same wrist. Sitting opposite him were DS Elan Jenkins and DC Ffion Morgan. The audio from the room, when heard from Reece's side of the glass, had an almost robotic sound to it.

Jenkins reminded Oughton he was under caution: meaning anything he said could be used as evidence against him in a court of law, if things were to progress that far. 'Are you sure you want to continue without legal representation?' she asked. 'You're entitled to it. Free of charge.'

Oughton lifted his chin off his fist and wiped his palms on the knees of his jeans. 'I've done nothing wrong.'

Reece pressed his head against the glass. It was cool, in an otherwise small and stuffy room. 'That's what they all say.'

Oughton rubbed his eyes and stifled a yawn. 'Can we get on with it? I've been up most of the night.'

Jenkins was quick. 'I thought you said you slept for most of it?'

'You ever try sleeping in a car seat?' Oughton asked. 'All you get for your efforts is a thumping headache and a crick in your neck. I catnapped at best.'

'Best not tell the dog that.' Jenkins was ready to begin. 'I can't imagine what you and your family went through after the assault on your son. It must have been an awful time for all of you.' Oughton made no comment and sat there chewing his bottom lip. 'Were you aware that Peter Larson had been released from prison and was living locally again?'

'He shouldn't have been anywhere near us. He wasn't supposed to be. That's what they said. That's what they promised.'

'But he was. I'm asking, were you aware of that?'

Oughton took a deep breath and brought his hands together in front of him. He looked like he was choking the life out of someone. 'We got a letter. The usual crap sent out to anyone like us. You'll know what I mean. It didn't say where he was, though.'

'That must have been a shock? Raking up all that pain and hatred you had for the man.'

'Who said any of that ever went away?' Oughton stared across the table. 'It's the first thing you think about when you get out of bed in the morning. The last when you go back at night. Some days, you don't feel like getting up at all. But you do it to keep the family together.' He knocked his knuckles against his temple, harder than was necessary. 'It's inside here, twenty-four seven.'

'When they told you Larson was due to be released, you saw that as an opportunity to exorcise a few of those demons.'

'If you say so.'

'Come on. The man who sexually abused your son is let out and you don't want to do him harm?'

Oughton rocked in his chair. 'You're barking up the wrong tree, lady, if that's what you think happened.'

'What *did* happen?'

'How should I know?' Oughton bared his teeth. 'I didn't go anywhere near him.'

'You sent a letter to his poor mother, telling her you were going to castrate him and let him bleed to death.' She spread a note in a clear evidence bag on the surface of the desk. 'I bet when the lab gets back to us, they'll confirm your prints are all over it.'

'I wouldn't be so sure of yourself.'

'Really?'

Oughton grinned. 'I wore gloves when I wrote it.' He sat back. 'It's just a letter, for fuck's sake. It doesn't mean anything.'

'It does when the recipient winds up dead only a few weeks later.'

'What would you have done if it happened to one of your kids, eh? You got kids?'

Jenkins shook her head. 'This isn't about me.'

'Look.' Oughton lay his hands on the table top, palms facing down. 'If I'd been left alone with him in a locked room, only one of us would have made it out alive.' He flung his arms wide open, making both detectives flinch. 'But that never happened. I never set eyes on the creep after they took him down at the court.'

'I don't buy that. You saw him,' Jenkins pushed. 'From your taxi. You watched Peter Larson over a period of days and got to know his routine. Then you shot him.'

Oughton turned his attention to Ffion Morgan. 'I think your colleague needs to quit reading crime fiction.'

'You're ex-military,' Jenkins said. 'Am I right?' She allowed no time for an answer. 'I know I am.'

'What – I was a soldier, so I'm automatically guilty as charged?'

'No one's charged you as yet.'

'You know what I mean.'

'Did you?'

'Did I what?'

'Did you bring a gun home when you left the army?'

'No.'

'Someone else did, then. You had them do your dirty work while you manufactured yourself a watertight alibi.'

'Is this the best you can come up with?' Oughton sniffed. 'Clutching at straws is what you're doing.'

'No one's clutching at anything.'

'I'm a taxi driver, not Al Capone's chauffeur.' Oughton looked towards the panel of glass in the wall. He wouldn't have seen Reece watching him. 'Clubbers and tourists are what I specialise in.'

'Did you pick up a fare and get talking when your guard was down? Said more than you intended to. A conversation with the wrong sort of person, maybe? Or the right sort, depending on how you look at it?'

'This is bullshit.'

'Is it?'

'You know it is.'

There was a knock at the door. It was Ginge. He waved a sheet of paper at the seated detectives. 'I've got what you wanted.'

Jenkins took the document and read from it while returning to her seat. 'Three thousand pounds is a fair amount of cash to withdraw in a single transaction.' She slid the document across the table away from her. 'Care to explain?'

Oughton picked it up without prompting. He put it down again once he'd finished studying the columns of figures. 'That was for Terry. The rest of what I owed him.'

Jenkins handed it to Morgan. 'Who's Terry?'

'Terry Mack Motorcycles in Barry.'

'You recently bought a bike?'

Oughton looked from Jenkins to Morgan and back again. 'You saw it outside my house. Under that grey tarpaulin next to the bins.'

Chapter 12

It had been a long and taxing day; the team not yet finished. Reece had sent a squad car to pick up the man from whom Lee Oughton claimed to have purchased a motorcycle. The bike itself had been seized and was getting a good going over at the local police pound.

Members of the forensics department were systematically working their way through the premises of Terry Mack Motorcycles in Barry. Ginge was checking sales receipts and the bank account activity of the business.

Reece had sent Ffion Morgan home for the night. She was clearly weary, and he didn't want her overdoing things so soon after her latest breast cancer scare.

When he and Jenkins entered the interview room, the environment smelled of cloying aftershave and body odour. Not unlike his days duelling with Billy Creed. He pulled two chairs from under the table and offered the first to his colleague. He lowered himself onto the other, studying the man opposite while getting comfortable. There was much a detective could glean through observation of a person's body language. Reece was a grand master of the art.

Terry Mack looked like a man not to be messed with. He carried a pad of excess weight around his middle, but otherwise had the physique of someone well versed in heavy manual labour. His hands were like pitted clubs. Stained with grease and used engine oil. Mack obviously liked to put a shift in at the garage as much he did the sales till and stockroom.

'Lee Oughton says he recently bought a second-hand motorbike from you.' Reece scratched his chin. 'Three thousand pounds. Do you often deal in such large sums of cash?'

Mack studied him before answering. 'Bikes aren't cheap, you know. Not the decent ones.'

'I can't imagine it would be the norm,' Reece continued. 'Wouldn't a bank transfer or some sort of finance agreement be a more common method of payment?'

'Usually. But a sale's a sale, right?' Mack's head jerked violently to one side. 'Hey, it wasn't a tax fiddle, if that's what you two are thinking. I've got an invoice and receipts.'

'I'm sure you have,' Reece said, reaching into a brown envelope. 'We're checking all the same.'

'You'll find everything's above board.' Mack caught Jenkins's attention. 'For twenty years, I've run that business and never put a foot wrong where the law's concerned.'

Reece placed four photographs on the table and fanned them out in front of him. 'Apologies. The photographer did try to get Larson's better side.'

Mack put a fist to his mouth and bucked in his chair. 'What the fuck?'

'Did Lee Oughton pay you to kill this man?' Mack's gaze was concentrated on the floor and not on the new exhibits. 'Did you kill him?' Reece repeated.

'No!'

'Let's end the bullshit. We know you've got form for violence.'

Mack stood and towered over them. He gripped the edge of the table, and for a moment, looked like he might be about to launch it across the room. 'Not for that sort of thing, I haven't.'

'Sit down.' Reece waited. 'Actual bodily harm, it says on this charge sheet.'

'Not with a weapon.'

'Doesn't matter what you used. You put a man in hospital for the best part of a week and escaped a custodial sentence by a hair's breadth.'

'The bastard deserved it. He was a . . .' Mack fell quiet and looked like he might cry if provoked any further.

'He was your abuser,' Jenkins said in a gentler tone. 'Your defence counsel entered that fact in mitigation of your violent actions.'

Mack's mood brightened. He raised his eye level to meet Jenkins's. 'Even the judge didn't blame me for what I did.'

'You were lucky not to go down for a couple of years, at the very least.'

'There'd have been riots round our way if I had. That judge knew it and let me go with a telling off and a community service order.'

Reece brought his hands together at his waistline and rolled his thumbs. 'Did the judge's leniency give you the confidence to go one step further this time?'

Terry Mack nodded at the photographs. 'I had nothing to do with any of that.'

'And yet you've made a name for yourself as a local paedophile hunter. You're something of a celebrity on social media.'

'I'm an *outer,* not a hunter.'

'What's the difference?' Jenkins asked. 'Both terms involve taking the law into your own hands.'

Mack took a swig from what must now have been a cold cup of coffee, if Reece's was anything to go by. He didn't seem to care. 'Me and my team expose predators, using adult decoys posing as young kids in online chat rooms.'

'That's entrapment?' Jenkins said.

'Not at all. The decoys pretend to be twelve or thirteen usually, and bring that up right at the start of the conversation. The nonce is given plenty of opportunity to back down and get out of there if they've made an innocent mistake.'

Jenkins closed her eyes. 'But they don't, do they?' She'd previously served time in vice and knew only too well that such knowledge only served to spur the offenders on.

'It's like a disease,' Mack said, clenching his fists on the table top. 'Only, it all goes to shit for them when it's me who turns up at the meet and not some innocent kid with braces and pigtails.'

'What you and your people do risks undermining ongoing police operations,' Reece said. 'It drives the major players in trafficking and child-porn further underground. Picking off the little fish is as ineffective as pissing into the wind.'

'We hold them until your lot arrives,' Mack said, justifying his actions. 'We even provide a file of evidence for the CPS.'

'It's still ineffective,' Reece said. 'And probably counter-productive.'

Mack brought the pad of his fist down hard. 'If we save one kid from going through what we did, then I'd take that as a victory.'

Chapter 13

THE SEARCH OF TERRY MACK's business premises came up empty, to everyone's disappointment. Cross-referencing sales receipts with stock information and serial numbers confirmed Lee Oughton's claims. The bike had been purchased some days earlier, using three thousand pounds in cash. The fact it was all black and chrome, with *sit-up-and-beg* handlebars, ruled it out as the bike used by the anonymous hitman.

But the fact remained: Lee Oughton was directly linked to the victim. He had obvious motive, if not clear means. He was also a known associate of a paedophile hunter, or 'outer' as Terry Mack preferred to describe himself.

Reece used wooden chopsticks to eat spicy noodles and caramelised chicken from a paper carton. Jenkins had long since given up on hers and resorted to shaking bits of the meal into an open palm. 'You look like you're feeding sugar cubes to a horse,' Reece told her.

'I can't use those things. I've tried loads of times.'

'Get a fork then.'

'I'm almost finished now. What's the point?'

There was nothing to be gained by arguing with her, Reece decided, munching on another chunk of chicken. 'No gunpowder residue found on either man,' he said. 'That almost certainly rules them both out as being our shooter.'

Jenkins picked bits of rice off her top like they were flecks of fluff. 'The gunman was dressed head to foot in leathers. It would have protected him.'

'True.' Reece put his carton to one side for a moment. 'But my gut feeling is, it's not them.'

'Mine too,' Jenkins agreed.

'And the money trail seems legit.' Ginge put his carton to his mouth and tapped out the last few morsels of whatever was left inside. 'That bike was bought and sold when they said it was.'

Reece stood and wiped the names of Lee Oughton and Terry Mack from the evidence board. 'The newsagent confirms Oughton was in there this morning. Bemoaning the heat and the havoc it was wreaking on his lawn. There's no way he could have got over to City

Road and back in the time he had available to him. Even with access to a superbike, he still wouldn't have managed it.'

'Are we going to caution him for sending the threatening letters?' Jenkins asked. 'For Mrs Larson's sake, if nothing else?'

'He's had his telling off,' Reece said. 'Besides, I can't say with any honesty I wouldn't have done the same, given the circumstances.' What Reece did know was, he'd have ended the life of Anwen's killer in the blink of an eye had he been offered the opportunity. 'I *do* want a list of the other players on Terry Mack's team, though. Find out who those people are and where they were at the time of this morning's shooting.'

'Given they're both innocent, why didn't Oughton just tell us he was waiting for a new debit card to arrive in the post?' Ginge asked. 'It would have saved him and us a load of bother.'

'Because he's a dick.' Jenkins lobbed a lump of caramelised chicken into her open mouth and chewed noisily. 'Some people like to create a fuss.' She pointed at Ginge's desk. 'Pass us that bottle of Coke.'

Reece stiffened. 'Be careful with it. I don't have another shirt with me.'

Jenkins stopped unscrewing the bottle top and frowned at him. 'What's that supposed to mean?' She looked to Ginge for an explanation. 'What's he on about?'

Reece moved a few inches further away. 'Fireman Sam's got nothing on you.'

'Ha, bloody ha,' Jenkins said, using a paperclip to pick between her teeth. She handed the bottle back to Ginge and winked at Reece. 'Panic over. Happy now?'

'Very.'

'Ffion would have enjoyed this,' Ginge said, running a finger round the inside of his empty carton until it earned him a single grain of rice. He licked his finger and repeated the manoeuvre. 'She did look a bit knackered, though.'

Jenkins glanced at Reece, but kept her thoughts to herself. She snatched the carton from Ginge's hand, much to his disgust. 'Give us it. Give! You're doing my head in.' She went across to the waste bin and dropped the carton inside. 'You need to check yourself for worms, my boy. It's not normal, the amount you eat.'

Ginge stood up straight and rested his hand on the crown of his head like a small child in a doorway. 'I'm a growing lad.'

Reece followed Jenkins over to the bin. 'You get any taller than you already are and Harris is going to stand you outside headquarters and hang a flag on you.' He returned to his seat and sat with it facing the wrong way round. 'Okay, team. One last run through what we've got so far and then it's home.'

Chapter 14

ONLY A SHORT TIME earlier in the evening, the smell of accelerant and burnt sausages had risen high above the stone walls and featherboard fences of middle-class suburbia. People washed and admired cars. Brushed pavements and cleaned windows. Kids squealed excitedly as dogs turned circles on manicured lawns. It was all the things a balmy summer evening should be.

But not for Archie Ives.

He had walked—and on several occasions, run—in something of a bewildered daze. Keeping mostly to the narrow lanes at the back of the red-brick terraced streets. He stopped frequently to check he wasn't being followed or manoeuvred into a trap. Keeping to a straight-line route on this occasion would not be a sensible option. Not with an itchy-fingered gunman about.

He circled the block and doubled back on himself several times until satisfied the biker wasn't returning.

The neighbourhood had long since quietened. Most kids were bathed and put to bed. Their parents winding down on patios cleared of clutter, a glass of something chilled gripped in their weary hands.

Archie stopped for a wee next to a garage door that needed its peeling paint seeing to. From the smell of it, he wasn't the first to have used the dark recess as a makeshift urinal. He drew a couple of fingers across his cracked lips, grimacing when he swallowed. If there had been a puddle of water at his feet—and not dark coloured urine—he'd have collapsed on all fours and lapped it up like the thirstiest of dogs. There wasn't. It hadn't rained in nine days and there was none forecast for the coming week. He'd have to wait.

There was little traffic on the roads, given the time of night. And it was marginally cooler. He was reminded of days as a child, sat watching television with the front and back doors open, his mum trying to encourage a cooling draft to pass through the sweltering house.

An occasional taxicab went by on jobs to and from local pubs. The buses were still running. That surprised Archie, given the events of the morning. Then again, everyone had a living to earn. The world didn't come to an end because someone got themselves gunned down on a city street.

But that particular street was in his home town. Not in New York, London, or Manchester, even. This was Cardiff. A place where shootings didn't often happen.

Archie had a worrying feeling that things were about to change.

Chapter 15

TWO WEEKS EARLIER. BILLY CREED'S SNOOKER HALL

Archie gave Coombsie a hefty pat on the back. 'I owe you one for getting me in. I know it wouldn't have been easy.'

Coombsie shut the entrance door to the snooker hall before they'd passed through it and stood firmly in the way. He looked unsure of himself. Like he might have had a change of mind, now they were there in person. 'You promised to behave yourself.' His fingertip was aimed at a point between Archie's eyes. 'You're not here to be sniffing about for a story for your newspaper.'

Archie raised both hands in surrender and backed off a yard or two. 'I'm not planning on landing either of us in any trouble,' he said, crossing his chest. 'Hope to die and all that.'

'Oh, you've come to the right place, if that's what you're wishing for.' Coombsie turned the door handle, looking no more convinced. 'What is it with you and Billy Creed, anyway? It's getting to be a proper man-crush.'

It *was* becoming something of an obsession. Partly driven by abject boredom most days at work. Donald Breslin—Editor of the South Wales Herald—had Archie covering junior beauty pageants and school fetes. What a pile of dog shite that was. The most serious crime he'd so far covered was the mysterious disappearance of a prize marrow from an allotment garden in the village of Gwaelod Y Garth.

Archie yearned to be an investigative journalist. *The* investigative journalist at the Herald. Move over Maggie Kavanagh, there's soon to be a new kid in town. 'Creed's an urban legend,' Archie said, following his best mate inside. 'I've always wanted to see where he hangs out and does his business.'

'A psycho is what he is.' Coombsie blocked the way again and leaned in close. 'If you're planning on walking out of here tonight, you'll do well to remember that.' The door slammed behind them with a heavy clank that echoed along the empty hallway like a shotgun blast.

There were two wall-mounted cameras directly ahead of them, their lights blinking as red as rat's eyes caught in torchlight. There was another camera at the foot of the stairs leading to the upper-floor snooker room. 'This place is kitted out better than Fort Knox,' Archie said, taking it all in.

Coombsie lowered his voice and spoke with a hand cupped over his mouth. 'Creed's paranoid that someone has ordered a hit on him. A few people round here are saying that bad knee of his has made him vulnerable to an attack. A liability to some of the people he does dealings with.' Coombsie made sure Archie was listening. 'You didn't hear that from me.'

Archie knew most of the details of the shooting at the Midnight Club. The stuff released to the public and maybe a bit more. Most of it was pinned to his spare bedroom wall, complete with Post-it notes annotated by his own hand. 'Who's your source?' He got his phone out and opened a new Google Docs file. 'Will they talk to me, do you think?'

Coombsie snatched the handset and shut the phone down. He tucked it away in his jacket pocket. 'What the hell are you doing? What did I tell you out there?'

Archie held out his hand. 'Give it back. Give me my phone.'

'Not until we're outside again.'

'Come on. It's off now. I can't use it.'

Coombsie handed it over. 'If I see you switch it on again . . .'

Archie slid the phone into the pocket of his jeans. 'I get you, loud and clear.'

'That's your last chance. Behave, or piss off home.'

'Charming.'

Coombsie opened the door to the snooker room. The escaping air smelled of furniture polish, cheap alcohol, and sweaty men. 'You're welcome.'

Archie felt more than a touch light-headed. It had nothing to do with his climb up the flight of steep stairs. Entry to Billy Creed's domain was closely regulated. An invitation came from trusted regulars only. That was Archie's way in. If a person was about to experience a very bad day, then the *invitation* came from the man himself. Creed's was a summons to be feared but never ignored.

There were several snooker tables in the room. Islands of green baize wallowing beneath prisms of white light. Motes of dust fell like fine snowflakes. Only a few of the tables were in use. The place rattled to the sound of cue against ball.

Some of the regulars raised their heads as the pair meandered past. One or two of them whispered a greeting. Others either nodded or ignored them altogether. This wasn't a place for conversation.

Coombsie led the way to his preferred table. 'Remember what I said about keeping your nose out of anyone else's business?' Archie was taking in the surroundings like a fee-paying tourist at a beauty spot. 'I'm talking to you,' Coombsie said through gritted teeth.

Archie broke free of his trance. 'What was that?'

'You're not listening.'

'I am. To every word.'

'Go get the beers in. Then park your arse on that and wait for me to finish my game,' Coombsie said, pointing to a faux-leather bench running the length of the far wall.

Archie was getting fed up with being ordered about like some fresh-faced squaddie. Still, if it wasn't for Coombsie, he'd be watching the place from his usual vantage point out in the street. 'Same as always?' he asked, looking for the bar. He hadn't seen it on the way in and still couldn't.

Coombsie lay his case flat on the edge of the table. He thumbed its metal catches and removed a two-piece ash cue. 'They only do cans,' he said, screwing the cue together. 'Fetch me a couple to be getting on with.'

Archie turned in a complete circle. 'Where from?'

Coombsie nodded towards a pair of gaming machines over in the corner of the room. They were brightly lit, but the sound they normally made had been disabled. 'You'll see it when you get there. Ask Big Babs to sort you out.'

Archie conjured a mental image. *Big Babs.* He liked the sound of her. Stopping next to what was little more than a tight cubbyhole, he hung his damp jacket among several others. There was a wall of glass behind the coats. One that turned a right-angle and swept round the front of what must have been an office of sorts. Occupants would have full sight of goings on in the snooker hall. Slatted blinds gave them almost total privacy whenever needed.

There were voices coming from inside. One of them was loud and angry. Archie recognised it from video footage he'd studied at home. Provocative taunts made to the police. Much of it delivered from the steps of the local magistrate's court. Billy Creed was in the building and sitting only a few feet away.

Archie was almost wetting himself with excitement. Without warning, the blinds shot up on one of the windows. Creed's inked face and forehead pressed against the glass, making it creak under the strain. The gangster's clenched fists supported his weight on the windowsill.

Archie smiled and raised a hand in greeting. Inappropriate given the audience. He brought his arm back down to his side, the smile quickly gone.

Creed's scowl deepened as he mouthed the words: 'Fuck off.'

Archie didn't wait to find out what might happen should he refuse. He quickstepped over to the bar – if a wobbly table with a money box set on top of it counted as one. He bought two cans of Brains Dark for Coombsie and a diet coke without ice for himself. Big Babs asked his name. Archie dragged his gaze away from what looked like a pair of heads fighting to free themselves from inside the woman's vest top. 'I'm Archie Ives,' he said. 'Daniel Coombs gave me the invite.'

Chapter 16

Archie waited patiently while Coombsie filed the tip of his cue, prepping it for his forthcoming match. 'I'm back,' he said, keeping his voice down.

Coombsie blew away dust and filings. 'What took you so long?'

Archie glanced in the direction of the office, deciding it was best not to mention anything of his *showdown* with Billy Creed. He put the cans on a circular table beneath the scoreboard and lay the back of his hand against one of them. 'They're as warm as piss.'

'We won't be making any complaints to management,' Coombsie said, pinging the ring-pull. He took a gulp of beer and stifled a burp. The door at the top of the stairs opened to reveal two shifty-looking men. They approached. Neither spoke. Coombsie turned to Archie: 'Make yourself scarce until I call you back.'

Archie went over to the bench on the far side of the room. There wasn't much to see from where he was and he soon got bored doing nothing. He attempted conversation with someone playing on the nearest table, hoping to get something useful for a story. The best he got for his efforts was a dirty look and the middle finger.

Hung on the wall behind him was an eclectic mix of framed photographs. Those were far less likely to punch his face in. Several of them would have fitted comfortably on an office desktop. Others were considerably larger.

There were pictures of fast cars. Powerful motorcycles. Black and white images of a local dog track he recognised. There was a snooker player wearing a green waistcoat and trilby hat. The man held a cigarette in one hand and a generous measure of whisky in the other. Billy Creed grinned next to him.

Archie leaned closer to get a proper look at the tattoos. Some had Celtic symbology. Running a hand over the crown of his own head, he wondered how much the needling would have hurt. He doubted it would have bothered Billy Creed.

In another photograph, Creed's thick forearm rested on the shoulder of a muscular boxer. Both men wagged clenched fists at the camera. Ridiculous as it was, Archie would have preferred to take a right hand from the man wearing the boxing gloves and knee-length shorts.

There were footballers. Golfers. Jockeys. Seemingly, none of them put off by the odious company they were keeping. Creed had reach and appeal. There was no doubting that. Archie wondered what the gangster was involved in and whose palms he'd greased to keep it that way.

On a potholed corkboard were business cards for local taxi firms, pizzerias, and a massage parlour. It didn't say massage parlour as such, but Archie suspected that *Fast-hand Fran* was unlikely to be found on any register of chartered chiropractors.

At table seven, Coombsie was head down and bent over, lining up his next shot. There were still a few reds left to pot. He wouldn't be finished any time soon.

Archie moved further along the wall and found himself not far from the cubbyhole and damp coats. The blinds were still raised on the office window, Creed and two other men sitting with their backs to it. The smaller man was getting the brunt of the gangster's mounting anger.

Archie inched closer and buried himself deep within the curtain of coats. If he kept still, there was no way he could be seen by those inside the office.

The heated discussion was mostly about a teenage girl. The very same one Maggie Kavanagh and every other crime reporter in the country were currently obsessed with. Isla Kosh. Archie recognised the name immediately. He'd seen the **MISSING** posters in just about every shop window in town. Isla was a local sixth-former feared abducted and murdered by a father who'd already confessed to the brutal slaying of his wife.

It sounded to Archie as though there might be far more to the story than was previously known. If what he was hearing from Creed's office was to be believed, then the father might be the perpetrator of neither crime. That thought alone had the young journalist's mind working overtime. For once, he knew something that Maggie Kavanagh didn't. There was a mother of a twist in this one, and only Archie Ives had knowledge of what it was.

The smaller of the three men was named Arvel. That's what Creed kept calling him. 'Where is she, Arvel? Where's the girl?'

Arvel was mostly keeping quiet. When he did speak, it was to insist he'd already killed the teenager, disposing of her body in some form of industrial furnace. Archie made mental notes. He couldn't risk the chimes of his phone's start-up sequence giving him away. What he was witnessing was gold. Career-making stuff. Sod the Herald. This was worthy of a slot on Sky News.

The topic of conversation within the office changed suddenly, Creed going off on a tangent without warning. He started ranting about how some in the city mistakenly believed he was a weakened man now he walked with the aid of a stick. A liability, even. The vultures were circling, according to the angry gangster.

The rumours Coombsie had heard were obviously true. A messy power struggle was on the cards. Creed's days as king of the Cardiff underworld might be shorter than was previously expected.

Creed limped over to a small grey safe in the corner of the room, returning only moments later, waving a small leather journal that was fashioned with a strap to keep it closed. '*There*,' he said, tossing it ahead of him. The journal completed several full rotations in the air before landing on the table with a dull thud. 'That's why they wouldn't dare fuck with me. Not if they know what's good for them.'

Archie pulled the sleeve of a coat to one side, straining his neck to get a better look. He couldn't miss a moment of this, whatever the risk to his health and well-being.

Creed lowered himself onto his chair, gripping the edge of the table for support. 'Take a butcher's,' he said, untying the leather strap on Arvel's behalf. 'Them's the names of bent coppers and what they've done for old Billy over the years.'

A man with a huge jawbone, who'd previously been shuffling through a deck of playing cards, paused to look up. 'We got ourselves an insurance policy in case things get hot.'

Creed puffed on a thick cigar. 'A quid pro quo arrangement,' he said, waving smoke from in front of his face. 'They thought they could drop me from the game coz I'm playing with an injury.' He leaned in his chair and looked towards the makeshift bar and the woman sat behind it. 'There's a loose tongue among us. One that's let slip about that journal and got this lot's sphincters twitching.' Creed loosened phlegm from his chest. 'That means I've got to strike before they do.'

Arvel wanted to know what any of it had to do with him.

'I'm recruiting,' Creed said. 'You're going to join us and help tidy things up. We need to move on. Make new contacts in the city and beyond.'

Arvel looked none too comfortable with that. 'Not me, Billy. I've got my own plans.'

'This ain't open for negotiation,' Creed told him. 'You're either with us, or against us.' The man with the huge chin put the playing cards to one side and cracked his knuckles.

Arvel handed back the journal with the strap trailing from it. 'I'm having nothing to do with killing coppers. No way.'

Creed leaned forward in his chair and worked his knee with the fingers of his right hand. A lump of silvered ash broke free from the cigar and landed on the thigh of his black trousers. 'You sound like a man who thinks he has two choices.'

Archie couldn't believe his good fortune. Isla Kosh. Corrupt police officers. A planned hit on Billy Creed. A counter strike by the gangster himself. This was the stuff of dreams.

Arvel got to his feet. 'I'm out of here.'

Creed went apeshit, screaming at big-chinned 'Jimmy' to 'chuck every fucker out!'

Archie made it to a place of safety with only seconds to spare. He was standing in front of a framed photograph of Billy Creed pointing both barrels of a sawn-off shotgun at the viewer. Archie told himself it wasn't a bad omen. When he reached to unhook his jacket from its peg, Jimmy threatened him with a 'proper kicking' if he even tried.

Coombsie was using his foot to wedge open the door at the top of the stairs. He had a jacket stuffed in an armpit. A snooker cue and case occupying both hands. 'Couldn't help yourself, could you?' He let go of the door before Archie got there and went hurtling down the stairs in a strop.

When Archie checked over his shoulder, Creed's thug was zig-zagging between the snooker tables like a hungry Pac-Man in search of its next meal.

Chapter 17

'Wait up.' Archie jumped when the outside door slammed behind him. It caught in the wind and opened again, knocking against its stop. There was no sign of Jimmy Chin, or Billy Creed, thankfully. Coombsie was already on the other side of the road, making a meal of forcing his cue into its case. He wasn't listening and had one arm pushed through the sleeve of his jacket. The rest of the garment trailed behind him on the wet tarmac. 'Hey,' Archie repeated. 'I said wait for me.'

Coombsie answered over his shoulder. 'I told you to sod off!'

Archie gave way to a minibus belonging to a local taxi firm and jogged across the road when it was clear. 'Whatever happened back there had nothing to do with me.'

Coombsie scoffed and was on his way again. 'You're a liability, mate. End of.'

'It was that little fella in the office,' Archie said, trying to keep up. 'Billy Creed had a right go at him.'

Coombsie spun on his heels. 'And you'd know that, *how?*'

'Because—' Archie swallowed.

'Because you were sticking your nose where it don't belong. That's how.'

'I was looking at photographs and minding my own business.'

'You were up to no good. You're always up to no good.'

'Says you. I saw those guys you were with. What did they want?'

Coombsie's eyes narrowed. 'You've gone too far this time. That's it between you and me.'

Archie looked away. 'Whatever.'

Coombsie took a step closer. He was the taller of the two and looked down on Archie. 'If you've got something else to say, then spit it out.'

'Look,' Archie said, trying to diffuse the situation. 'They were all shouting in there. Arguing. You must have heard them?'

'Nobody hears anything in Billy Creed's gaff. That's why we go there.' Coombsie wedged the snooker case between his knees and got his jacket on properly. 'He saw you, didn't he? That's what happened. Creed caught you listening in on his business.'

Archie shoved his hands in the back pockets of his jeans. 'Do you think he'd have let me out of there if I'd been doing something I shouldn't?' Archie took a deep breath. 'Creed and that Arvel guy got into an argument and then it all kicked off.'

Coombsie started walking along the pavement. 'And you just happened to be standing next to the office door the whole time?'

'Why won't you believe me? Where are you going?'

Coombsie checked his watch. 'Anywhere away from you.'

The distance between them widened rapidly as the rain drummed on the roofs of parked cars. Archie was already wet and needed his coat. Getting it back was going to be no easy feat. Not with Billy Creed on the warpath.

Without warning, the door to the snooker hall swung open. There was a commotion coming from the foyer. Voices. Shouting. More banging of the door.

Archie moved a few car-lengths further along the street and ducked out of sight when Arvel appeared in the doorway. He was in a violent push-n-pull duel with Billy Creed. The gangster collapsed in a heap when his knee gave way. Archie went to draw Coombsie's attention to the scrap as proof of his innocence, but his friend was already gone.

Arvel took his opportunity while Creed was down and went sprinting along the wet pavement without looking back.

Creed screamed obscenities from his position on the floor. He was trying to get up but having little success. He called for Jimmy to 'bring the motor round the front.' His other thugs stepped over him. One of them chased on foot.

The BMW pulled up with its engine growling, Creed and the doorway temporarily obscured from view. There was more shouting and plenty of swearing before the vehicle set off again with grey smoke spewing from its tyres.

A motorist travelling on the same stretch of road braked hard and sounded his horn. The BMW honked back but didn't stop. It wouldn't have been a fair fight.

Archie emerged from the shadow of a parked van. The evening was getting crazier by the minute and he'd have to work hard to remember every detail of what had happened. He waited for the BMW's red tail lights to disappear before stepping off the pavement.

The door of the snooker hall caught on the wind and hit against its stop, calling to him. Creed's lot hadn't locked it before chasing after Arvel. It bounced and hit again.

Fate?

Coincidence?

Either way, re-entering the building wouldn't be without its risks. He checked one last time, reassuring himself he was alone. There was no sign of Billy Creed and the black BMW. Would going back inside turn out to be the dumbest decision he'd ever made?

With the question left unanswered, Archie Ives set off across the road.

Chapter 18

ARCHIE PUSHED HIS HEAD through the open door. The hallway reeked of cigar smoke and patchouli oil. Anyone familiar with Billy Creed would have recognised its significance. 'Hello. Anyone about?'

The regulars were gone, obviously. None had waited to be asked a second time. Creed and his crew were otherwise occupied. That left the woman selling warm beer from the makeshift bar. Archie hadn't seen Big Babs leave.

He went inside and was at the bottom of the stairs before remembering the cameras. How could he have forgotten already? He turned to flee, but didn't. Billy Creed had no idea who he was. To him, Archie was nothing more than an unfamiliar face from beyond the office window. It wouldn't matter if Creed ever reviewed the security tapes. He'd be none the wiser.

Besides, the lure of what lay upstairs was too much to pass up on. 'I've come for my jacket,' he called. 'It's raining outside.'

At the top of the stairs, he stopped to steady his breathing, a hefty dose of adrenaline coursing through his body. The door opened when he pushed on it. There had been no time for Creed to lock up. The creaking noise was ear-splittingly loud in an otherwise empty room. Nothing stirred. Maybe Big Babs *had* left with the others, using a different exit.

A few of the snooker tables had their overhead lights on still. The ones for which the wall-mounted coin slots hadn't yet time expired. Archie chose to keep well within the boundaries of darkness for as long as he was able.

The only other light source came from Billy Creed's office. The blinds were down now, but the door was wide open. An invitation to enter, if Archie had ever seen one. He was shaking with fear. Excitement. A combination of both. People wound up dead for what he was about to do. Got themselves buried in shallow graves, or weighted down and dumped out at sea.

The leather journal was on the table where Arvel had left it. Archie could see it from where he was. He peered into the shadows lurking in all four corners of the room. Nothing moved. No one challenged him. Yet he had the unnerving feeling of being watched the whole time.

He followed the light.

Not another bad omen? The thought refused to go away. What would he find at the end of it? Billy Creed beckoning him with that sawn-off shotgun he'd been wielding in the photograph?

The office stank like the foyer downstairs. Worse, even. Archie had often heard the scent referred to as junkie-juice. The stuff old hippies dabbed on their skin and clothing. Billy Creed was no hippy, but wore patchouli oil all the same.

There were five white plastic chairs and a table at the centre of the office. Cheap patio furniture that served its purpose. Archie's eyes were fixed on the journal. A warts-and-all tale of illegal collaboration between the criminal underworld and any number of corrupt police officers.

Archie used the strap to drag the journal towards him. The pages were loose. Like a scrapbook of research notes kept safe for a school project. He pressed them flat against the table and loaded the camera app on his phone.

'You've got some balls helping yourself to Billy's business.'

When Archie jumped, the camera clicked. Keeping hand movement to a minimum, he pushed the phone into his front pocket. 'I came back for my coat,' he said, turning to face Big Babs. The woman stood with her arms folded and her head tilted to one side. It was an accusing pose for sure. Tattooed in green ink along her forearm was the claim: **BORN TO RUN.** Archie tried to undo the sight of her trying. Born to crush skulls, more like.

'You're not going to find it in there.' Babs said. Her eyes were on the journal.

Archie's mind was a fog of thoughts. 'Um. Yeah. No. You're right.' His way out of the office was blocked. 'My mistake. It's over on the peg. I can see it now.' He moved. Babs stepped aside and didn't follow when he passed in front of her. Her gaze hadn't left the table.

It took all of Archie's resolve not to barge his way back inside the office, to grab the journal and run. Despite what it said on Big Babs's forearm, her being anything of an Olympic sprinter was highly unlikely.

He checked his watch. Billy Creed could return at any time and would take his frustration out on him. Survival mode kicked in. He glanced at the journal and then at Babs. Two poker players trying to out-bluff the other. He weighed up his options and decided he had few. 'I'll be on my way then,' he said, walking towards the door.

Chapter 19

THE LONELY WALK HOME took Archie the best part of forty minutes. By the time he reached the top end of Glenroy Street, the weather had gone full circle and it was pouring with rain again.

He closed the front door behind him and removed his wet jacket before switching on the hall light. The decorating elves had chosen not to visit while he was out.

Running a hand along the cracked plaster, he knew things wouldn't be progressing much any time soon. He'd started the project several weeks ago. With enough enthusiasm to get the paper stripped and the woodwork wiped down, ready for painting. That's when he ran out of steam – redirecting all his efforts on what clung to the walls of the tiny spare bedroom instead.

He tossed his jacket onto the bare boards of the stairs before going through to the living room. There was an empty pizza box obstructing his way, a blob of tomato ketchup congealing at the corner of its lid. Two empty cans of cheap lager and an open pod of garlic dip rested among a pile of dried crusts. He took the mess through to the kitchen and searched for enough clear space to put it down. On top of a pile of dirty dinner plates was as good as it got. He'd see to them after work the next day. That was the plan.

He'd left his Coke untouched at the snooker hall and couldn't remember having much to drink since his lunchtime Starbucks at work. Not surprising then, he felt like he was wearing someone else's teeth.

Settling at the table with a tall glass of water, he put his phone in front of him and navigated to the photographs folder. He wasn't holding out much hope of having captured anything worthwhile. Damn that Big Babs for interrupting him. He saved the image to Google Drive before studying it. He'd previously lost stuff and had learned his lesson the hard way.

There was camera blur. He enlarged the picture, but that didn't help much. He reduced it to normal size again. There were eleven digits. The first was a zero. Almost certainly a mobile phone number.

But whose?

A rogue officer?

One of Billy Creed's thugs?

Or did it belong to the man himself?

That thought alone almost freaked him out. He stared at the number, drumming his fingers on the table. His heart was racing. He could ring it and claim it was an accident, if challenged. What harm would that do? People rang wrong numbers all the time.

He thumbed the first few digits before abandoning the call. 'Think, Archie. Think.' He licked his cracked lips. 'This might be your only chance of ever making it big.'

It was while hanging about in corridors at the Herald – lurking next to photocopying and fax machines, that he'd first learned of Billy Creed. According to Maggie Kavanagh, the gangster was untouchable. Some in the print room used the word *Teflon* to describe him. Archie now knew why that was.

Juggling the phone in the palm of his hand, he read the mystery number out loud for no one's benefit but his own. His thumb hovered over the keypad. 'What's the worst that can happen?' He dialled the first four digits—one more than last time—then deleted them. He brought the phone to his mouth and nibbled the edge of its plastic case. 'Come on. This is how it's going to be as an investigative journalist.' He dialled the full number. It rang while he waited. Someone answered, but didn't speak.

'I've seen Billy Creed's journal,' Archie said. 'I know who you are,' he lied. 'Did you hear me?' he asked when there was no response. 'I'm going to expose you.' The silence made him wonder if the recipient of his call had already hung up. 'I'm going to expose you and Creed.'

There was movement on the other end of the line. Shuffling as well as a scraping noise. Then a voice that cut through both. 'You're a dead man.'

Chapter 20

THE NUMBER 22 BUS into Cardiff came to a halt with a lurch and a loud hiss of its air brakes. When the front-end doors *whooshed* open, Archie caught hold of the chrome handrail and climbed aboard. 'Morning Doug. A better day after last night's rain.'

The driver was a short, ruddy-faced man with an untidy brush of a salt and pepper moustache. He pulled a stunted tie over a swollen belly and leaned an arm on the steering wheel. 'But what a shit-show on the weekend,' he said, picking bits of psoriatic skin from his elbow. 'Just as well it was only a preseason friendly.'

'You're not wrong there.' They were talking football as usual. The woes of Cardiff City, specifically. Archie put his bus pass away unchecked. He took the 22 every day, and most times, it was Doug who drove it. 'It's enough to make a fan want to switch allegiance to another club.'

'Never a Swansea Jack, though.' Doug shook his head firmly.

Archie laughed his way along the narrow aisle. 'A Bluebird until the day I die.'

'Getting the bad games out of the way before they count,' Doug shouted after him. 'That's what they're doing.'

Archie wasn't at all convinced and shifted across the worn fabric of his usual seat. He leaned against the glass and put his baseball cap on the seat next to him. A silent, yet effective, *sod-off and let me be* statement to anyone who might otherwise have wanted to sit there.

Despite his show of joviality, Archie was tired and more than a touch jumpy. There had been little sleep gained following the previous night's phone call. He'd checked the window locks several times before going to bed and propped chairs against the front and back doors.

He reached into his shoulder bag and sat quietly unravelling the tangled charging cord for his battered phone. The morning ritual for the short commute to work was to check the overnight happenings in the city. That way, he could submit an early request to go and cover anything of real interest to him.

Not that it ever worked out that way. Maggie Kavanagh always managed to hoover up the good stuff. Archie was as sure as he could be that Kavanagh and Donald Breslin were doing each other favours.

Things were about to change at the South Wales Herald. Archie—not Maggie Kavanagh this time—had the mother of all stories. Two stories, if the Isla Kosh development was run by the newspaper. Breslin couldn't possibly turn either down. The man would be a complete fool to do so.

Archie was skimming the news headlines when he almost dropped his phone through the narrow gap between his knees. **Local Gangster Dies in Clifftop Plunge,** it said in a bold typeface that filled most of the screen. '*What the?*' The woman opposite glanced at him. He nodded a silent apology and went back to reading the article.

It was written by Maggie Kavanagh, of course. Archie couldn't imagine her having that many miles left in the tank. The woman chugged through enough cigarettes most days to kill a small community. It was only a matter of time before the Reaper came calling for Maggie.

In truth, Archie admired the senior crime reporter. She had a nose for a story and shot from the hip, which was something he liked in a person. There were no airs and graces where Maggie Kavanagh was concerned. She treated everyone with the same spadeful of coarse grit and honesty.

He re-read the headline several times to be sure. It didn't change things. Billy Creed was dead. Splattered on the rocks of a fast-flowing river, surrounded by a forest of trees.

It was the end of an era. Or perhaps the beginning of a new one.

The stubborn Arvel Baines—Archie hadn't known the man's full name before now—had met with the same fate as the gangster. The Reaper had been otherwise engaged. Lucky Maggie.

The article suggested Baines had been acting on the command of people he'd met in prison. He'd lured Billy Creed to a remote spot with the intention of carrying out a hit that had somehow backfired, killing them both.

An interesting angle. But Archie knew otherwise. Baines was little more than collateral damage in something bigger and far more dangerous. The Isla Kosh story was intertwined with the one about Creed. The girl had been found safe and well. There was even a photograph of her with a police detective named Reece.

Archie wondered if the rogue officers had been first on the scene. Had they taken out Creed and Baines, cleaning up before more reputable colleagues arrived?

Which camp did DCI Reece belong to? He looked a bit rough and ready to Archie's eye.

His mind was in overdrive. What did last night's threat now mean in the context of Billy Creed's death? The perpetrators had not only succeeded in killing the gangster, but also looked as though they'd avoided any suspicion being cast in their direction. Would they risk changing all that to pursue a nobody like him?

He hoped not and relaxed a little. But what if they'd been caught in the act and got themselves arrested? What if his number came up in a check of their phone records? He'd been a fool to use his own. Would he too be implicated in Billy Creed's death? Would he end up in jail alongside them?

He should make another call. Better still, get down the police station right away and speak to someone in person. DCI Reece, maybe. Explain everything he knew and how he'd come by it.

It took him no time at all to realise the flaw in that particular scenario. He'd first be expected to explain his attendance to whoever was manning the front desk. He wouldn't know who he was talking to and could wind up as dead as Creed and Baines.

The woman opposite was looking at him again. Had he been thinking out loud? Saying things he shouldn't have done? He turned away from her and hunched his shoulders self-consciously.

Chapter 21

When the bus pulled into Archie's stop in the city centre, Doug had to shout to alert him. 'I thought you'd nodded off,' he said as Archie went past the front cab. 'You burning the candle at both ends?'

'I was reading.' Archie held his phone at an arm's length. 'Have you seen the news? Billy Creed's dead.'

Doug leaned towards the screen and squinted. 'Who did he play for?'

'He wasn't a footballer.' Archie recognised a look of total bewilderment when he saw one. 'Never mind,' he said, dropping to the pavement below. He sidestepped a crowd of people waiting to get on and broke into a fast walk, headed towards the South Wales Herald building.

He lost count of the number of times he turned to check he wasn't being followed. The number of times he moved out of the reach of anyone waiting in a shop doorway.

People walked ahead of him. Some faster than others. Several of them stopping to chat, or to read from the screens of mobile devices. Had they too seen Maggie Kavanagh's article? Would they even care that Billy Creed was dead?

Archie very much doubted it. The British public was more likely to be engrossed in televised dross featuring narcissistic wannabes sporting blinding dental veneers and orange tans.

He brushed against a man stood dawdling at the opening in the railings of a pedestrian crossing and made it to the holding-point at the centre of the widened road only a few seconds later. Not waiting for the green light to show itself, he was on his way again, raising a hand in apology to the sounds of blaring horns.

That got people staring. He'd have to get used to it. They'd soon be pointing and shouting, 'There he goes. That's Archie Ives off the telly.'

Not yet though. Not before he knew the streets of Cardiff were safe.

He was soaked with sweat by the time he got to the Herald building and swiped in at reception using an ID card dangling from a lanyard draped round his neck. He said good morning to Moira on the front desk. Gestured, would have described the interaction more accurately. Too dry-mouthed to speak, it was all he could manage to raise a hand in greeting.

'Are you okay?' Moira looked genuinely concerned for his welfare. 'Shall I call the first aid rep?'

Archie shook his head. 'I'm fine,' he said, bent over and dripping sweat on the tiled floor. The buttons next to the lift were lighting up in ascending order. It was going the wrong way. He rapid-pressed the call-button like he was playing an arcade game. The lift ignored him and continued its upward journey. 'Great. The stairs it is.'

Chapter 22

ARCHIE CROUCHED AT THE foot of the stairwell, gazing through the space between the wooden handrails until his neck and back ached. He adjusted the strap of his shoulder bag, psyching himself for the upward climb. It was a long way to the top. Undeterred, he grabbed hold of the polished rail and used it to propel himself onto the second step.

He'd have walked barefoot over hot coals for a chance to work on the story he had. The difficulty would be to convince the Herald's editor to let him have it and not hand it over to Maggie *bloody* Kavanagh.

How would Maggie react to being left out of something that began on the worn keys of her own laptop? She'd be rightly pissed off, was Archie's best guess. But hey, journalism was a dog-eat-dog environment. *She* knew that. Had probably written the rule book. All tactics were fair game, as long as they led to a story.

Archie's thighs burned under the onslaught, and he wasn't yet halfway there. He massaged them as he went, with little effect.

He pushed on with only one more floor to go. Couldn't have managed another and used his arms and the handrail as much as he did his legs. When he got there, he waited, slumped over the rail, fighting for breath. He grasped his canvas bag with both hands and used its rough surface to wipe his face. All that did was smear sweat from one area to another. It had little, if any, drying effect.

He was dizzy. Nauseated. Such extreme exercise couldn't be good for a person. He opened the landing door and stepped into the corridor. It was bright and airy compared with the stairwell. That was a good thing.

He was rehearsing what to say when the lift pinged, its door opening with a judder. It was Donald Breslin. Immaculately dressed in a sand-coloured linen suit and light blue shirt. He'd combed his silver hair back and away from a tanned and super-smooth forehead.

'Archie, isn't it?' Breslin smiled, showcasing an expensive set of dental work.

Archie wondered if he should be pleased with the editor's ability to put a name to a face. Or irritated because the man had to check to be sure. 'That's right, sir. I'm Archie. Archie Ives.' Shuffling awkwardly, he tried again. More clearly this time. 'That's Archie Ives, not *Archie-Archie Ives.*' He lowered his head and blushed. 'I didn't need to tell you that, did I?'

Breslin cleared the lift area and rested his briefcase on the tiled floor. 'Are you okay? You look unwell.'

Archie used the cuff of his shirtsleeve to wipe sweat from his face with more success than he'd earlier had with his bag. 'I'm trying to get more exercise, sir. I've started taking the stairs in the morning.' He doubted he'd ever use them again.

'Good for you.' Breslin played an imaginary backhand pass down the corridor. 'You ever play tennis?'

Archie resisted the urge to play a forehand return. 'Not on what you pay me.' He instantly wished he'd gone for the return instead. 'Sorry. I didn't mean that.' He did. Being on the wrong end of the career ladder paid peanuts. 'I'm a Cardiff City fan. A match day pie and a pint is my spending limit most weekends.'

Breslin laughed off the remark and patted a trim abdomen. 'Tennis gives a great calorie burn if you put the effort in.' He lifted his case and walked. 'And they've made it a lot more affordable these days.'

Archie followed along the corridor. 'I really didn't mean what I said about my pay, sir.' He banged the side of his head. 'I must have suffered a lack of oxygen to the brain after doing those stairs.' Breslin's office was only another ten metres away at the very most. The opportunity was almost gone. 'Sir, I—'

Breslin wagged a finger. 'The big bucks come with the big stories. There's no secret or magic pill to swallow.'

'That's just it,' Archie said excitedly. 'I've *got* the story.' It wasn't how he'd wanted to do things. Standing in a corridor where anyone could walk past. Maggie Kavanagh included. 'And this one's as big as it gets. Can we talk?'

Breslin slowed to check a weighty wristwatch. 'I don't know. I'm due to meet with someone very soon.'

'It's about Billy Creed's death last night.' Archie blurted it out. 'There's more to it than Maggie knows.'

Breslin's keys rattled against the wood of his office door. 'Archie—'

'Really, sir. It's true. I promise you.'

The editor checked his watch for a second time. 'I can spare you five minutes. No more.' He went to his desk and lay his briefcase flat on its polished surface. The air conditioning was doing a sterling job of keeping the room cool. Yet still, he opened the window. He took two bottles of water from a refrigerator concealed in the oak panelling of the office wall. 'Catch,' he said, tossing one in Archie's direction. 'You look like you could do with a drink.' The bottle hit Archie's sweaty hands like a wriggling trout. He dropped it after a fair fight and squatted to pick it up. Breslin unscrewed the plastic cap on his and settled into his chair. 'Four minutes, thirty seconds remaining.'

This was Archie's big chance. He'd never forgive himself if he were to mess it up. 'What if I told you Billy Creed was silenced before he could expose a ring of rogue officers working for the South Wales Police?'

'By rogue, I'm guessing you mean corrupt?'

'Bent.' Archie could think of no more similes and left it at that.

Breslin tapped the plastic bottle against his teeth. Then rinsed his mouth with cold water before swallowing. 'Says who?'

'Billy Creed himself.'

'From the grave?' Breslin gave Archie a sceptical look.

'Before that. A lot earlier in the evening.'

'Archie, this is making no sense.'

How best to get the hook across without giving too much away? 'I've a source who overheard Creed talking about a planned hit on him.'

'Last night's hit, you mean?'

'Not exactly.'

Breslin slumped against the upright of his chair and sighed. 'You're wasting my time.'

The opportunity was slipping away. 'The police killed Billy Creed. Arvel Baines had nothing to do with it. Maggie's got it wrong this time and you're missing out if you won't believe me.'

Breslin put the bottle next to his briefcase. 'Time's up.'

'But it's not five minutes yet?'

'I've heard enough.'

'What proof did Maggie Kavanagh give you before you let her run the story?' Archie knew he was well out of order, but it did little to deter him. 'Why is it only me who has to jump through hoops?'

Breslin was on his feet and rounding his desk. 'Maggie has it on good authority that it was Baines who killed Creed. She and the DCI on the case go way back.'

Reece? Archie wondered. 'Who's to say he isn't one of them? He could be throwing her a red herring for all you know.'

'Archie.'

'Give me a chance. Please.'

Breslin was almost at his office door. 'It's not your enthusiasm I'm struggling with.'

'What then?'

'I need proof. No proof. No story.' Breslin turned the handle and opened the door. 'Goodbye.'

A fuzzy photograph on Google Drive wouldn't be enough. 'What if I gave you a journal full of evidence?'

Breslin pushed on the door but didn't quite close it. 'You can do that?'

'Some of it's in here.' Archie tapped his shoulder bag. 'I'm working on the rest.'

The door opened. This time wide. 'Come back and see me when you're done.'

'We've got a deal?'

'Not yet. Evidence first.'

Archie started up the corridor. 'You won't regret this. I promise you.'

Breslin called after him. 'Let's keep this between you and me for the time being.'

Chapter 23

PRESENT DAY. GLENROY STREET, CARDIFF.

Archie knew that going home so soon after the shooting on the bus posed a real risk to his life. The gunman might already have realised his error and be looking for him again. Home would be the obvious place to start the hunt.

But Archie needed money, as well as his passport. The stuff pinned to the walls of the spare bedroom could stay there, ingrained as it was in his memory. He'd take his laptop. A phone was good for keeping abreast of the news, but it wouldn't harm his cause to have something as a backup should the need arise.

Besides, he was sure that using the phone was the cause of his current predicament. He'd made one call only—albeit a stupidly naïve one—and already they'd used their vast resources to track him down. They'd have triangulated his position using available telecoms masts. But how could they have known about his seat on the bus? That would have required the help of someone. Someone who knew his comings and goings. The thought worried him as much as any of it did.

It was difficult to believe that almost seventeen hours had elapsed since the shooting. That's what his wristwatch claimed. He had little reason to doubt it.

He'd need an alternative place to stay for a few days before moving on again. Somewhere safe. Coombsie was the only real friend he had, but their paths hadn't properly crossed since that fateful night at the snooker hall.

When he entered Glenroy Street, he paused to check that nothing looked out of place. What should he be looking for? He wasn't entirely sure. A car that wasn't normally parked there? Or a hooded figure leaning against a lamppost, smoking, waiting, screwing a noise suppressor to the end of a gun barrel?

Archie quit with the over-thinking and squatted behind a parked car. It was something he was getting good at. There were no lights illuminating the windows of the houses behind him. No twitching curtains, nor shouts for him to clear off elsewhere.

He didn't need the unnecessary hassle of someone thinking he was trying to steal their vehicle. Someone who'd inadvertently draw attention to him, or batter him senseless with a short length of heavy pipe.

The pavements were deserted on both sides of the road. The siren of an emergency vehicle wailed somewhere way off in the distance. Another joined in. Like a pair of tomcats fighting over an unsettled dispute of territory.

Archie moved from his temporary vantage point with a muted groan and risked another look both ways before scarpering across the road. If anyone had been watching him, he'd have resembled a slapstick comedic act, zig-zagging towards his own house. They'd probably think he was drunk. Or drugged. There was already one pisshead living a couple of doors further down. Geoff was his name?

Archie freed the latch on the front gate and pushed it, half expecting a hand to reach out of the shadows and grab a hold of his shoulder. When one didn't, he got going again, leaving the gate standing in its open position. His hands were trembling so badly it took three attempts to get the front door key in the lock. He waited in the hallway. Listening. Sniffing the air for a waft of unfamiliar aftershave or anything else that might give away an intruder's presence.

The kitchen clock was ticking. As were the water pipes in the attic. Satisfied he was alone, he passed through the hallway without turning the lights on. He would have used the torch function on his phone under different circumstances. Not today. He was quickly learning from his mistakes.

The first step complained under his weight. As did each of the next three. The others were good until he rounded off on the landing. He put a finger to the bathroom door and stuck his head inside. Empty. He went in and threw cupped handfuls of cold water on his face and finger-combed his hair. It felt good for such a simple act of grooming.

He checked his bedroom next. Empty, unless someone was hiding beneath the mountain of clean laundry piled on the floor. He rummaged among them. Jeans, T-shirt, and trainers swapped for the trousers and shirt that clung to the sweat on his grubby body. He grabbed a hoodie in case the weather proved the forecasters wrong.

At the window, he stood out of view from the road and couldn't see anything glaringly obvious in the street below. Ducking lower than the sill, he moved to the other side of the reveal to check in the opposite direction.

There was a car parked at the top end of the street. One he hadn't noticed earlier. Its lights were off and there didn't appear to be anyone sat inside. He willed himself to calm down. That was easier said than done.

Under the mattress was a few hundred pounds he'd saved since beginning his job as a junior reporter. There wasn't much point in putting it in a bank. Not when interest rates on savings accounts amounted to near enough a zilch of a percent.

He shoved the envelope of money into his jeans pocket, along with his passport. Having it gave him options. If things got any hotter than they already were, then he could flee the country for a few weeks and get a summer job to live on.

The spare bedroom was Archie's control centre. A place where he studied the goings on of Billy Creed and his underworld empire. There was all manner of clutter strewn across a desk pushed against the wall. The laptop was on a trickle-charge, ready to go. Archie reached for it and promptly froze. Someone was moving in the living room downstairs. At first, he blamed it on his heightened imagination. When the noise repeated, he knew it was for real.

Chapter 24

Someone had their foot on the bottom stair. Slow to move now that they'd made a noise. Archie cocked an ear to it. There it was again. The sound of weight shifting slowly to the next tread.

Someone had followed him inside. Or had been there all along, lying in wait. Had they used the spare key *hidden* under the bucket next to the back door? The same key he'd meant to move following the telephone threat to his life. The oversight was one that might cost him dearly.

Counting the steps, he estimated the intruder being not far from the top already. A few more to climb and the short landing would be the only thing separating him from whomever they were. He raised the sash window – several layers of thickly applied paint causing it to judder in its runners. It went only a third of the way up before getting stuck.

He poked his head out into the night air. It was a fair way down to the garden below. He could be seriously injured or killed if he got it wrong. He'd be killed for sure if he didn't give it a go. Staying put was no longer an option.

When the bathroom door banged open, he ducked and dangled a leg outside. When the floorboards creaked not far from the bedroom door, he stretched for the downpipe. It shifted in his hand and rattled in its rusted fixing. There was no time to test its structural integrity. He was going whether he liked it or not.

The bedroom door flew open as Archie hoicked himself out. The downpipe made a worrying noise as it took his full weight, but didn't pull away from the wall altogether. His foot slipped on the stonework, leaving him dangling above an untidy-looking bush, stamping in search of any sort of grip.

A face appeared in the open window. Not a *face* exactly, but a head covered with a black balaclava. Then what might have been a gun with streetlight reflecting off it as it swung from left to right.

Here it was. Archie's punishment for getting involved in something he shouldn't have. He shut his eyes and let go of the drainpipe, crashing into the bushes feet-first. It hurt. Granted, not as much as a bullet would have done. He forced his way out of the bushes as a chunk of turf exploded next to him. The gunman had opened fire; the stuck window making it more difficult to get a clear shot.

Archie hurdled the dwarf wall, crying out when a fragment of stone broke free as a second shot skimmed off the top of it. Something—bullet or stone, he didn't know which—took out the side window of the neighbour's parked car, setting off its alarm.

Archie ran for his life, using the cars on his side of the road as a shield.

Chapter 25

REECE COULDN'T SLEEP. NOT because of nightmares of Anwen bleeding to death on the cobblestone road in Rome. Or the sight of Peter Larson's brain leaking through the hole in the shattered bus window. He just couldn't sleep.

He'd tossed and turned for what seemed like an age, listening to a silence that only people like him knew. He read a few pages of a book. Put it down and picked it up again. Bored with the clunky prose, he gave up on it and went downstairs to get a glass of cold milk.

His stomach burned. An increasingly frequent occurrence of late. That and belching more than usual. His GP put it down to stress and lack of sleep. 'What right did a murder squad detective with a dead wife have to be stressed?' Reece had asked with more than a hint of sarcasm.

The doctor hadn't answered.

Reece was physically fit, and for the most part, ate healthily. He took the occasional whisky, but mostly when joined by a friend or colleague. He wasn't one of those alcohol dependent detectives described in the novel he'd given up on. He looked after himself. Ran every day. Sometimes more than once. His blood profile was spot on. As was his blood pressure, heart rate and rhythm.

But still, the GP had seen fit to lecture him on the benefits of lowering the levels of stress in his life. 'Get yourself a pet,' she'd told him. 'They're great for helping you unwind after a busy day.'

Reece took a gulp of milk straight from the bottle. Having no one to share it with meant it didn't matter much. He screwed the lid tight and returned the container to the fridge.

Chief Superintendent Cable had earlier that day insisted he get back to the counselling sessions with Dr Miranda Beven. The last time they'd met, he'd had made a complete idiot of himself, babbling incoherently and running off into the night.

He wished he could have been honest with her. Or accepted her gift of theatre tickets for what they were: a thank you for him having saved her life. But he'd read more into the kindly gesture. Had over-complicated things. Unrelenting guilt over his wife's death being too much to bear. He couldn't go out on a date. Couldn't spend the evening in the company of another woman.

Not yet.

Probably never.

If only he'd been able to find enough courage to tell Miranda he wouldn't be showing up that night. Instead, he'd let her arrive at the venue and wonder where he was. Refusing to answer her calls, he'd sat in the darkness of his living room, staring at a phone that spoke to him in voicemail. He didn't pick up for worry of not being able to speak. He felt ashamed and wholly inadequate.

He was as much a failure of a man as he was a failure of a human being. That was his brutal and self-deprecating assessment.

The wall-clock showed 1.12am. Should he return to bed and fight for sleep, or go out and run for as long as it took to clear his mind?

That was a question easily answered.

Chapter 26

It was just after 2am when Reece shut the front door behind him. The night air was warm and dry. The streets bathed in a soft orange glow from roadside lamps.

There was a fox on the pavement opposite. It stared at him. Reece stared back. There was an instant connection between them. He couldn't remember the last time he'd seen one in the City of Llandaff. There were plenty to be had lying dead at the side of the roads he travelled to and from work. Badgers too. It always put a dampener on his day to find them like that. He didn't like to admit it, but he was a pushover where animals were concerned and preferred them to most humans.

A couple of late-night revellers rounded the corner, singing while scraping deep inside foil takeaway trays. The fox ran off, clearly unimpressed by the interruption.

'Pick it up,' Reece called when one of the men crumpled his tray and tossed it into the gutter.

The man looked surprised to see him and was quite obviously struggling to focus. 'What's it to do with you?' His speech was slurred. His gait unsteady.

'I live here.' Reece crossed the road, heading for them like an unleashed torpedo. 'There's a bin further along.' He pointed up the street. 'On the lamppost over there.'

The fox had stopped to watch.

The second man threw his tray to the ground and clapped his hands together. It landed upside down, spilling a few uneaten chips and a small pile of rice. 'Whatcha going to do now, fuckface?'

Reece grabbed him by a handful of shirt collar and forced him against the glass of the bus stop. He kept his eyes on the other man, who was now rolling up his sleeves, ready to start a fight. Reece glared at him. 'You don't want to go there, mate. Believe me.' There was a brief standoff between them before the man squatted to pick up his tray. When he got low, he fell onto his haunches. Then flat onto his back. Reece let go of the other man's shirt. 'Help him clean it up.' It took far longer than it should have done, Reece watching over them until satisfied the pavement was clear. 'Bin.' They needed reminding and didn't object to him walking them along the pavement. 'Easy, wasn't it? Night, night, fellas.'

With the drunks almost out of sight, he pressed a finger against each ear bud in turn and selected a Spotify playlist Jenkins had set up for him. His choice of music, not hers. He hadn't a clue how to do it for himself.

"It'll save you having to strap a record player to your back," she'd joked. The memory made him smile. Lots of things made him smile these days. The fox, especially. Some things made him cry, still. But the balance was certainly shifting.

The playlist kicked off with 'Wild Horses' by *The Rolling Stones*. One of his favourites. It wasn't what many would consider music to exercise to, but for Reece, it was just about perfect. *Bob Seger* pushed 'Against the Wind.' While *Tom Petty* was 'Learning to Fly.' Reece was lost in the narrative. The gradual incline of the cracked pavement negotiated with the ease of a man twenty years his junior. No coincidence then it being done to *Don Henley's* 'Boys of Summer.'

Reece did some of his best thinking while listening to music. Countless hours sat in an armchair with his eyes closed, searching for the clues that were always there if a detective looked hard enough.

"I need peace and quiet, myself," Jenkins had remarked when he first took her onto the team. Not that she was ever quiet for long. Even that made him smile.

Music cleared his mind and cleansed a soul that was in dire need of a deep clean. Running was something he'd taken up only after Anwen's murder. He'd promised her father, Idris Roberts, he wouldn't throw himself under a bus, or train, or something equally terminal.

At times, he'd come very close to breaking that promise. But Reece was a man of his word.

His thoughts wandered to events aboard the Cardiff-bound bus. He'd always cautioned himself, and his juniors, against jumping to early conclusions in a case. Regardless, he had been guilty of thinking this might turn out to be one of his shorter investigations. The paedophile angle had some legs. Larson was killed soon after his release from prison. The man whose son he'd abused had withdrawn a large sum of cash and paid it to a known vigilante. Reece could see how he'd let himself get sucked in.

But Peter Larson's death had nothing to do with Lee Oughton and Terry Mack. Larson was killed for reasons, as yet, unknown.

A blaring horn cut rudely through the early morning air. Rising well above the sound of the music. Horn, brakes, and a worrying amount of metallic screeching coming from a flatbed lorry bearing down on him. Its lights were flashing. The horn not stopping to catch its breath. Reece was only halfway across the road, caught like a squirrel wondering whether to go back or forward. Left or right. He did none of those things and instead came to a full stop with his feet planted together. His upper body bent forward with the sudden loss of momentum. Then it came upright again. Not before his head was only inches from what would have been a very short scrap with several tonnes of speeding metalwork. It ruffled his hair and shoved him rearwards.

The lorry went on its way with a final blast of its horn. No real harm done.

'Whoa, that was close.' Reece removed the ear buds and kept them safe in the palm of a clenched fist.

He'd run the remainder of the route in silence.

Chapter 27

Archie Ives hadn't been killed by the returning gunman. He'd avoided death twice already that day. Good going by anyone's standards. A better geographic knowledge of the surrounding area, and keeping to dark alleyways where possible, had undoubtedly aided his escape. His assailant would have expected him to move in a straight line, putting as much distance as possible between them. That's what Archie didn't do, and so far, it was working.

Fleeing abroad was becoming increasingly appealing. He could book a seat on a flight or ferry. Destination didn't matter. Being well away from Cardiff, did.

He tapped his pocket and immediately entered panic-mode. His passport was gone. He slapped himself down like an ape having a tantrum. Then got up to check the surrounding floor. 'Jesus, no.' He must have dropped it on his way down the drainpipe. Or while hurdling the garden wall.

It could be anywhere. Picked up or flushed down a storm drain. Should he go back and check the pavements and gutters? Reverse-walk every step of the route he'd taken? The gunman wouldn't believe him to be stupid enough to do that.

Archie sank onto his buttocks and pressed his back against the cool upright of the cemetery headstone. 'Help me, Mam.' He blinked tears and ran a hand over the smooth granite surface, taking some comfort from the fact his mother's mortal remains were close by. 'You'd know what to do.'

Archie was only fourteen when Molly Ives keeled over dead while frying him an egg to go with his chips. He'd got home from school—all acne and attitude—shouting: *"How long before grub's ready?"* When first he suspected there might be a problem, he forced a shoulder against a kitchen door that refused to budge an inch.

He called to Molly with increasing levels of anxiety. Banged on the door and gave it a hefty kick when he got no answer. When the unmistakable smell of burning made its way through the downstairs, he rushed out the front and ran around the block to the lane and back entrance. He'd known as he sprinted along the garden path that his life was about to change beyond all recognition.

Molly was lying flat on her back. Fitting. One pupil several sizes bigger than the other. Archie hadn't known what the twitching was until a doctor explained it to him. The same doctor who stood with an arm on his shoulder as he turned off the power to the breathing-machine. A teacher from school was there too. Archie had no one else.

Mam was gone. His rock and soul mate. Best friend and confidant.

Molly Ives had bled into her brain because of something Archie couldn't pronounce. It began with an 'A' and might have had an 'ysm,' somewhere in the word. Many medical terms did. Something had burst in Mam's head. That was the long and short of it. She was dead and wouldn't be coming back.

He'd sat next to the bed once the nurses had given Mam a freshen up wash. Held her hand and noted with waves of crippling grief how quickly it turned cold and stiff. 'Was it my fault?' he'd wanted to know. 'If I'd gone to the chippy instead of bugging you to cook me something, would you still be here with me?'

Mam hadn't answered.

Archie used his school tie to wipe his eyes. When he took it off, he called to a nurse waiting on the other side of the curtains. 'Can this stay with her?' he asked. 'Mam always said it made me look smart.'

The young nurse was unable to speak as she took it from him. One wrong word and she'd be sobbing like he was. 'It's okay,' he told her when able. 'I'll be all right.' The nurse had backed away silently, tie in hand.

'*So*, Mam,' Archie said, running a finger over Molly Ives's name. 'How the bloody hell do I get myself out of this one?'

Chapter 28

Wiggley-Jones Funeral Directors was a single-storey building in dire need of a lick of paint and a tidy up. The roof leaked from the valley above the front entrance. The external cement rendering was stained green in places and cracked like the shell of an egg.

On a broken tarmac forecourt next to the main building was parking for four or five cars. In front of an open garage door were two chauffeurs wearing white shirts and black ties. One of them was polishing a behemoth of a car.

Marma Creed was starting the new day early. Catching up with several of her late brother's business associates. *Negotiating* new terms and conditions wherever she saw fit.

When her bodyguard, Husam Kahn, swung the Gold Lexus SUV in off the road, both chauffeurs stopped what they were doing and gave the new arrivals room. The Lexus braked, coming to a stop with a short skid. The front passenger door opened. Marma stretched a leg and stood almost six-feet three inches tall on doorstep heels. 'Let's get out of this sun,' she said, making her way to the cover of the overhanging garage door. 'It's not good for my skin.'

The chauffeurs looked nervous. Marma Creed paying them an impromptu visit meant someone was in for a bad day.

Kahn got out of the driver's side door. His skin was so black it looked ink blue. When he stood, he trumped Marma's height by a full two inches.

Marma took a polishing cloth from the hand of one of the chauffeurs and tied a small knot in it. She flicked it to the right, then left of his head as though swatting flies. 'Decisions, decisions.' The cloth came to rest on the man's shoulder. 'I have room for only one of you,' she said, stepping well within the boundaries of his personal space. 'But which one shall it be?' She handed the cloth to her companion and took a Stanley knife in exchange. Moving to a spot equidistant between the two chauffeurs, she offered the knife in an open palm. 'Which of you wants to go first?' The men glanced at the knife. Then straight ahead again. Neither spoke. Both looked bewildered. Marma moved her hand slightly left. Nearer the man who'd originally held the cloth. Thumbing the blade to the open position, she said: 'Cut his throat.'

The man took a rearwards step and made a poor attempt at a smile. His lips were quivering and stuck to his teeth. 'Marma, I—'

'Not up to it?' Marma offered the knife to the second man. 'What about you?' She grabbed his groin with her other hand and squeezed hard. 'Do *you* have the balls?'

The first man had a sudden change of mind and seized his opportunity. Snatching the knife, he gave himself space and swung his arm in a wide arc, careful to keep well out of the way of the pulsing red jet. He retracted the blade into its housing and held it at his side.

His victim staggered towards the opening at the front of the garage, both hands gripping a gaping slit at the front of his neck. It was useless. His white shirt was already soaked red. His face pale and waxy. He got one foot on the broken tarmac before Kahn grabbed him from behind. As the pulsing arc dwindled to little more than a feeble trickle, Kahn's arm shook with the effort of holding the dying man upright. Kahn let go. The man went down with a sickening thud when his head struck the ground. He groaned. Convulsed. Then went still and died without further fuss.

Marma buttoned the surviving man's collar and tightened the knot of his tie. She pressed a painted fingernail to his bottom lip and dragged it along his chin, breaking the skin. 'That's the only time I'll allow you a second chance.'

They entered the main building, leaving the chauffeur to deal with the body and spilled blood. A woman dressed in receptionist's garb appeared in a doorway leading to a narrow corridor behind her. She stepped out of the way when first Marma and then Kahn marched past.

The corridor smelled of damp; its carpet in need of lifting to check what lay beneath. The receptionist followed at what she must have considered being a safe distance. Marma didn't knock on the office door when she got there and barged straight in.

Wiggley-Jones was picking fluff from his suit jacket. He looked up and lowered a phone from his ear. He raised it again and said, 'I'll call you right back.' When he returned the handset to its place on the desk, it clinked against a half-empty glass of water. 'This *is* a pleasant surprise.'

Marma twice-clicked her fingers at the receptionist. 'Last year's accounts. Make it snappy.' She took a seat on the other side of Jones's desk with Husam Kahn standing behind her.

Wiggley-Jones glanced at his phone as though tempted to pick it up and call someone. He left it where it was and looked away.

Tapping out a tune on the desktop, Marma awaited the receptionist's return. The sound was annoying. Jones didn't complain. The only other sounds came from the traffic on the road outside, and the rasp of the funeral director's heavy breathing.

They hadn't waited long when the receptionist returned, carrying a black ledger that was more than an inch thick. Marma thumbed through the pages. Jones lowered his head and exhaled slowly. 'Don't be nervous,' Marma said. 'I'm sure there's a perfectly reasonable explanation for why my Billy's share of the takings isn't what it should be.'

'Your brother never complained.'

Marma looked up only fleetingly. 'You're dealing with me now.'

The undertaker put the flat of his hand against the side of his face and closed his eyes. When he opened them again, Kahn had moved to a position behind him. Jones used the armrests of his seat to push himself more upright. His head turned to the front again when Marma slammed the ledger shut.

She dropped it onto the desk. 'Looks like you've been open for business as usual.' She swivelled in her chair, taking in the drab furnishings. 'You've not spent the money on décor, that's for sure.' Then she leaned forward and pointed accusingly. 'That means someone's been squirrelling money away for a rainy day. *Your* doing?' she asked the receptionist. The woman shook her head. 'I didn't think so,' Marma said with a thin-lipped smile.

'I can explain.' When Jones went to stand, a firm hand pressed him into his seat. 'I was going to ring you.'

Marma put a finger to her lips. 'I'm taking over full ownership of the business.' Kahn took a document from a large brown envelope and put it on the table. Marma handed the funeral director one of his own pens. 'Sign here. And again, just there.'

'I—' Jones faltered. 'Look—'

'It didn't need to be like this,' Marma said, watching the pen scratch its way across the page. 'I want the code for the safe.'

'Marma. *Please.*'

'I know it,' the receptionist said, making her way across the room.

'*Justine!*' Jones whined the name.

Marma pointed the receptionist towards a washing-machine-sized chunk of metal in the far corner of the room. 'Over to you.' When the safe door clicked open less than thirty seconds later, Marma got up and went over to it. Squatting, she removed one of several envelopes. All as thick as paperback novels. Each stuffed close to bursting with fifty-pound notes. She counted out ten notes and handed them to the woman named Justine. 'Consider yourself hired as the new manager of this establishment.' Marma went back to the desk and sat on its edge, looming over Jones. 'But first we have to create a vacancy.'

Kahn lowered a clear plastic bag over Jones's head and pulled a drawstring tight to the skin, cutting off all possibility of incoming airflow. Jones moaned. Growled. Rocked side to side, fighting to get out of the chair. He sucked the bag into his mouth and gasped for breath, condensation obscuring a full view of his face.

Marma stared into the funeral director's eyes. The whites were already marbled with the red lines of burst blood vessels. 'My Billy's waiting for you downstairs,' Marma joked, as Jones took his last breath and slumped over the desk. 'Be sure to look him up.'

There was a knock at the office door. Two taps followed by the squeak of the handle turning. Kahn reached for something hidden under the strap of his belt, his hand coming away again when the chauffeur entered.

'What shall I do with—' The man paused when he saw the deceased Jones.

Marma spoke to Justine. 'Do we have much on for the rest of the week?'

The newly appointed funeral director checked the ledger. 'A half-dozen booked in so far.'

Marma took four fifty-pound notes from one of the envelopes and handed them to the chauffeur. 'Get yourself over to the garden centre for a chainsaw.'

The chauffeur folded the notes and put them away in his trouser pocket. 'Why a chainsaw?'

Marma had her back to him and was busy searching through the safe. 'How else do we make eight bodies and six funerals work?'

Chapter 29

Reece hadn't gone back to bed after his run. He'd showered and slumped in a chair downstairs for what was left of the night. Then found, to his annoyance, that the Peugeot was going to play silly buggers and make him late for work. Thumbing his eyeballs, he phoned Yanto in Brecon. 'It's properly had it this time. Can't get it started, no matter what I try.'

'That's because it's only good for scrap.'

Reece's attention was drawn to a small dog playing chicken with the morning traffic. There was no owner to be seen. The animal wagged its back end as he walked towards it. Then it had a change of mind and scarpered towards the white centre lines, where it promptly rolled onto its back. 'No, you stupid sod.'

Yanto coughed. 'Are you talking to me?'

'Not you. The dog.' Reece waved an arm like a traffic cop and stepped in front of the nearest car. He went further into the road, reacting angrily to the comments made by waiting motorists. 'Stay where you are. *Stay*, I said.'

'Brân. Are you pissed?'

Reece inched towards it, worried he might scare it off again. 'I'm talking to the dog.'

Yanto wasn't following. 'What dog? What are you on about?'

'*This* fucking dog!' Reece dropped his phone on the tarmac as he bent to scoop the animal out of harm's way. He used his foot to drag the handset into the gutter. The dog shifted in his arms like it was having an epileptic fit. It tried to lick him. Tried to get down on the floor. 'It's not mine,' Reece told a couple of pedestrians when they stopped to watch. He reached one-handed for the phone. The glass screen had a crack along its full length and plenty of new scratches. He stared into a pair of shiny black eyes. 'Don't look at me like that.'

He hadn't known what to do with the puppy after saving it from certain serious injury. He spent a good twenty or thirty minutes walking the pavements of Llandaff, asking if anyone recognised it. Nobody did. It wore no collar and refused to answer to any of the names he tried.

He was left with no option but to take it home—leaving it roadside wasn't a viable option—and feed it a few slices of raw steak he'd earlier earmarked for his tea.

Everywhere he went, the dog followed. Wagging its tail and rolling onto its back, insisting he tickle its tummy. 'What am I going to do with you?' Short of a sensible answer, and concerned for the welfare of his carpets, he took it to work.

Reece passed through the foyer of the police station with the puppy squirming underarm.

George, the desk sergeant, chewed more slowly and leaned on an elbow. 'Whatcha got there, then?'

Reece stopped in his tracks. He had an idea and went over to George's window. 'A puppy.'

'I can see that. What I meant was, what are *you* doing with it?'

Reece put it down on the counter, a hand resting against its back end in case it decided to jump off. 'I found it.'

George straightened and tucked his shirttail under his belt. 'Where?'

'Does it matter?'

'It does if it belongs to someone.'

'Christ, I didn't nick it. It was in the middle of the road, trying to get itself killed.' Reece watched the desk sergeant roll the wheel on a computer mouse. 'What are you doing?'

'Checking no one's reported it lost.'

Reece waited, feeling suddenly anxious.

George looked up from his screen. 'Nope. Not yet, anyway.' He patted the puppy and offered it a bit of rind from the bacon roll he'd been munching on. 'Happy little thing.'

'Have a proper hold,' Reece said, manoeuvring the puppy away from him.

George pressed the animal to his chest, giggling when it nuzzled into his neck. 'What are you going to do with him while you're at work?'

'Funny you should ask,' Reece said, backing away.

'Oh, no you don't.' The animal was going nuts now that it had lost all sight of Reece. 'Brân. Get back here.'

'He likes you,' Reece called from the foot of the stairwell. George disappeared momentarily. By the time the doors to the stairs closed behind him, Reece could just about hear the desk sergeant screaming his name from the foyer.

When Reece reached the landing on his floor, he slowed and almost turned and left. Assistant Chief Constable Harris was talking in the incident room. Even with the thrum of activity layered over it, Harris's voice was the dominant one. He looked up when Reece came through the door. 'Ah, here's the man himself. Get in here.'

Reece shoved his hands in his pockets and went no closer than he already was.

'Here,' Harris said, clicking his fingers. 'I want you to meet someone.' Chief Superintendent Cable, Jenkins, and Morgan were all there. Plus a stranger.

Reece couldn't place the man and made *what's going on?* eyes at the chief super. Cable shook her head. 'What's up?' Reece asked.

'There's nothing *up*,' Harris said, wringing his hands. 'Come here, man. Meet Inspector Brogan.' The name was more familiar than the face. Reece came forward and reluctantly stuck out a hand and introduced himself. 'Mike knows who you are.' Harris rolled his eyes at Cable. 'Every bugger in the Force does.'

Reece pointed at his office and went to manoeuvre around the assembled group. 'I'm busy, so I'll be off.'

Harris stepped in front of him. 'Stay put.'

'With all due respect, sir—'

'Stay!' Harris went red and patted his shiny combover. He took a breath. 'I've brought Mike in as an adviser on this bus shooting.'

Reece's hands went to his hips. 'You've done what?'

'You'll remain in charge, obviously—'

'Too bloody right I will.'

Cable got in between them. 'Brân, listen to what the ACC has to say.'

Reece craned his neck to see round her. To Harris, he said: 'What is it with you and this department? Why can't you let us do our jobs in peace?'

Jenkins took Morgan by the elbow and walked her sideways towards the door to the landing.

'Where are you two going?' Harris demanded to know. 'It's like herding kittens.'

'I'm not here to interfere,' Brogan said, playing peacekeeper. 'Just to give an opinion on the ballistic side of things.'

'Now that you've dropped the vigilante angle,' Harris added. 'It makes things more complicated than they previously were.'

'I know how to run a murder investigation,' Reece said. 'You *do* know that, don't you?'

Harris donned his service hat and readied himself to leave. 'Mike's staying until that shooter is under lock and key. Like it or lump it.'

Chapter 30

IT WAS CLOSE TO 9am and Detective Constable Owain Evans—aka Ginge—was running a few minutes late. Literally running. Along hospital corridors, looking for any clue where the mortuary might be. Ffion Morgan had told him it was downstairs. But downstairs from where or what?

A nurse shrugged when he stopped her for directions, and quickly went back to texting without suggesting a useful alternative.

He asked a man who was pushing a cage full of cardboard boxes.

'Don't have the foggiest,' came the reply. The man went further along the corridor before stopping to point at someone wearing a yellow polo shirt with black trousers. 'Ask him. The porters know where everything is in this place.'

Ginge did as suggested and got directions and an escort who kindly swiped him through a series of locked doors on the lower ground corridor. 'I owe you one,' Ginge said, bracing himself outside a door labelled **MORTUARY - AUTHORISED PERSONNEL ONLY.** He went inside, following the signs for the **VIEWING GALLERY.**

The darkness of the gallery contrasted with the harshly lit environment on the cutting side of the glass. There were several rows of seats and a central stairway running the full length of the room. It was uncomfortably warm. Ginge's short-sleeved shirt stuck to his back and underarms. He was making his way down the steps, a finger pulling at his collar, when the PA system clicked into life.

'Afternoon, Owain. Very nice of you to join us.'

Ginge checked his watch. It was nowhere near afternoon. 'Morning Doctor Frost. I took the wrong corridor upstairs.'

'Is that the best excuse you have?'

'Oh, it's not an excuse. This place is like a maze.'

'You're here now.' Frost turned her back on him. 'Is it all right with you if we begin?'

Ginge wiped the sweat from his forehead. 'Definitely. Sorry again, Doctor Frost.'

The pathologist positioned herself on the right-hand side of her patient and began her external examination with a slow and deliberate circuit of the body. She stopped occasionally to get a better look at areas of interest, scribbling on a proforma attached to a clipboard. She took Peter Larson by the wrist and spoke in medical terms. Larson was missing the distal phalanx of the first finger. The distal and middle phalanxes of the second finger. 'A defensive wound,' Frost said. 'A hand raised as an instinctive act of self-defence.'

Ginge couldn't blame Larson for trying. He'd have done something similar himself. Not that it had done any good.

Frost had her patient rolled onto his side. Areas of his back and buttocks were stained with the bruise-like appearance of blood settling after death. Ginge had seen it before. What was new to him was the ragged hole in the back of the victim's skull. It was many times bigger than the entry wound in the forehead. Much messier too. Larson's hair was matted with blood, brain, and fragments of shattered bone.

Frost described the awful injuries. The likely trajectory of the bullet, and the damage it inflicted when passing through Larson's head. There were no exit holes to be found on his back, Frost concluding that the bullets were still lodged somewhere inside. That was a good thing, because the one responsible for shattering the bus window was still unaccounted for.

With her external examination complete, Frost waited for photographs, nail scrapings, and hair samples to be taken. Next, she took a post-mortem scalpel—a larger blade and heavier handle than the standard surgical version—from a tray of other instruments. She hovered it close to Peter Larson's shoulder. Pausing to check the viewing gallery, she said: 'Owain, why don't you come down and take a closer look?'

Ginge had seen plenty of horror films begin with the same innocent suggestion. The pathologist would be standing over the corpse, keen to get started. The lights would blink, then go out, throwing the room into total darkness. There would be noise. Banging. Screaming. Then silence. Suddenly, the lights would come on again, but with a strobing effect. A fog would part to reveal the pathologist's face squashed against the glass. Her fingernails clawing at it. The camera would pan to an empty examination table. It was only then they'd show themselves. Aliens. Or zombies.

'Owain.' Frost was watching. Knife in hand. No aliens or zombies as yet. 'I asked if you'd like to join us?'

It was the young constable's punishment for being late. 'What? Over there with you?'

'Are you squeamish?'

Punishment definitely. Ginge puffed his cheeks and fiddled with his ear. 'No.'

'Okay then . . .'

Ginge hadn't moved. 'You mean now? Today?'

Frost tapped the blade against her open palm. 'Yes, Owain. Today.'

Chapter 31

Ginge was asked to change into scrubs and full PPE, not to risk the transfer of DNA from himself to the deceased man. Unlike Reece and Jenkins, he hadn't attended the City Road crime scene, and so his involvement wouldn't yet have been logged as a matter of formal protocol.

His chaperone pulled a tube of mints from his pocket and offered them. 'It helps,' he said with his arm held outstretched. He thumbed a mint loose and waited for Ginge to take it.

'Is it that bad?'

The man offered the packet a second time. 'It's not going to help much if you crunch them.'

Ginge helped himself to another and popped it under his face mask. 'I'm a bit nervous,' he said, making a hash of getting his gloves on.

'No need to be,' the chaperone replied, leading the way into the cutting room.

Even with the aid of the mint, Ginge could smell it. Disinfectant, rot, and death. Not a pleasant mix. He edged his way towards the table and its unflinching occupant. 'Am I okay just here?'

'Closer,' Frost said, patting her hip. 'The dead don't bite.'

'What about here, then?'

Frost caught him by the elbow and had him stand next to her. 'That's more like it,' she said. 'Now you have a ring-side view.' She lay the blade of her knife somewhere near Peter Larson's shoulder and drew it towards the breastbone. Then repeated the movement on the other side. Next, the blade cut its way effortlessly towards Larson's groin, leaving a Y-shaped incision in its wake.

Ginge closed his eyes and couldn't help but crunch down on his mint. When he next opened them, Frost was snipping through the ribcage with something resembling a set of garden secateurs.

'The sternum is fractured in several places,' Frost said. Ginge was unable to respond verbally and nodded instead. 'You see this?' Frost had her hand inside Larson's chest, snipping at the pericardial sac with a pair of sharp scissors. 'The right side of the heart faces outward and often sustains the most damage in these types of injury.' She reached inside the sac and lifted the heart. 'It's actually rotated in the chest, unlike the front-on images you see in school books.'

She lowered the organ. 'In this case, the left ventricle has been torn open. That's the main pumping chamber.' She withdrew a bloody hand. 'It wouldn't have mattered which came first—the head or chest-shot—either in isolation would have killed this man.'

'Can you feel the bullets?' Ginge asked, trying to get a better look inside the chest. His initial queasiness had quickly passed. Being *ring-side* was fascinating.

'We did an x-ray examination before you got here.' Frost came away from the table and went over to a light-box viewer on the opposite wall. There were four images to be seen. 'Let me show you.'

Ginge had a bash at working out for himself what some of the white bits were. He was able to identify the bones of the upper arms, shoulders, and rib cage. 'What are those?' he asked, hovering a finger over the viewer.

'When a bullet enters a person's body, it'll often strike against a solid structure, like bone, causing it to fragment. The impact causes the bullet to change its course of direction and repeat the process of collision and fragmentation until it runs out of kinetic energy.'

'This here is bone?' Ginge asked.

'Exactly. See that? One of the bullets is lodged in the spine.'

'Oh, yeah. I can see it now. Bloody hell, that's brilliant.'

'Not for Peter Larson, it wasn't.'

'No. Sorry.'

Frost moved to the image of Larson's left shoulder. 'The other bullet deflected upwards off the edge of the sternum, passed through the lung, and got stuck in the joint of the shoulder.'

Ginge shook his head and tutted. 'That's a right mess.'

'Indeed. It's just as well he won't be needing the use of it.' Frost went back to the table, skilfully removing the remaining contents of Peter Larson's chest and abdomen. She took a forceps to the exposed vertebra, turned, and held a flattened bullet under the young constable's chin. 'Gotcha.'

'Will ballistics be able to give us anything to be getting on with?' he asked.

Frost dropped the bullet into a metal kidney dish. 'I'd be surprised if they couldn't.'

Chapter 32

THERE WAS SILENCE IN the incident room. All eyes alternating between DCI Reece and Inspector Brogan. 'Pull up a chair,' Reece said. 'I'll brief you on what we have so far.'

'I think you're right to assume this was a contract killing,' Brogan said once Reece had finished. 'You can't be absolutely positive, obviously. Not until you've got the shooter in custody.'

'Where would the average Joe find themselves a hitman in Cardiff?' Jenkins asked.

'Down the local pub.' Brogan didn't look like he was joking. 'There's always some nutter who'll do just about anything in exchange for a few grand in cash.'

'That's a worrying thought.'

'They'll be amateurs in most cases,' Brogan said. 'Resorting to using a knife or baseball bat to get the job done.'

'A knife's as good as anything.' Reece's mind flooded with unwelcome images of Rome. 'Larson wasn't killed by someone desperate for a few quid.'

'He still had his wallet on him.' Jenkins explained. 'Several witnesses say the killer took his shoulder bag. Maybe whatever he had inside that was the motive for the hit?'

Brogan nodded. 'The truth is, we don't have any idea how many elite hitmen there are out there. Their type doesn't often get caught.'

'Are you saying we're likely to get nowhere with this?' Jenkins asked.

Reece answered before Brogan could: 'Not if I've got anything to do with it.'

'I'm afraid your sergeant's right,' Brogan said. 'The chances of you finding—'

'Can we move on?' Reece went to the evidence board. 'I want to know how we catch this killer, not fanny about with why it might be difficult.'

Brogan joined him. 'Okay, let's start at the beginning. There are firearms brought into the country by service personnel. It's an age-old problem. But these don't account for many. Not in the bigger scheme of things. The bulk of them arrive from central and eastern Europe. Concealed in vehicles using channel ferry and tunnel routes. They'll have been sent to Belgium and the Netherlands before transiting to the UK via France.'

'What about the so-called Dark Web?' Reece asked.

'That's real enough. But again, numbers-wise . . .' Brogan's face contorted as he gave the question more consideration. 'The Dark Web can be an option for people who aren't part of an organised criminal network. They can buy and sell single items there. Typically, these purchases enter the UK as parcel post.'

'You're kidding?' Jenkins stared, wide-eyed. 'They've got the local postie delivering guns?'

Brogan chuckled. 'Not knowingly. And not often, I'd imagine. But it does happen.'

'Bloody hell.'

'Then you have the gun club weapons and farmer's shotguns that go missing every year.'

'Those will have been reported?' Reece said. 'As part of the license conditions?'

'Yes, but many of them are never recovered.' Brogan put his hands in his pockets and came away from the evidence board. 'There's also the lone wolf working from home. They convert decommissioned weapons and even make their own bullets, if they're skilled enough. I'm not sure if what I've said so far puts you any closer to knowing who's involved.'

'Let's come at this from another angle,' Reece said. 'Let's ask ourselves *why* it happened.' He turned to Jenkins and Morgan. 'What else might Larson have been into? Did he owe money to the wrong crowd?'

'I know someone working in drugs,' Jenkins said. 'I can find out if he was known to them.'

Morgan nodded. 'And Ginge can do his usual wizardry on the bank account.'

'Did I hear someone bigging me up?' Ginge asked, bursting into the room, all limbs and a wide smile.

'Where have you been?' Reece asked.

'Peter Larson's post-mortem.'

'Oh, yeah. What came up?'

Jenkins put an arm around Morgan's neck and pulled her close. 'Most of his stomach contents if he's anything like Ffion.' She finished with a loud encore of retching sounds.

Morgan pushed her away. 'Stop it.' She slapped Jenkins's hand. 'You're an evil woman.'

'It was brilliant once I got into it,' Ginge said, laughing at them.

Morgan gawped. 'Are you for real?'

The young detective slid a leather strap off his shoulder and hung his satchel on the back of a chair. 'Doctor Frost even let me hold what was left of the brain.'

Morgan hurled her bag at him and reached between her legs for the waste bin. 'For Christ's sake, someone shut him up.'

'I hear the canteen's doing jelly and blancmange,' Jenkins said. 'I'll go and get us all a bowl, shall I?'

Morgan put her head in the bin and heaved.

'Can you lot remember we've got company,' Reece said. 'Ginge, this is Inspector Mike Brogan.'

Ginge shook Brogan's hand. 'I'm Owain Evans. Detective Constable.'

'Pleased to meet you, Owain.'

'Inspector Brogan is here to help with the firearms' side of things.' Reece was no less annoyed by the outsider's presence on the team. His statement was intended for more than Ginge's ears. It was a clear reminder to the AFO that his remit on the case was limited.

Ginge took a seat. 'While I remember, George reckons there's dog crap on his floor. You're taking liberties, boss.' Ginge blushed. 'George said that, not me.'

Jenkins swung on the back legs of her chair. 'How come there's dog doo-da behind the front desk?'

'The new puppy did it,' Ginge said. 'Cute little thing he is, too.'

'A puppy? With George?' Morgan looked deeply concerned. 'Who thought that was a good idea?' She turned to Jenkins and whispered: 'Did you take that bag of shit out of the boot of the car yesterday?' Jenkins shook her head and put a hand to her mouth. 'Me neither.'

'The dog's mine,' Reece said, sounding exasperated.

'Yours?' Jenkins and Morgan spoke like a well-scripted double act. They glanced at one-another.

Reece closed his eyes. He didn't want to be doing this. 'I found it this morning. It was going to get itself killed on the road outside the house.'

Jenkins brought the legs of her chair to rest on the carpet tiles. 'I didn't have you down as an animal lover.'

Reece looked surprised. Hurt, even. 'Why not?'

'No reason.'

'There must be a bloody reason. You wouldn't have said it otherwise.'

Jenkins looked away. 'Wish I hadn't now.'

Reece let her be. He took a marker pen and removed the top with his teeth. 'Right, Ginge. Post-mortem.'

Chapter 33

Jenkins found Mrs Larson sitting in a cramped hospital waiting room, accompanied by two bored-looking police constables. The woman resembled a cardboard cut-out of a real person. Speechless and bereft of any facial expression. She wore a plain beige dress. Not black. Jenkins was unsure if she should read anything into that. A pair of flat shoes completed, but in no way complemented the outfit.

'Afternoon,' Jenkins said, wishing she'd rehearsed something on the way over. 'I'm Elan. Do you remember me?'

Mrs Larson's hands fiddled with a clutch bag held in her lap. She nodded, though it was barely noticeable. 'Yes.'

'You got here okay?' Jenkins was floundering. The older woman was making nothing easy for her. 'It won't be long now,' Jenkins said, taking a seat and reaching for Mrs Larson's hand. She wondered how it must feel to bring a child into the world, showering it with love, instilling it with one's own ideals and morals, only to have it reject everything it's been taught and become a monster.

But was that the reality of Peter Larson's childhood? Such awful behaviours were very often self-perpetuating. Had the boy been loved and protected, or was he too a victim of sickening abuse? Jenkins had seen no evidence of a father figure at the house and wondered if he'd been sent on his way by a wife who'd refused to turn a blind eye to such things.

A hospital waiting room wasn't the place to ask such searching questions. But there *were* answers that needed to be had. Peter Larson deserved justice like anyone else.

'I know there were several serious threats made towards Peter,' Jenkins began, 'but was he in any other trouble that you were aware of?' Mrs Larson didn't answer and withdrew her hand. Jenkins didn't resist. 'Did Peter owe anybody money? Were there gambling debts? Did he ever mention being witness to something he shouldn't have been?' Mrs Larson's eyes moved. Not her head. Just her eyes. Jenkins took a breath. 'We're trying to piece together who would do this to your son and why.'

A tall, thin man entered the room after a single knock on the door. He wore green scrubs with a knee-length white coat over the top. He bore more than a passing resemblance to John Cleese. For an awful moment, Jenkins imagined him goose-stepping his way to the viewing room. It was a coping mechanism of sorts. Searching for humour in situations that were otherwise dark and distressing. She knew her colleagues in other emergency services did it all the time. How else would they be able to go home at the end of a shift to live out a normal existence with their families?

Mrs Larson stood. 'Peter is better off dead.'

Chapter 34

When Reece got back from the canteen, it didn't escape his notice that Ginge was avoiding all eye contact. The young detective constable was busy at his desk. He had his back to him; his left shoulder lowered to the side.

Reece surveyed the room. The door to his office was shut. He was certain he'd left it open before going downstairs for lunch. When he turned to ask why, Ginge lowered his head and put a hand against his ear.

Something was up. 'What's that smell?' Reece pushed on his office door. When only two strides inside, he stepped on something soft and slippery. 'Holy Christ!' He raised his foot and let it hang there while he stuck his head through the open doorway.

Ginge was gone. Nowhere to be seen. A mug of coffee left steaming on his desk. Curled up on the swivel chair in the office was the black-and-tan pup. It hadn't woken. Its legs were twitching as it chased cats—or something far less dangerous—in its sleep.

Reece removed the soiled shoe and went to the window and opened it. He took a few lungfuls of fresh air while he could. On his way back, he put his stockinged foot on a wet patch of carpet. He was on one foot again. The offending shoe held at an arms-length.

Jenkins appeared in the doorway, a finger and thumb squashing her nostrils flat. 'My God, what did you have for lunch?'

'It's not *me!*' He crouched to get a better look through the slatted blinds. 'Where's that lanky string of piss? Did you see him on your way in?'

'Who?'

'Who do you think?' Reece hopped through the room, using a filing cabinet to keep his balance. He looked for somewhere to put the sock and shoe. 'I'll have him back on the beat for this.'

Jenkins pointed when a whiskered face yawned over the top surface of the desk. 'Is that him? The puppy. Aw, he's lovely.'

By the time Reece realised what she meant, the dog was all over him. He dropped the shoe on his trouser leg – shit-side down. 'It's peeing on me!'

Jenkins doubled over and hung on the door, banging her chest, willing herself to breathe. 'Don't!' she shrieked. 'I'm wetting myself.'

The dog was just about welded to Reece. 'Help me, then. Oh, Jesus Christ, he's going again.'

Ffion Morgan's head came over Jenkins's shoulder. 'What's that horrible smell? Have you stepped in something, boss?'

Reece limped past in one shoe and a wet shirt. He prowled up and down the incident room, the wriggling animal held under his arm in a vice-like grip. '*Ginge!*'

Reece had since showered and changed into clean clothes. He'd calmed down and almost saw the funny side of the situation.

'George said he'd break my legs if I didn't go down and collect it pronto,' Ginge explained, still giving the DCI a wide berth.

Reece's eyes widened. 'Who are you most scared of – him or me?'

'George is a fair bit bigger than you are, boss.'

Reece lobbed a half-eaten biscuit at the young constable. 'I've obviously been far too soft on you.'

Ginge caught the biscuit one-handed and broke it in two. He shared one half with the puppy.

'What are you going to do with it?' Jenkins asked. 'You can't keep it.'

Reece leaned to stroke the back of the animal's neck. 'Why not?'

'You're at work most days. It wouldn't be fair for him to be stuck inside all that time.'

'When I move out to Brecon, I'll have far more outdoor space. I can even fence off a bit of the field for him to run about in.'

'That's then. What are you going to do in the meantime?'

'You could always get someone to pet sit,' Ginge suggested. 'I've seen people advertising on Facebook.'

Jenkins nodded. 'That's an idea. Pay someone else to have him during the day.'

Reece shook his head. 'I don't need Facebook. I know just the man.'

Chapter 35

Reece knocked on the back door of the Brecon farmhouse and went in without waiting to be invited. 'You're looking as lovely as ever, Ceirios.'

Yanto's wife blushed and dabbed her lips with the edge of a paper napkin. 'Brân.'

Yanto looked up from a lamb chop dinner, his fork already loaded with the next juicy mouthful. He returned it to the plate, untouched. 'What have you got there?'

Reece glanced behind him. Then turned to the front again. 'Where?'

Yanto folded a pair of thick forearms across the chest of a grubby Barbarians rugby jersey and sat up straight in his chair. 'You know what I'm on about.' He pointed, reaffirming the statement. 'And don't be trying to buy yourself any more time.'

'The dog, you mean?' Reece lifted the wriggling puppy and went slowly towards the dinner table. 'What I was thinking was—'

Yanto waved his arms. 'Nah, nah, nah. Not happening. End of.'

'He likes you,' Reece said, shoving the puppy closer. 'I can tell.'

Yanto pushed his plate to the centre of the table, knocking over a wooden pepper pot. 'I said it's not happening.'

Reece put the puppy down on the flagstone floor and watched it zig-zag about the kitchen with its nose pinned to the ground. It cocked its leg against the Aga stove.

'Christ Almighty!' Yanto got to his feet and hooked a thumb towards the back door. 'Outside, you. Now!'

'I don't know what else to do with him,' Reece said, as they crossed an area of gravel at the side of the farmhouse. 'I found him on the road in Llandaff.'

'Take him to a rescue. Don't bring him here to me.'

'I'm not doing that. Look at him.' The animal was oblivious to the discussion that would soon determine its fate. It chased sparrows as they took sand baths. 'They'll put him to sleep.'

Yanto took a swipe at the early evening midges. 'Brân, you're killing me. You know that, don't you?'

Reece gestured towards acres of land and hills. 'Look at all the space you've got here. You'd hardly notice him.' There was a long silence between them. 'A few days is all I'm asking. Until I can find something more long term.'

Yanto arched his back and scoffed at the clear sky. 'Where have I heard that one before?'

'Straight up, this time.' Reece promised. 'Scouts honour.'

'If I had a pound for every time you gave me that load of bull.'

'*Please.*' It was how it had been when they were kids. Reece knowing which buttons to press and which to stay well clear of. Yanto always came round in the end. He needed to make an almighty fuss beforehand. 'Want to hold him?'

'You named him yet?'

'I was thinking of calling him Gelert. After the dog in the Welsh legend.'

'I know the story,' Yanto said. 'Bloody stupid idea.'

'Why do you say that?'

'Naming it after a dog slaughtered by a medieval knight. Why would you want to do that?'

'Because Gelert got a hero's burial when the prince realised his mistake.'

'He still cut the thing in half, though, didn't he?' Yanto held the pup to his chest. 'Don't worry. I'm not letting this one name you after a butchered dog.'

'Come on then,' Reece said. 'What have you got as an alternative?'

Yanto gave it some thought. 'Redlar,' he proudly announced.

'I wanted something Welsh,' Reece said. 'That sounds more like a marauding Viking's name.'

'It's a strong name,' Yanto argued. 'If he's staying with me, then he's Redlar from now on.'

Reece knew when to give in. 'Redlar it is, then.'

When they got back inside the farmhouse, Ceirios had already scraped half of Yanto's dinner onto a spare plate. 'I thought you might be hungry, Brân.'

Yanto slid into his chair, glaring, and mouthing silent obscenities at the detective. 'Where have my lamb chops gone?' he asked in a high-pitched whine. 'I had three left when I went out the back.'

'I gave two of them to Brân,' Ceirios said. 'And the other one to the dog. Ooh, he's enjoying it, too. Look at him licking his lips.'

Yanto gave Reece a hefty kick under the table.

Chapter 36

The barn doors swung open after pudding and the best part of an hour's chit-chat. Reece joked that the creaking noise they made sounded like his knees before he got them going in the morning.

Once inside, Yanto heaved them closed again, using a short length of rope attached to a rusting bracket on each of them. 'Are you sure about this?' he asked, wiping his hands on the seat of his jeans. 'It's much bigger than that French thing you had.'

Reece was preoccupied, trying to keep Redlar in sight and out of harm's way. He called the dog's name, for all the good it did. 'Yeah, I'm sure.' He went over to the other side of the barn to collect him and stood him on a hay bale when he got back.

'They don't need that amount of fussing,' Yanto said in a gruff voice. 'You'll ruin him.'

Reece tickled Redlar under the chin. 'He's meant to be a pet, not a working dog.'

'They still don't need fussing.' Yanto caught hold of one corner of a dirty tarpaulin, poised to drag it off whatever was lurking beneath. 'Do something useful and grab the other side of this.'

Reece fought for floorspace when Redlar bounced in tight circles around him. 'Move,' he kept saying. 'I'm going to step on you.' Pulling in synch with Yanto, they wrestled the tarpaulin to the floor, both of them descending into fits of coughing when it threw up a cloud of dust. Reece banged his hand against the vehicle's bonnet once he had full sight of it. 'That's exactly what I'm looking for.'

It was a twenty-year-old Toyota Land Cruiser. Navy blue, with grey plastic moulding running along the lower part of the doors and up around the wheel arches. The trim was loose in places. Nothing Yanto couldn't fix with the slap of an open hand. The chrome bull-bar at the front came with a pair of bolt-on lights. Essential for winter commutes through dark country lanes in the National Park.

'Still sure now you've seen it?' Yanto asked.

'I should have got myself one of these years ago,' Reece said enthusiastically.

'You'll get rubbish mileage with the city driving you do,' Yanto warned. 'And parking's going to be a pig compared to that toy car you're used to.'

Reece made his way round the Toyota, opening and closing doors. The creased and cracked leather interior matched the dashboard moulding for colour. It smelled musty. A few hours outside with everything open would remedy that. There were dirty footprints on the mats. He got in the driver's side and gripped the steering wheel, grinning like a kid left to sit in their father's place. 'Redlar.' Reece whistled and patted his hip. 'Do you like it?' he asked, holding the dog's paws to the steering wheel. Redlar wagged his tail enthusiastically and barked. 'Looks like you do.'

Yanto watched from the open door. 'You soppy sod.' He turned and went to the far side of the barn and a desk that was full of clutter. Returning with a near-blunt pencil and a scrap of yellowed paper covered with oily thumbprints, he said: 'We'd best make a snag list and start ordering fluids and parts.'

'What does it need?' Reece had little clue himself.

'A full service and MOT,' Yanto said, kicking a tyre. 'The walls on these are cracking. You'll need new on all four sides, plus the spare.'

'What about the brakes?'

Yanto crouched and ran a finger over the disks. 'Lipped. I'd change those and you might as well put new pads on while you're at it.'

Reece tapped his chest. 'Me? I can't do any of this. I thought you'd sort it out when you had a minute?'

Yanto paced the barn, attacking the air overhead with his clenched fists. 'I knew it. I *bloody* knew it.'

'You'll have it finished in no time.'

'Brân, something's gotta give, man. I told you before, you're sending me to an early grave.'

'Stop being so dramatic. You said yourself, there's not much to do.'

Yanto folded the paper and tucked it away in his shirt pocket. 'You're a right royal pain in the arse.'

Reece cuddled Redlar. 'Hear that, boy? Uncle Yanto's going to fix our car.'

Chapter 37

THE DAY HAD BEEN a productive one. Marma Creed had visited several of her dead brother's business partners and saw fit to kill only one of them. The others had accepted—albeit reluctantly, in some cases—to honour the new terms offered.

Only Wiggley-Jones had taken the piss. Squirming while he denied creaming off profit that was rightfully Marma's, as Billy's heir. The funeral director had squirmed one hell of a lot more with a bag over his head. He'd gagged and flailed like someone with a cattle prod stuck up their arse. Marma had never trusted Jones. There was no such thing as honour among thieves. She'd warned Billy, for all the good that did him.

Her brother had long been stuck in the past. Living off old loyalties and friendships that quickly became one-sided once the knee injury weakened him. People had a habit of trying it on whenever they thought they could. Marma had offered to return home and co-run the Cardiff side of the business. Things were changing. The city was no longer a safe place to be a Creed. Billy had warned her to stay away.

The Creed family had grown up in abject poverty. Many living in Tiger Bay had. Maria was the youngest of three children. Roxie, Billy, then Maria. In that order.

The nickname Marma was self-applied and stuck with her through thick and thin. It was constructed using a mishmash of letters taken from her own name and the yeast extract, *Marmite.* 'You either loves or hates me,' she'd explained when asked. No one at school, or ever since, had dared admit to the latter. And so Maria Creed became known as Marma.

Their father was mostly absent from the children's lives. Repeatedly locked away in prison for thieving, fighting, or whatever else the police could nick him for. Those were the good times Marma remembered – whenever Charlie Creed was nowhere to be seen.

When not incarcerated, Charlie would think nothing of coming home drunk at night, demanding food, money, or sex from a mother who'd taken to drinking cheap gin like others did tea. Young Billy would sit on the windowsill, wrapped in grubby net curtains to keep himself warm, surveying the street outside like an early warning system. 'He's coming,' little Billy would shout on sight of his father at the entrance to the lane opposite.

Charlie would stop there to pee—not thirty yards from the house—an orange dot dancing in the dark as a cigarette hung from the corner of his mouth. He'd zip himself up with a shoulder pressed against the damp wall. Stare up and down the street, as though deciding whether to go home or return to the pub and drink until he could no longer stand or speak. With his decision made, he'd stagger across the road. Fists thrust deep inside the front pockets of a black, knee-length coat. Two steps sideways for every one taken in the correct direction.

Billy would slide off the windowsill and take Marma by the arm. They'd scarper upstairs and hide on the bare boards under Billy's bed with their hands held to their ears.

Charlie would bang the front door against the wall of the hallway, its handle carving an ever-deepening groove in the crumbling lath and plaster. 'Where's my supper?' he'd demand to know. Quickly followed by: 'I can't eat that shit!' He'd smash plates and put his knuckles to his wife's ribs, where the bruising didn't show.

There was screaming. Crying.

Crying. Screaming.

Banging. Thumping.

Thumping. Banging.

Marma would grab Billy's leg when he crawled from under the bed, pleading for him not to go downstairs. Billy never listened. Regardless of the severe beating he knew he'd get. He'd ride Charlie's back, but not like a *normal* father and son playing horses and jockeys. This was no game. There was no laughter in the Creed household. Only tears, pain, and broken dreams.

Billy was only twelve-years old when he killed their father. Marma, nine. Roxie knew nothing of the plan hatched by her two younger siblings and would likely have stopped them if she had.

Billy had lain face down, sobbing on the kitchen floor after his latest beating. His mother not daring to comfort him. No loving hugs for young Billy. "*It'll turn him into one of them poofs*," Charlie announced with spit and fiery eyes. Billy didn't blame his mother for doing as told. She'd earn herself another pasting if she went against her husband's word.

The Creeds had taken their last ever beating from Charlie. While the drunk slept in an armchair next to an open coal fire, Billy set him alight, using the contents of a brandy bottle prised from a clenched fist. By the time Charlie woke up, screaming his last, it was already too late. Billy had smiled and given his father the middle finger, keeping well out of reach until the man keeled over, dead.

They put the flames out using wet towels and positioned Charlie's corpse in the hearth. Billy was sent out into the street to call for help. There were no household telephones to be had in Tiger Bay. It mattered not. Billy was in no rush. He sat on a wall, kicking his feet and laughing his head off for a good five minutes before he could be bothered to knock on the first door.

Chapter 38

Reece stopped in the middle of the incident room to check his watch. It was a little before 7am and the cleaning staff had only just finished their night's work. The heady mix of coffee, body odour, and off-the-shelf fragrances were not yet in attendance. A weak sun peeked through the window on the other side of the room, stirring the gulls into a morning ballet on rising thermals. 'What are you doing in so early?' Reece asked.

Ginge got up from his desk and yawned. His creased shirt suggested he'd slept in it. 'Making amends for yesterday's cock-up with the dog.'

Reece took a sip of coffee and put the paper cup down on the nearest desk. It needed more sugar, not to mention heat. 'Forget it. I have.'

'George wasn't messing when he insisted I go down there and fetch the thing. I've never seen him so angry.'

Reece belly laughed. 'Scared you, did he?'

'I wouldn't want to get on the wrong side of him, that's for sure.'

Reece opened and closed desk drawers in a continued hunt for sugar. 'It's not the size of the man that matters. Being a big lump doesn't necessarily make you tough.' He gave up looking and stirred the pale contents of his cup with the blunt end of a Biro. That made it slightly more palatable. But not by much. 'What's at stake makes all the difference. Fighting for survival can turn the smallest man into a superhero.'

'You do all right in a scrap,' Ginge said. 'That's what people say.'

'People?'

'Other officers. Word at the station is to stay well clear when you lose your shit.'

Reece put a hand to his chin and gave it a slow scratch. 'I've said and done things I shouldn't have, that's for sure.' He felt saddened and was in no way proud of the reputation he had.

'I didn't mean only since your wife's death.' Ginge paused. He opened a case file and started turning pages. It was obvious he wasn't reading them.

'Go on,' Reece said. 'It's okay.' That surprised him. Twelve months earlier, there would have been a real risk of him breaking down and having to leave the room. As it was, his head was now clear enough to go there, if that was the direction the conversation was being steered.

The young detective closed the file and pushed it to one side. 'When you were rising through the ranks, you got into a lot of scrapes and scraps. That's what they say.'

'Most of them were Yanto's fault,' Reece joked. 'Now there's a man to fear.'

'I've only met him once,' Ginge said. 'He seemed friendly enough.'

'He must have liked you.' Reece leaned closer. 'A word of warning though: if you ever do get on the wrong side of him, run, and don't you dare stop.'

Ginge nodded like a plastic dog on a car dashboard. The to and fro motion stopped suddenly. 'I meant your hard man reputation at work. That and you not always doing things by the book.'

'Why are you asking me this? Has ACC Harris got you up to something?'

'Not at all, boss.'

Reece kept his eyes on the younger man. 'Are you sure?'

Ginge opened the file again. It was the wrong way up, but he didn't seem to notice. 'I shouldn't have asked. I'm sorry.'

'Will you stop saying that?' Reece pulled a chair. He sat down and wiped his nose with a loud sniff. 'I was schooled in policing by the likes of Idris Roberts. No-nonsense coppers who were out to get results. We kicked in doors and weren't afraid to dish out a bit when someone deserved it. I'm not saying that was right. It's just the way it was back then.'

'Do you think things have swung too far the other way?' Ginge asked. He put a hand to his belly when it grumbled loudly.

Reece puffed his cheeks. 'You had breakfast yet? Your guts sound like the drains in my first flat.'

Ginge pulled a box of Jaffa Cakes from his desk drawer and shook it. 'Do these count?'

Reece took it off him and tossed it into the open drawer. 'Come on. I'll buy us both a good fry-up in the canteen.'

Chapter 39

Archie's pleas for maternal assistance had gone unanswered. He'd fallen asleep with his cheek pressed against the hard headstone and awoken a few hours later with a neckache so bad he was frightened to move his head. Slowly, it loosened up enough for him to stop worrying.

He didn't dare risk going to work. And calling in to report his absence wasn't a viable option. That was how they kept finding him. By tracing his calls. The phone was a poisoned chalice. He went to the path that meandered through the cemetery, checked no one was watching, and smashed the handset underfoot. Not yet content, he removed the SIM and tossed it towards a pair of magpies, watching with interest as they fought over it. 'Let's see you find me now,' he said as the winner flew off with the broken SIM gripped in its beak.

He needed something to eat and drink. Not to mention access to a lavatory. There was a café only a couple of hundred metres from where he was. He checked his watch. It would be open by now.

Despite his change of clothes the previous evening, he felt grubby. His teeth were furry and his underarms smelled as bad as those of *Stinky Simmonds,* his overweight maths teacher at school.

The café was doing a roaring trade. Archie decided on a breakfast roll with lots of ketchup and a large coffee to go. With his order placed, he used the GENTS while he waited. It was a one toilet, one sink basin, type. He did what he needed to, then stood in front of a cracked mirror while he washed his hands and face. His eyes were red through lack of sleep, and he carried the stubble of a few days without shaving. He dragged his T-shirt over his head and did his underarms. That would have to do for now.

Someone tried the door. Archie watched the handle turn for a second time before he spoke. 'Give me a minute.'

'Hurry up. I'm busting.' It didn't sound at all threatening. The hitman was unlikely to bother with niceties once he had him trapped.

Archie would have gone out of the window had it been any wider than the arrow slit it was. 'I'm nearly done,' he said, smoothing the creases out of his T-shirt.

'Me too, mate. And it ain't gonna be pretty.'

Archie opened the door a few inches and peered out. A hand grabbed him by the arm and forcibly heaved him against the wall opposite. He was about to scream for his life when his *assailant* tossed a yellow helmet onto the tiles and hoicked his jeans down to his knees.

'You don't want to be standing there when this lot goes off,' the man warned. 'I've got toxic guts.'

Archie left him to it and collected his order on the way out. The walk to Coombsie's place was a little under two miles. Archie merged with the shadows thrown by the trees. Keeping off the main thoroughfare wherever he could. He was a fugitive. A man on the run.

Chapter 40

Coombsie wasn't at home. He was rolling about the boot of Marma Creed's car like a can of beans set free from a spilled bag of shopping. He hit his nose against the metal wheel arch and let out a muted grunt of complaint. His wrists were bound tightly behind his back and he could do nothing to stop himself bleeding into the carpet.

There were voices coming from the front of the vehicle. Competing with the thrum of rubber tyres on the asphalt road. Coombsie couldn't, with any certainty, make out what was being said.

He'd earlier responded to a heavy knocking at his front door, believing it to be Archie Ives come to say sorry for the umpteenth time. When he released the safety-chain from its runner, the door almost flew off its hinges. It hadn't been Archie standing there on his doorstep. It was a huge Arab fella with Marma Creed at his side.

The photograph on the wall of the snooker club hadn't fully captured the threat the woman carried in person. She was every bit as menacing as her brother.

One word from the front of the vehicle sounded loud and clear above the traffic noise. "*Kill*." It sent cold shivers through Coombsie. Was *he* the topic of conversation? If his hosts meant him no harm, then he'd be travelling on the rear seats, listening to music while sucking on a boiled sweet. As it was, they had him rolling side-to-side on a car mat with no clue where he was going or why. When he heard "*Kill*," repeated, he shrunk into a ball, trying to block out the voices.

Drawing his knees into his chest earned him little in the way of comfort. When the vehicle leaned while cornering, he was pushed against the metal tailgate. He arched his body away from it. The vehicle rolled the other way as it came out of the bend, thrusting him forward against the back of the rear seats, striking his nose for a second time.

He'd heard of kidnap victims being marched into the woods to be executed in graves dug with their own hands. Others had been dismembered and scattered in remote fields for the local wildlife to feast on their rotting remains.

But not usually ordinary folk like him.

The vehicle slowed and turned in a wide arc, coming to a full stop without warning. Coombsie hushed his breathing and listened for clues. There was no cooing of wood pigeons. No spade cutting its way through sod and grit.

That had to be a good thing.

A car door opened.

Then a second door.

Both slammed shut again. One behind the other. Like a volley fired from a pair of ships' cannons. There were voices. The words mostly lost on the wind. Then footsteps approaching in stereo. His captors were walking on both sides of the vehicle, offering him little chance of escape.

The boot mechanism clicked with the sound of someone cocking a handgun. The tailgate lifted open above him, letting in much needed fresh air. There was daylight, but not much. When Marma Creed reached for him, he turned his head the other way and squealed.

Chapter 41

ONCE SUITABLY FED AND watered at the station canteen, Reece and Ginge made their way upstairs. 'What did you find on the CCTV from the bus?' Reece asked once they'd exhausted his memories of the *good old days*.

'Not sure yet,' Ginge said. 'I'm still working through the witness statements, trying to match them to who sat where and so on.'

Reece gave him a pat on the back. 'If anyone can do it, I know you can.'

'That's the thing, boss. I'm struggling a bit.'

'Do you need another pair of eyes?' Reece asked. 'Ffion will be in soon. I'll have her come over and give you a hand.'

'There's definitely a missing statement. I've checked the number of passengers more times than I can count. It's not there.'

They climbed the last flight of stairs. Reece held the door open on their level and let his junior duck under his outstretched arm. 'Everyone at the scene was questioned by uniform.'

Ginge nodded. 'And you and Jenks spoke to the most reliable of them. Nineteen adults in total. Including the driver. Plus twelve pedestrians who got sight of the gunman arriving and leaving the scene.'

'What about the old man who was taken off to hospital?'

'I've accounted for him. It still doesn't tally up.'

'Are you sure?' Reece asked.

Ginge stopped in the doorway to the incident room. 'Let me show you something that's been troubling me all night.'

Reece clapped his hands to get everyone's attention. 'Listen up. Ginge is on to something.'

The detective constable went over to a viewing screen and pointed a remote control handset at it. The screen came to life without the usual flickering; the picture quality excellent. He rewound the colour images and turned to face the team when ready. 'Apologies if anyone has only just eaten,' he said, singling out Ffion Morgan. 'This gets a bit messy towards the end.'

She waved him off. 'Go for it.'

Reece sighed. 'We're waiting.'

Ginge thumbed the handset and gave a running commentary throughout. 'There's no sound, but with information taken from witness accounts, we can safely say the motorcycle arrives any time now.'

'Lime green,' someone called from the back of the room.

'That's what the majority of people said. We had two claim it was black. One red. But lime or bright green was the overall winner.'

'Why draw attention to himself?' Jenkins asked. 'That colour would have stuck out like a sore thumb in any line of traffic.'

Ginge looked at Reece. 'I've a theory for that, boss. Can I?'

'Go on.'

'Everything about this hit is unnecessarily over the top. The shooter choosing a lime green bike, when, as Jenks says, he could just as easily have used a nondescript one. And shooting a person on a bus in a busy street, instead of lying in wait somewhere quiet suggests—'

'That your shooter was sending a clear message to someone.' The interruption came from the back of the room. From the same person who had shouted out the colour of the bike.

All, including Reece, turned to look over their shoulder. It was Brogan and the ACC. Brogan raised a hand in apology. 'I didn't mean to interrupt. Carry on.' He and Harris stayed where they were.

Reece was the last person to face the front again. He nodded at his junior.

'I think Inspector Brogan might be right,' Ginge said. 'It looks like the shooter meant to draw as much attention to the killing as possible.'

'A terrorist?' asked one of the uniforms. 'That's what they do, isn't it? Go for all the exposure they can get.'

'Larson's talking to someone,' Morgan said, pointing at the screen. 'Who's that? Do we know?'

Jenkins said she thought they might be arguing.

Ginge looked momentarily flustered and didn't answer the uniform's question. 'I'm coming to that in a minute. Bear with me. The bike was taken from a back garden in Church Village sometime during the night. The owner only realised it was gone when he went to leave for work that morning.'

'Have we still not found it?' Reece asked.

'We know it used Penarth Road, before entering the Ely Trail, next to the river,' Ginge explained. 'Once it turns off there, we lose it. No more cameras.'

'That's a rough spot, right there,' Reece said. 'What about this argument, or whatever it was?'

Ginge restarted the recording. 'This is just prior to the bike arriving. Larson gets into a spat with this guy.'

'Is this the passenger you were telling me about?' Reece asked. 'The only one not to leave a statement?'

'I thought everyone was held at the scene?' Jenkins said, questioning the uniforms. A few of them shrugged in response.

'The pair of them were arguing over the seat, according to the nearest passengers.' Ginge's thumb alternated between the *pause* and *play* functions of the handset. 'This guy claimed he always sits in that particular seat and made a right fuss when Larson refused to move.'

'And look at the resemblance between the two of them,' Reece said. 'They could be brothers.'

'Are you thinking what I'm thinking?' Jenkins asked.

Reece nodded. 'The gunman got the wrong man. Larson wasn't the intended victim.'

'He's your back seat puker.' Again, Ginge glanced at Morgan. She was concentrating on the screen and not on him. 'Here he is, making his way down the aisle and off the bus. The external camera then shows him skirting round the other passengers.'

'He didn't wait,' Jenkins said. 'Look. He's making off down a side street before uniform turned up.'

Ginge closed the monitor screen. 'That's the owner of our missing statement right there.'

'I want to know who he is,' Reece said, getting to his feet. 'Who he is and where we find him.'

Chapter 42

MARMA CREED WASN'T MESSING about. She barked orders and dragged Coombsie out of the boot by a handful of his hair. He let out another high-pitched squeal and collapsed onto the concrete hardstand with a deep groan. Kahn gave him a swift kick to the ribs as he went past. It wasn't overly forceful, but did establish who was in charge.

Coombsie rose on unsteady legs when told to do so. Marma clamped her hand to the back of his neck and steered him towards the side entrance of the snooker hall. An overhead bulb sensed their presence and blinked into life, illuminating the hallway with bright white light. He lost his balance as they reached the first tread of the stairs and slumped against the wall.

Marma pulled him off it and propelled him forward, sending him stumbling to his knees. The ritual repeated itself until they reached the top, where she bent him over the drop to the hallway below. 'Can you fly?' she asked without a trace of humour.

Coombsie shrunk away from the edge. 'Please. Don't.'

Marma slapped him hard against his right ear. 'We're only just getting started,' she said when he cried out in pain. 'You'll need to be a braver man than that.'

Kahn opened the door to the snooker room and let them pass. Marma flicked the light switch. A half-dozen neon tubes stuttered overhead. One of them illuminated along only a third of its length, the rest of the tube glowing a dull orange.

Marma directed him between the tables, towards the office, and made him sit down. When he tried, she pulled the chair away, sending him crashing to the floor. He hit his head against the leg of the table, pushing it from its position at the centre of the room.

Kahn grabbed him by his clothing and lifted him onto the chair. Marma was busy fiddling with a TV monitor. The monitor came to life, displaying grey images of what looked to be the hallway at the foot of the stairs. There were three white lines of interference running across the width of the screen, each of them travelling slowly from top to bottom.

'You're going to like this,' Marma said, positioning the monitor for Coombsie to get a better look. Two figures came into view. One of them carrying a cue case. 'That's you,' she said, tapping the glass. 'Agree?'

Coombsie nodded and chose not to speak.

Marma thumbed the remote control, making everything on the screen move in treble-time. She twisted to look at him. 'And then there's this guy. He came back after my Billy and the boys left.'

Coombsie groaned as he watched Archie Ives enter the snooker room all alone. The fuckwit even looked directly into the camera.

'Who is he?' Marma asked.

Coombsie was slow to answer and buckled when Kahn drove a fist into the same ribs that had only minutes earlier taken the kick. Coombsie gripped them and sucked air through his teeth.

Marma held out her hand. 'Knife.'

Coombsie sank in his chair. 'Please.' The blade twisted against his lips, drawing blood.

'The next thing coming out of that mouth of yours is going to be a name or your tongue.' Marma winked. 'Your choice.'

Coombsie lowered his head. 'Archie Ives.'

'A friend of yours?'

'Not anymore.'

'That's good to know.' Marma released the pressure on the knife and sped the recording on to the bit when Archie wandered into the office and lifted Billy Creed's journal off the desk. The recording ended there. 'Because you're going to help me find whatever that was.'

Chapter 43

Reece was informed that the press room was ready and waiting for him. He put on his suit jacket and straightened his tie. Taking a file and paper coffee mug from his desk, he stepped round the stained carpet tiles. The smell hadn't yet fully gone and he couldn't with any honesty claim the cleaning fluid used by the housekeeping staff had made it any better. The window was already open. He went over and pushed it another couple of inches.

They made their way down the stairs, coffee in hand, Jenkins walking on one side of him. 'I'm hopeful we'll soon have a name for our absent commuter,' Reece said, pulling on the heavy fire door at the bottom of the stairwell. He ushered Jenkins through ahead of him and left the door to squeak closed behind them.

He gave George a wave; the file in his hand bending like a sapling in the wind. Only when it threatened to fall open and deposit its contents on the floor did he lower his arm. 'Catch up for a chin-wag later?' he asked.

The desk sergeant waved back. In his hand was a half-eaten scotch egg. 'Righto. You can give me an update on Redlar.'

Reece stopped where he was. 'That reminds me. You're not off the hook yet for that prank you pulled with Ginge.'

George pointed to the floor behind his desk. 'We're at one all, as far as I'm concerned.'

'Fair point,' Reece conceded. 'But yours was a fair bit easier to clean than mine. The office still smells like a public bogs.'

'I wouldn't know,' George said, pulling a bemused looking junior into view. 'I had this one do it. Character building for him,' he said, giving the younger man a playful shove. The junior disappeared from sight. 'They're not a patch on us at that age,' George continued.

'Tell me about it.'

Jenkins nudged Reece's arm. 'I hope you're not including me in that?'

Reece pulled a face. 'You've started something now, George.'

Jenkins dared either of them to keep their conversation going.

'I'd best be off,' the desk sergeant said, munching on the remains of his Scotch egg. 'I can see you're busy.'

Chief Superintendent Cable took her place at the centre of the table.

She tapped her watch. No one else in the room would have noticed. Reece did and was meant to. He ignored her and went over to speak to someone at the back of the room. Cable sent Jenkins to fetch him.

'I needed a word with Maggie Kavanagh,' Reece said, settling next to the chief super.

Jenkins sat down and leaned forward on the edge of her chair. 'It's a shame Mrs Larson refused to join us. I think the public would have had sympathy with her.'

'I'm sure you tried your best,' Cable said.

'It's like she's pretending her son never existed.'

'It's a pity he ever did,' Reece said, staring out into the room. 'The bastard should have been strangled at birth.'

Cable gave him a look of warning. 'Promise me you won't say anything like that during the press conference.'

Reece showed his crossed fingers. 'I promise.'

'I mean it.'

He faced the front again and watched the goings on in the room. There were journalists just about everywhere. Talking. Laughing. Even eating, in some cases. There were sound checks. Lighting checks. Checks of makeup and breath. Events like these were always something of a free for all. *A day at the zoo* was how he often referred to them.

'The images of the missing passenger are pretty good,' Jenkins said. 'I'd be surprised if someone doesn't come forward to tell us who he is.'

'That's why we're here.' Reece wrung his hands. 'Can we get started now?'

Cable called the room to order and carried out general housekeeping instructions.

Reece yawned and rubbed his eyes during most of the preamble. 'The victim's name, as you already know, was Peter Michael Larson,' he said when it was his turn to speak. A twenty-five-year-old local man.'

'Was this an act of vigilantism?' someone shouted. 'The victim was a convicted paedophile, wasn't he?'

'Is the abused boy's father still a person of interest?' asked another.

Reece stood. Cable pulled on his sleeve. 'We can do this one of two ways,' he said. 'You won't like the second.' He lowered himself slowly, alternating his stare between the two offenders.

'Why?' Cable asked without moving her mouth. 'Just for once. Be nice to them.'

'You're lucky I didn't go over there and smack their sodding heads together.'

'*Reece.*'

'If we let that pair carry on as they are, they'll have the public celebrating Larson's death instead of trying to help us find his killer.'

'I'll deal with it,' Cable said. She called everyone to order for a second time. With further instructions clearly communicated, she handed back to Reece.

'We know the killer used a bright green Kawasaki Ninja,' he said. 'That's a high-performance sports bike to the likes of you and me.' Still images of the exact make and model appeared on the screen behind him. 'We know it headed along Penarth Road after the shooting. Maybe the killer lives locally.' He shrugged. 'It's more likely he was trying to avoid any surveillance cameras in the area. We're appealing to anyone who might have seen this bike. Did the rider lift his visor while he waited at a traffic light? Was there anything distinctive about his leathers or mannerisms?' None of the witnesses at the crime scene had mentioned any such thing, but it was worth a try. 'This is where we really need your help,' he said, waiting for Ginge to load the images of the missing passenger. 'Who is this man? Someone must recognise him.'

Chapter 44

Archie had long since given up banging on Coombsie's front door. Squinting through the letterbox, he called his friend's name repeatedly, but to no avail. He put his head against the downstairs window, looking for any movement inside. He checked the bedroom windows. Front and back. Nothing. Coombsie was either doing an impressive job of hiding from him, or was simply not at home.

Archie came away. His movements were drawing the attention of neighbours. Some peered through gaps in their curtains. Others opted for standing on doorsteps, blatantly watching him. Only one of them approached him directly.

He couldn't blame them. He was beginning to look like he lived on the streets. Actually, he *was* living on the streets. They must have thought he was gearing up to break in and squat. 'I'm worried about Daniel,' he said, backing away from the neighbour. 'Have you seen anything of him these past few days? Do you know if he's okay?'

'Clear off or I'll call the police,' was the only response he got.

He wondered if his friend had fallen foul of the same people he had? Coombsie knew things about Billy Creed. More than mere rumours, as it turned out. He had insider knowledge that might very well have got him killed.

Archie wished he could turn back time. If his journalistic career was destined for nothing more interesting than teeny-bopper beauty pageants and thefts from village allotments, then so be it. What he was currently mixed up in was some serious shit. He had no way of knowing what was going on. Or who was involved.

If he was to track down the perpetrators and save himself from certain death, he'd need a new phone to make calls when he needed to. One that wasn't registered to him. He counted the money in his trouser pocket. Luckily, that hadn't gone AWOL, along with his passport. He'd get two phones. Models that were throwaway cheap.

He found a small independent store not too far from where he was. They were likely to ask fewer questions and would be grateful for the passing trade. The door opened with an electronic buzz to alert the owner. He went in and couldn't help but look over his shoulder as it closed behind him. He needed to relax. He'd already caught the attention of the Indian couple standing behind the serving counter. 'Morning,' he said, initiating a response in kind from both of them. 'I'm after a phone.' It wasn't a daft statement. There were rows of cases and other bits and pieces on offer.

'What did you have in mind?' the man asked. 'We have the latest iPhone—'

'The cheapest you've got,' Archie interrupted. The owner looked disappointed. 'Two of them,' Archie said with a forced smile. If the couple thought they were having a bad day, then they should step into his shoes for a few hours. 'With ten pounds credit on each.'

The handsets looked like toys. 'Do they come with a charger?' he asked. The shop owner rifled through one of the boxes and confirmed that they did. It was a stiff length of lead with an integrated plug. 'No lightning charger?'

'For this money?' The man shook his head at his wife.

'Fair enough.' Archie pulled the boxes towards him. 'How much?'

The woman took them back to her side of the counter and scanned their barcodes. 'Forty pounds each,' she said. 'Eighty pounds in total.'

Not the *throwaway* price he'd been hoping for. 'Is that the best you can do? I did buy more than one.'

The couple discussed it in a language Archie didn't understand. 'Seventy-five,' the man said. 'That's the best I can do.'

'With credit on both, right?'

The man nodded.

Archie thumbed seven plasticky banknotes onto the counter. They refused to flatten out, no matter how hard he tried. He reached inside his trouser pocket and paid the rest with an assortment of coins. 'There's another ten pence for a bag.' He took one charger and both phones, and left the other bits and pieces, including the boxes on the countertop. 'Are the sims ready to go?'

'Yes,' said the store owner. 'But I'd charge the handsets soon, if I were you.'

Archie thanked the couple and left. It was so hot outside. Like the balmy summers of yesteryear described by his late mother. "*We always had snow in winter. Droughts during the summer months,*" she'd tell him, staring into some distant memory.

Archie didn't believe her, but never said anything to spoil it.

He found a dwarf wall beneath the overhanging branches of a sycamore tree. Its gigantic roots had lifted and split a section of tarmac on the pavement. He had to be careful not to catch his foot on it and trip. The temperature was several degrees cooler now that he was out of the sun's glare. When he started one of the phones, its battery icon flashed. He wasn't completely sure, but took that to mean he might manage part of a call before it gave up on him completely.

At first, he couldn't remember Coombsie's number. Why would he? He'd never previously had to manually input it. He wracked his brain and tapped his foot. When that didn't work, he turned and swung his legs over the other side of the wall. It was only when he entered a form of daydream state that the number came to him. The keypad was clunky. The buttons so close together he twice dialled incorrectly and had to start over again. All the while checking the environment for potential threats. 'Daniel?' he asked when his call was answered. 'Are you there?' There was silence on the other end of the line. 'Answer me.' Archie held his thumb over the *end call* button. This felt unnervingly familiar. 'Your last chance before I go.'

'Where are you?' It was Coombsie.

'Thank God. You're not dead.'

'No.'

Archie thought that an odd response. Coombsie hadn't questioned why he'd said such a thing. 'Is everything okay?'

'Where are you?'

'I could ask the same. I went round your house earlier and . . .' Archie paused. His friend was acting strangely. Even making allowances for him still being pissed off, Coombsie didn't sound himself. 'Are you with someone?' Archie asked.

'No.'

'Are you sure?'

'Yes.'

This didn't sound right at all. Archie slid off the wall and paced up and down a short stretch of pavement. 'I've got to ask you this. Have you been speaking to anyone about me? Anyone at all?'

'Like who?'

'I don't know. The police?' He cupped a hand over his mouth and whispered into the handset: 'That dead guy on the bus. That was supposed to be me.'

'Right.'

'Is that the best you can do? My world's gone to shit. I've got the police trying to kill me because of something I overheard at Billy Creed's place.'

'Can we meet?' Coombsie asked?

Archie wiped a hand across his forehead. 'Are you sure you're all right?'

'Yeah. I'm sorry we argued.'

'Me too, mate. Life's too short.' Wasn't that the truth.

'So, we can we meet up?'

This time it was Archie who delayed his answer. 'Where?'

'Come over to my house. Have a few beers and you can tell me all about it.'

That didn't appeal to Archie one bit. 'I want to be somewhere with lots of people,' he said. 'Like in front of the main gates of the castle.'

Chapter 45

It was Maggie Kavanagh who gave them Archie's name. Away from the other journalists. Knowing better than to throw chow to the sharks. She waited until Reece was packing up his things and approached the long table, dry-smoking a lipstick-stained cigarette.

Reece stopped what he was doing and made eye contact without raising his head any more than he needed to. 'That's it, Maggie. We're all done here.'

Kavanagh brought an end to her latest bout of coughing. 'That's where you're wrong. How about you and me go upstairs for a quick one?'

Reece pinched the bridge of his nose. 'Maggie.'

Kavanagh leaned towards Jenkins. 'Look how red he's gone.' She reached for Reece's cheek. 'You should be so lucky. I meant for a cuppa and a chat.'

He grabbed his suit jacket from the back of a chair and hurried towards the exit. 'I really don't have time for this.'

'I'll make it worth your while.' Kavanagh pouted her heavily made-up lips. 'There he goes again, look. Like a beetroot every time.'

Reece came back and leaned across the table. 'What do you want?'

They used the lift to get upstairs. It was either that or carry Kavanagh's corpse most of the way. 'You're not smoking in here,' Reece said, holding his office door open.

'What in hell's name have you been eating?' the reporter asked with a hand pressed to her face. 'You need to get yourself checked over by a doctor. Smells like you're rotting from the inside out.'

'It's not me,' Reece said, settling into his squeaky swivel chair.

Jenkins followed them in. 'He's got himself a dog.' Reece shook his head, but it was too late. The secret was out.

'Dog?' Kavanagh was laughing. And coughing. 'You've got yourself a dog. *You?*'

Reece closed his eyes. 'Why shouldn't I?'

'Because you're a miserable git, that's why.' Kavanagh took another deep drag from the unlit cigarette. 'The poor animal will be on antidepressants before he knows what's hit him.' She turned to Jenkins. 'Is it a him or a her?'

Jenkins turned to Reece. 'Can't say I know.'

'It's a *he.* Or whatever they call them these days,' he answered. 'Maggie, I'm losing the will to live.'

'All right. I know. Dry your powder.' Kavanagh jerked her chair closer to the desk. 'I know who your missing passenger is.'

'Really?' Jenkins leaned and closed the door.

Reece told her to open it again and made a mental note to submit a maintenance request for new carpet tiles. He took a pen and hovered its nib over a piece of scrap paper. 'Fire away.'

'Not so quick.' Kavanagh took another drag on the cigarette. 'I want an exclusive.'

'A night in a cell downstairs is what you're getting if you don't stop messing me about.'

Kavanagh tutted. 'It's Archie Ives.'

'And you'd know this, how?' Reece asked.

'He's a junior reporter at the Herald. A bit wet, but his heart's in the right place, bless him.'

'Address?'

'Dammed if I know,' Kavanagh said. 'You'll have to contact the newspaper for that.'

'Any idea why someone would want him dead?'

'Like I said, he's a bit wet.'

'*Maggie!*'

Kavanagh shrugged. 'I've no idea.'

Reece stood and spoke to Jenkins. 'Go book us out one of those pool cars.'

'Don't forget the exclusive,' Kavanagh called after him. 'It's the least you can do for little old me.'

Chapter 46

By midday, Reece had an address for Archie Ives and an appointment with the Herald's editor booked for later that afternoon. He pointed to the open bedroom window in Glenroy Street. 'Looks like he might be at home after all.'

Jenkins knocked on the front door and rang the bell. 'I wouldn't bet on it.' She went to the downstairs window and held her head against the glass. 'It's a right mess in there.'

'Any sign of him?'

'Not that I can see.'

'That gives us justification to force an entry.' Reece nodded to the officer carrying the *Big Red Key*. 'Open it.' The officer hammered the short length of steel against the wooden door. 'Good man,' Reece said, entering after only two strikes.

The hallway was thickly carpeted with paper flyers for local supermarkets and takeaways. The stairs were bare.

'Someone's in the middle of decorating,' Jenkins said, nodding at the wall.

Reece was first into the living room. Even with the curtains open, the place had a depressingly dull feel to it. 'It's hard to know if this is a crime scene or not,' he said, standing amongst the clutter.

Jenkins followed him in. 'I'd say someone's had a good rummage about. Why else would all the drawers and cupboards be open?'

'Get a forensic team sent over.' Reece went through to the kitchen and viewed it from the safety of the open doorway. 'It's no better out here. Worse, in fact.' Jenkins was already on the phone to Sioned Williams.

Reece ventured further in, carefully picking his way through the kitchen. He stepped on a pedal bin and looked inside. There wasn't much to see in there. Donning a pair of gloves, he squatted and had a poke about.

'Anything of interest?' Jenkins asked, putting her phone away.

'Nope.' Reece tried the handle of the back door. 'It's not locked.'

'Looks like Ives might have left in a hurry.'

Reece raised his gaze to the ceiling. 'We haven't checked upstairs yet.'

Jenkins copied him. 'Do you think the gunman realised his mistake and came here looking to finish the job?'

'Peter Larson's name was only officially released at the press conference.'

'But some of those reporters knew beforehand,' Jenkins said. 'A leak at the station?'

'No change there,' Reece told her. He knew it was pointless them even trying to pursue that angle. The press wouldn't give up their sources. Not without a court order forcing them to do so. He led the way upstairs and pushed on the first door they came to on the landing. There wasn't much in the way of free space available. He edged his way into the spare bedroom. There was a bed-settee pushed against one wall. A small desk and an overturned chair. There was a dust-free rectangular space on the desk, large enough to accommodate a laptop.

'What is it?' Jenkins asked, squeezing around him. 'Jesus.'

'I'd say it was more the devil himself.'

'Looks like our Archie Ives was a Billy Creed fanboy.'

'Maggie did say he wanted to be a crime reporter.'

Jenkins moved from one newspaper clipping to the next. 'If he was hoping to get anything on Creed, then he's a few weeks too late.'

'Maybe he already got his story,' Reece said thoughtfully.

'Could that have put him in the line of fire, do you think?'

Reece shrugged. 'It's an angle we haven't explored.'

Jenkins came away from the clippings and gave him her full attention. 'Come on then. Run with it. What's your best guess?'

Reece went to the window and looked along the length of the back garden. 'What if Ives somehow got close to Creed's business and started asking questions in the wrong places?'

'But like you said, Creed's gone. What would it matter?'

'It matters if what Ives discovered implicates others in some serious crime.'

'And that's why they'd want to silence him?'

'Exactly. But the million-dollar question is: who stands to lose the most by Ives knowing what he does?'

Chapter 47

'Relax, we're police officers.' Reece stepped off Archie Ives's doorstep and presented his warrant card as proof. 'And you are?'

'I live two houses up.' The neighbour pointed in case the detectives were struggling to work it out for themselves. 'Can't believe you lot came back for a smashed window?'

Reece held a hand to his forehead, shielding his eyes from the sun. 'Say again.'

'Geoff's car. Someone put the window through. Kids if you ask me.'

'Who's Geoff?' Reece asked.

'Next door down.' Again, the man pointed. 'He swore blind the thief ran off waving a gun.' He motioned like he was holding a glass of something to his mouth. 'Likes a drink, does Geoff.'

Reece lowered his hand and squinted. 'A gun?'

'Not that your lot took much notice. They reckoned it was more likely to have been a phone he was carrying.' The neighbour shifted position, standing with one foot on the road, the other on the pavement, making him look bandy-legged. 'I'm with them on that. There can't be many guns round here.'

'You *do* know there was a shooting on City Road a couple of day's back?' Jenkins asked.

'Hang on a minute,' Reece interrupted. 'There were police officers in attendance?'

The neighbour nodded. 'A van full of them. All helmets and machine guns.'

Reece glanced at Jenkins. 'An armed response team.'

'If that's what you call them,' the neighbour said. 'And some miserable so-and-so from CID.'

'Do you remember his name?' Reece asked.

'He flashed one of those cards you've got. I can't remember what was on it, though.'

'What did he look like?'

'You all look the same to me. Suit, shirt, tie.'

'Get Ginge onto it,' Reece told Jenkins. 'And let the people at the newspaper know we're going to be a few minutes late.'

It was still little more than a hunch. An irritating niggle that refused to go away. Reece needed to see the car with the broken window. He let Jenkins drive while he gave thought to what they knew so far. Things were slowly clicking into place. Archie Ives was the intended victim, not Peter Larson. Reece now knew that with absolute certainty. Ives knew it too. That's why he'd fled the scene after the shooting.

The motive was something Reece hadn't fully worked out as yet. But he was satisfied it had something to do with Billy Creed's death and those involved in it. Even from the grave, Creed was messing with his head. 'Sorry. What did you say?'

'The dog?' Jenkins asked. 'How's he settling in with Yanto?'

'He's having a whale of a time.'

'He's obviously forgiven you for leaving him there?'

'Pretty much.'

'But you're going to have him back?'

'Just as soon as I'm living out in Brecon myself.'

'I can't believe you're actually going to move out there.'

'It'll do me good,' Reece said. 'All that fresh air and beautiful scenery. Besides, I'll be closer to Anwen and Idris.'

Jenkins turned off the main carriageway. They weren't too far from the garage and Geoff's car. 'You and Yanto are good friends.' There was an emptiness in the tone of her statement.

'We're more like brothers. Always have been.'

'I wish I had someone like him,' Jenkins said. 'A friend I could go to if needed.'

Reece couldn't ever remember hearing her speak of close friends. 'You and Ffion get on well.'

Jenkins gave way to a cyclist. For once, Reece didn't hurl abuse at the man in Lycra. He did tut, though. 'It's not the same,' Jenkins said. 'Ffion's a colleague.' She took one hand off the steering wheel and grabbed Reece's arm. 'I love her to bits and all that. But it's not the same as having a real friend you've grown up with.' She returned her hand to the wheel. 'Does that make sense?'

Reece went back to people watching. 'I didn't have you down as the lonely type?'

'I'm not lonely.'

'What then?'

'It doesn't matter.'

'Is everything all right?' Reece asked.

Jenkins wiped a tear from the corner of her eye. 'Hay fever, that's all.'

Chapter 48

HIGHSTREET GARAGE WAS wedged into a space at the far end of a narrow lane riddled with potholes. Its name was professionally written in black paint on a once-white background.

'Pull over,' Reece said, indicating a space in front of a recovery vehicle.

'I'll never get it in there.'

He took another look. 'Swing the front end in and leave the arse sticking out.'

'It's still too tight,' Jenkins said, inching their Vauxhall Astra past the lorry.

'Trust me. It'll be all right.' Reece had his door open before the car came to a full stop. 'It's not like we're abandoning it to go to the beach for the day. If they want it shifted, they'll know who to ask.'

Jenkins put the car in reverse and gave it her best shot. 'What do you think?'

'Looks good to me.' With the car parked—its arse-end sticking out—they crossed the forecourt in front of an open shuttered area. There was an employee squatting to change a car tyre. Another stood under a vehicle supported by a lift. He was draining oil into a bowl on a tall stand.

'Who's in charge?' Reece asked, with his ID in hand.

The man with the air gun repositioned a long length of rubber hose. 'Tony's in the office. It'll be him you want.'

Reece nodded and went in search of the proprietor. 'Are you Tony?' he asked no sooner had he entered. There were several calendars pinned to the drab walls. Mostly of Formula 1 and rally car scenes. There was a yellowed photograph of a family, as well as a crayon drawing of a rainbow. The tiled floor was chipped and cracked. One of the walls was missing a length of skirting board. Tony wasn't ploughing much of his profit into the décor.

'Guilty as charged.' The owner was dressed in a navy one-piece overall, unbuttoned to reveal a hairy chest and a Saint Christopher medallion hanging from a chain. He took his feet off the desk and put a half-eaten pasty to one side. 'What can I do you for?' he asked, wiping his mouth on his sleeve.

Reece swapped his ID for a scrap of paper with a registration number scrawled on it. 'Have you still got that car here? It's a grey Ford Mondeo.'

Tony nodded. 'The driver's window was put through.'

'You've not touched it yet?' Reece asked.

'Only to get it on and off the truck.' Tony was beginning to look worried. 'What's this about?'

'Why didn't you fix it at the property?' Jenkins asked. 'Simple enough job these days, isn't it?'

'The insurance company wanted the locks changed as part of the settlement.'

'But you've not started the work yet?' Reece repeated.

'The parts are out of stock. It's going to be another couple of days before they come in.'

'I want that vehicle impounded,' Reece told Jenkins. 'Every inch of it needs a good going over.'

Chapter 49

'How did the newspaper react to you telling them we'd be late?' Reece asked as he negotiated the midday traffic.

'The editor's secretary said it wouldn't be a problem.' Jenkins checked her watch. 'We're only twenty minutes behind time.'

'Fair enough.'

'You haven't forgotten about tonight?'

Reece had. 'Remind me.'

'I did. Yesterday.'

'Remind me again. You know how I still forget things.'

'You don't listen in the first place. That's your problem.' Jenkins huffed. 'You're supposed to be coming over for drinks and something to eat. Ffion and Ginge will be there as well.'

'Aw, that. Look. I was going to—'

'You promised.'

'No, I didn't.'

'Yes, you did. Ffion was a witness.'

Reece gripped the steering wheel. He didn't need a telling off. 'She'll say anything you tell her to. Thick as thieves, you pair.'

Jenkins folded her arms. 'Please yourself. I knew you wouldn't come.'

'Don't be so touchy.'

'One evening. That's all I asked. The team together. Letting off steam and having a laugh. Why couldn't you do that for me?'

'Because I'd spoil it for everyone.'

'Spoil it. How?'

'I haven't done that sort of thing in a long while. Not since . . .' He couldn't finish the sentence.

'Now's the time to start up again.' Jenkins adjusted her seat belt. 'Bring Miranda along. It would be lovely to see her.'

Reece took his foot off the accelerator pedal, a gap opening between them and the vehicle ahead. 'Is that what this is about? You and Ffion trying to set me up on a date?'

'Don't be daft.'

'She's married, anyway. I've met her husband.'

'That was her brother.'

'How do you know?'

'She told me about it.'

Reece took his eyes off the road. 'When?'

'What's with the twenty questions? When the two of us got talking at the hospital.'

Reece tapped the accelerator pedal. 'She wears a wedding band.'

Jenkins nodded. 'Her mother's.'

'On her ring finger?'

Jenkins opened her arms wide. 'Ask *her*, not me.' They didn't speak again until they'd entered the underground car park from the rear of the South Wales Herald building. 'They've given us bay three in the visitor section,' Jenkins said.

Reece grunted and searched for it.

They shook Donald Breslin's hand in turn; Reece introducing them both. 'Apologies for being late,' he said. 'You know how it is.'

The editor said he did and showed them to a leather sofa. 'No problem at all. Tea, coffee, or can I get you something cold?'

'Coffee would be good,' Reece said, sitting down. It wasn't as comfortable as it looked. But was very expensive if the rest of the office was anything to go by. He estimated his own would fit in there a dozen times over. There were white marble floor tiles and walnut panelling. It smelled of freshly cut flowers and not of festering dog shit.

'What about you, sergeant?'

'Nothing for me, thank you.' Jenkins gave Reece one of her *happy now?* looks.

He ignored her. 'Did Maggie mention why we wanted to speak with you?'

'Only briefly.' Breslin brought a coffee over and handed it to Reece. 'Something about Archie Ives?'

'That's right. A junior reporter, isn't he?' Reece asked, stirring in two heaped spoons of brown sugar. He took a sip. The coffee was good. Very good.

'He *was*.' Breslin went back to the percolator and fixed himself an espresso. 'Can I get you a biscuit to go with that?' Reece declined the offer. 'Archie hasn't been in for the past couple of days,' Breslin said. 'We assumed he's decided to leave without giving due notice.'

Reece took another sip of his coffee. 'Why would he do that?'

Breslin took a seat opposite and sat with his cup and saucer held between open knees. 'Archie was angry with me the last time we met. He didn't say so exactly, but I could tell.'

'Can I ask why?'

'He came to me with a fanciful story about there being a rogue element among the local police. Officers who'd protected Billy Creed for their own financial gain. The same officers Archie now claimed to be responsible for the man's death.'

'Did he mention any names?' Jenkins had her pocketbook and pen at the ready.

'I'm afraid not,' Breslin said. 'Archie fancies himself as the next Maggie Kavanagh. Only, Maggie's not ready to retire and hang up her typewriter just yet.'

'When did you have this conversation?' Reece asked.

'The week before last, maybe.' Breslin sat up straight. 'The morning we knew Billy Creed was dead. Archie was adamant Maggie's story was flawed.'

'Did he give you any proof?'

'There was nothing but promises and fanciful claims. I wasn't going to run with that.'

'I thought that's how newspapers worked?' Jenkins said. 'Get the story out. Then go looking for something to back it up.'

Breslin lowered his cup. 'Not this one.'

Reece finished his coffee and looked for somewhere to put his cup and saucer. Breslin stood and took it from him. 'Do you know where we might find Archie? He's not at home. We've been there.'

Breslin poked his head through the office door and spoke to his secretary. He left it open when he returned; a clear indication the detectives' time with him was drawing to a close. 'Sandra will get hold of Archie's line manager. They'll do all they can for you.'

Reece stopped in the doorway and turned to ask: 'Have you ever heard anything like this before?'

'There are always rumours,' Breslin said. 'But I expect you'd already know that, Detective Chief Inspector?'

Reece did. Over the years, he'd started several of them himself.

Chapter 50

Reece heard laughter. He knocked on the front door and let himself in when it inched open. 'Hello.' He moved sheepishly through the hallway. When he reached the living room, there was music and the sound of rattling crockery.

'Hey, the boss is here.' Ginge was over by the fridge. He had one hand inside, like a child caught helping itself to a forbidden midnight feast. 'Jenks. I said the boss is here.'

Jenkins appeared from the garden, wiping her hands on a tea towel. 'Look what the cat dragged in. Or should that be, *dog?*'

'I never said I wasn't coming.'

'You're full of shit.' She aimed a playful kick at him. 'Get out there with the rest of them.'

Ginge closed the fridge and handed Reece a bottle of Peroni. 'Try one of these, boss.'

Reece put a box of wine on the counter and followed Ginge into the garden. There was a large, circular table laid out with candles on saucers. Coloured lanterns and fairy lights hung from the trees. There were more candles on the patio. It was just turning dark, the area of sky above the distant hills taking on a lilac and orange appearance.

'Brân. You made it.'

Reece turned towards the voice. It was Miranda Beven. She held the stem of a cut flower in her hand and looked stunning set against the backdrop of soft lighting. 'Hello.' Reece didn't know what else to say. 'Nice to see you,' he added as an afterthought.

Beven raised the flower to her nose and took in the scent of its petals. 'I'm so glad you came. Elan said you were in two minds.'

Jenkins whispered as she went by, laden with empty plates. 'We bumped into each other in Waitrose.'

Reece knew his junior was an Aldi shopper. Never Waitrose. Strangely, he didn't feel angry. In fact, he wasn't sure how he felt.

'Come sit by me, boss.' Ffion Morgan tapped the seat next to her. 'We don't get to talk enough at work.'

Jenkins glared at her. 'He's supposed to be sitting here, remember?'

Morgan put a hand to her mouth and giggled. 'Oh yeah. Next to Miranda.'

'Shush.' Jenkins leaned across the table. 'What's wrong with you?'

Morgan rolled her eyes. 'As if he hasn't cottoned on already.'

Jenkins wagged the bread knife. 'One more word. I swear to God. I don't care how many people are watching.' Morgan poked her tongue out and poured herself another glass of Prosecco. Jenkins came away from the table. 'Is everyone ready to eat?'

Ginge sat with his knife and fork gripped in both hands. 'I thought you'd never ask.'

Cara Frost appeared, carrying a tray of food. 'Spicy chicken wings, or stuffed mushrooms?'

Ginge licked his lips. 'Can I try both?' He glanced at Jenkins. 'If that's okay?'

She told him it was. 'You must have eaten your poor parents out of house and home,' she said, placing another couple of trays on the table. 'Watch your fingers. They're hot.'

'My dad reckons I ate more than my three sisters put together.'

'I don't doubt it.'

Sinatra, Crosby, and Dean Martin took turns to croon among the shrubbery. Reece imagined the choice of music to be Frost's doing, not Jenkins's. Axl Rose and Alice Cooper screaming into the night would have given the event a quite different ambience. He offered everyone more wine. 'There were a few bottles left over from my wedding reception,' he explained. 'This seemed as good a time as any to shift some of it.'

Ginge was content with the bottled Italian lager he'd brought with him. Ffion Morgan was every bit a Prosecco girl and said she'd stick with that. Jenkins didn't drink alcohol. It sent her 'bat shit crazy,' she reminded him. That left Cara Frost and Miranda Beven.

Beven held her glass while Reece poured. 'Thank you,' she said, holding eye contact for longer than was necessary.

'You're welcome. What about you, Cara?'

'I'll have some with the pasta.'

Ginge approved. 'Pasta. That's sounds good. Are we having garlic bread as well?'

They all fell about laughing.

'Are you sure you're not pregnant?' Jenkins asked.

Ginge felt his waistline. 'I don't think so,' he said, laughing with them.

Cara Frost rested her empty glass on the table. 'Elan tells me you're a whisky man.'

Reece returned the bottle to the centre of the table. 'I'm the bereaved detective, right?'

'Oh, I didn't mean that.'

He ran his finger round the rim of his glass, stopping when it began to sing. 'I rarely drink at home these days. Whisky doesn't complement meals served from the popty ping.'

'The what?' Frost looked confused.

'Oh God. Here he goes again,' Jenkins said, spooning mounds of spaghetti onto Ginge's plate. 'Ffion, you speak proper Welsh. Tell him popty ping isn't a real word.'

'It is,' Reece said. 'It means *microwave*.' He forced the word.

Morgan leaned on her elbows. 'He's right.'

'It's made up,' Jenkins insisted. 'It's what we Welsh do when we haven't got an equivalent for an English word.'

Reece fired up his phone. When he'd found what he was looking for, he turned the screen towards Jenkins and Frost. 'See. *Popty ping*. Microwave. Told you.'

Frost took the handset and checked for herself. 'That's hilarious,' she said, giving it back. 'Have you got any more of those?'

'*Igam ogam*, is zigzag.' Reece laughed when Frost repeated it. 'And my own personal favourite is, *pili pala*. Butterfly.'

'We have to learn Welsh,' Frost told Jenkins. 'It would be so much fun.'

'I can speak it already,' Jenkins protested.

'No, you can't,' Reece said. 'You make do with what little you remember from school. Our language would die out completely if it was left to people like you.'

'That's unfair.' Jenkins insisted. 'I can speak Welsh.'

'Go on then,' Reece challenged. 'Prove it.'

'I will.' Jenkins put the pot of pasta down and cleared her throat, readying herself in front of her audience. 'There's a pili pala doing igam ogams on my popty ping.'

Reece let his head bang against the table top. 'Save me, someone.' Ginge coughed, spraying his Peroni everywhere. 'Jesus!' Reece wiped froth off his shirt sleeves. 'Don't *you* start as well.' He turned to Miranda Beven and offered his napkin. 'Did it get you?'

'It's actually popty microdon, now I think about it.' Morgan was deep in thought. 'The popty ping thing only caught on lately. To make the Welsh sound stupid, no doubt.'

Jenkins gawped. 'And the igam ogaming pili palas don't?'

Morgan returned a forkful of spaghetti to her plate. 'I'm just saying.'

'Popty ping for me. Definitely,' Frost said.

Jenkins agreed. 'The microdon thing makes it sound like we keep dinosaurs in our back gardens.' She pointed a finger of warning at Morgan. 'Now that *would* be stupid.'

Reece closed his eyes, listening to what it was like to be in the company of good people. When he opened them again, Cara Frost was handing him an acoustic guitar.

'Elan says you play.'

He took the instrument and turned it over in his hands. 'A Taylor. Nice.' He drew his thumb lightly across the strings, playing an open chord. 'Very warm and resonant.'

Frost watched him, her elbow resting on her knee, a clenched fist supporting her chin. 'A present to myself when I got my final exams out of the way.'

'You should buy one,' Jenkins said. 'Instead of hording your money like Scrooge.'

'Are you calling me tight?'

'You're hardly the last of the big spenders. Look at the clapped-out deathtrap you drive. How old is that thing?'

'Twenty-four. Twenty-five years maybe.'

'See what I mean?'

'I've just got a new one,' Reece said. 'Didn't know that, did you?'

'New?' Jenkins looked surprised. 'On order?'

'You could say that.'

She leaned towards him; the initial look of surprise already replaced by one of deep suspicion. 'New, as in delivery miles only on the clock?'

Reece ran a hand across his mouth. 'Not exactly.'

'How many miles?'

'I don't know. I didn't ask.'

'How many?'

'I can't remember.'

Jenkins turned her chair round the wrong way and sat down, facing him. 'I can do this for hours. Until I break you.'

Reece bit his lip, fighting the urge to laugh. 'I know.'

'Last chance.' She brought her face to within inches of his. 'I asked you how many miles it has on the clock?'

Reece could hardly speak. 'A hundred and eighty-seven thousand.'

Jenkins flew to her feet. 'That's more than halfway to the moon!' She put her hands to her head. 'How can it be new?'

'It's less mileage than I had on the Peugeot.'

Jenkins pointed at Ffion Morgan. 'How many miles on your car?'

'I dunno. I'd be hard pushed to tell you how many wheels it's got.'

'Yours?' Jenkins asked Cara Frost. 'What about you, Ginge? Miranda? There you go,' she said once she'd done the maths. 'It's got more miles on the clock than the rest of ours put together.'

'What does it matter?' Reece asked.

'It matters to me because I have to drive the thing. We're like the Keystone Cops most days. It's embarrassing.'

'You won't be embarrassed driving this.'

'Why? What is it?'

'A Toyota Land Cruiser. The Amazon version.'

'What's one of those?' Jenkins looked round the table for help.

'It's pretty big,' Ginge said. 'A four by four.'

'Get a picture up on your phone,' Jenkins told Morgan. 'Shit, it's the size of a bus.'

'You won't be able to reach the pedals with your little legs.' Ginge stopped laughing almost immediately. 'Sorry.'

'When are you getting it?' Jenkins asked.

Reece sounded confident. 'Yanto reckons it'll be ready over the weekend.'

Chapter 51

Coombsie needed a stiff drink once Marma had released him. Several drinks, in fact. There were times during the afternoon when he was sure they were about to kill him. They probably would have done had Archie not chosen the perfect moment to make his phone call.

Archie hadn't said much. But what he did say had Marma needing to know more. She'd been the one prompting Coombsie to ask for a meet up that evening.

With a few pints under his belt, he checked his watch and left the Westgate pub for the short journey on foot to the gates of the castle. He'd only just stepped onto the pavement when he felt a hefty shove in the small of his back. It bounced him off the unforgiving upright of the junction's traffic lights and onto the floor. 'You again,' he managed, before taking a savage kick to the head. He raised his hands in an attempt to defend himself, but a second kick caught him full in the face. Someone came out of the pub to check what was going on. They went back inside without getting involved. It wasn't their problem. Not their fight.

'Get up,' his attacker commanded.

Coombsie rolled onto his front and pushed against the pavement for leverage. He was on his feet but unable to straighten. His ribs still hurt from the beating he'd taken that afternoon. 'What do you want? I've told you all I know.'

'You warned him I'd be on that bus. I know you did.'

'I didn't tell him anything. I swear I haven't spoken to Archie since you and me first met.'

'Where is he?'

Coombsie reached for the pub windowsill and rested his arm along it. He had an idea. If he could somehow lead his attacker to where Marma Creed and Hussam Kahn were waiting, then maybe he and Archie could get away while the three of them thrashed it out. It was worth a try. 'Archie's meeting me by the castle gates, ten minutes from now. That's where I was going.' He pointed across the road. 'We should—' The punch caught him in the midriff, taking his wind. He spewed four pints of lager into the gutter. Another shove in the back had him stumbling along the pavement. He managed to stay on his feet, but only just. He thought about calling out. His assailant must have read his mind and clamped a hand to his mouth, rendering him mute.

They were close to the bridge over the River Taff. The lights of the Principality Stadium shone brightly on the opposite side of the water. This wasn't going to end well. Coombsie knew. Mumbling under the grip of the other man's hand, he tried to strike a deal. It was useless. He held his ribs and walked like an old man while his assailant steered him down Coldstream Terrace, towards the Fitzhamon Embankment. There was a wide stretch of black water off to their left. On another night, the stadium lights reflecting off it would have looked beautiful. Tonight, they'd lost their lustre.

Neither of them spoke until the police officer drew a knife and held its blade to Coombsie's throat. 'You warned him. That's why he wasn't in his usual seat.'

Coombsie shook his head and felt the cold steel bite into his skin. They knew he'd taken Archie to the snooker hall. There was so much they'd wanted to know after that. Archie's full name and address. His telephone number, as well as his place of work. It was like something out of a spy film. And the true reason for him giving his mate the cold shoulder for so long. If this had anything to do with what had happened to Billy Creed, then Coombsie wanted no part of it.

'And you've been speaking to Marma.'

How could they possibly know that? 'I didn't tell her anything about you and what was going on.' He knew he didn't sound convincing.

'You can't be trusted. You're a liability.'

Coombsie was already too close to the water's edge to back away. Throwing himself into the river was his only chance of escape. Even as a non-swimmer, it had to be better than staying put. The knife hit him in the middle of his upper abdomen. Just below the sternum. He doubled over and slid further onto it. The blade re-routed up and into his chest, its razor-sharp tip searching out his thumping heart. It stung and burned and wasn't at all what he'd previously imagined being stabbed would feel like.

He stared into the other man's eyes and groaned as the blade was twisted and withdrawn. A firm kick to the groin sent him on his way down the river, towards the waiting sea.

Chapter 52

Archie had waited outside the main entrance to Cardiff Castle for the best part of twenty minutes. It was looking like Coombsie had stood him up. The place was crawling with people having a good time. He envied them and couldn't remember when he'd last properly enjoyed himself.

A group of six women, all of them dressed as police officers, stopped and asked him to take a photograph of their hen group. When he reluctantly agreed, they hitched their skirts to mid-thigh and waved phallic truncheons at the camera. They promptly put him under arrest on a charge of "*being a dirty perv.*" Archie nervously laughed it off, foolishly allowing them to handcuff him to a woman wearing a *Bride-to-Be* banner.

He immediately knew it was bad judgement on his part. 'You're going to have to let me go,' he said, trying to free himself from the cheap metal attached to his wrist. 'I'm supposed to be meeting someone back there.' The castle doors were already ten metres away as they dragged him along the pavement.

One of the women stopped to kiss him full on the lips. 'Not scared of us, are you?'

Archie turned to look over his shoulder. Coombsie was still nowhere to be seen. 'A bit,' he said with a nervous laugh.

'Bend over.' It was the same woman.

'You what?'

'Jail or six lashes? The choice is yours.'

Archie shut his eyes and wondered if things could get any worse? 'And then you'll let me go?' he asked.

'We might.'

'Aw, come on. I've been a good sport so far.'

'You're gonna be our sex slave,' said one of the others. She waved her *truncheon* in his face like it was a wizard's wand.

Archie did his best to avoid it. 'I've really got to go.'

'Bend.'

'And then we're finished?'

'I said, bend over!'

He bent at the waist and took six of the best from the pissed-as-a-fart bride.

Free of restraints, but not yet his blushes, he made his way back to the meeting point in front of the castle.

'Spare any change?'

There was a man sitting upright against the door, his legs hidden inside a scruffy sleeping bag. Archie checked his pockets. Fives and tens in notes. He pushed a few coins round the palm of his hand. 'There's almost three quid there,' he said. 'Sorry, but I need the rest.'

'God bless you, son.' The man held out a grubby hand and took the coins.

'I'd give you more if I could.'

The man was already burrowing back inside his sleeping bag, singing a reasonable enough rendition of Waltzing Matilda.

Archie saw a face in the crowd. There were plenty of faces. This one was different. It belonged to a man who was paying him way too much attention.

He turned to flee in the opposite direction and saw Marma Creed. She was almost on him and would have been had he not got spooked by the man making his way through the throng. Instinct alone told Archie the man was a police officer. The same basic instinct that had him run for his life. He went straight into the road with no concern for the traffic. It was his best option if he wanted to put any real distance between them. Coombsie had sold him out. Had lured him into a trap.

He slowed on the centre lines of the road to let a couple of taxis whizz past. That gave Marma and the police officer an opportunity to close the distance on him. Even so, they both appeared completely oblivious to the other's presence and were not working as a team.

He sprinted down Queen Street. Past the statue of Aneurin Bevan, founder of the National Health Service. The entrance to the indoor shopping centre was closed; the shutters fully drawn and locked in place until morning. There were a couple of tents pitched outside it. Belonging to homeless people and a sad-looking dog. He thought about asking if he could hide inside one of them, but the officer had him firmly in his sights.

There was a police van parked at the front of the Marks and Spencer store a bit further along. Its blue lights were on, but there wasn't much activity around it. The uniformed occupants were advertising their presence to would-be troublemakers.

Archie made his way towards the van. Not every member of the South Wales Police could be bent. The officer behind him slowed and then turned away, disappearing from sight. When he next looked, Marma Creed and her towering accomplice had also made off and were nowhere to be seen.

Archie waited a while, making sure he was safe before he made a call. Things were getting way out of control. But now he had a face for one of the major players.

'Which service do you require?' the operator asked.

Archie stalled. The woman repeated herself. 'Police,' he said when he next answered.

Chapter 53

'Can you hold the fort while I go talk to a couple of people downstairs?' Reece asked. Jenkins was at her desk, talking on the phone. When Reece asked for a second time, she turned her back on him. He went closer, picking up on aspects of the conversation. It sounded like she was speaking to someone from ballistics. There might be a lead, and the new day was only just beginning.

Jenkins thanked whoever was on the other end of the line before hanging up. 'You won't believe this.'

'Don't be telling me someone's mislaid the bullet casings from the bus?' Reece said, readying himself to play merry hell.

Jenkins rose from her seat. 'Relax. It's good news for once. They found a small fragment of bullet lodged in the dashboard of that

Mondeo we seized from the garage yesterday. That's what put its window through. Not a car thief.'

The size of the find was what caught Reece's ear, and it didn't sound much like good news to him. 'Is it big enough to get a match with the ones taken from Larson's chest?'

'Sioned said that no matter how small the sample, it'll still show the same rifling marks as it rotates down the barrel.'

'Did you tell her to let us know as soon as she's got anything?'

'Of course I did.' Jenkins watched as colleagues came and went in the busy incident room. 'You don't think this Archie Ives really was onto something, do you?'

Reece made a move for the door. 'That's what I intend to find out.'

He found Detective Sergeant Arthur Moles—CID—in an almost empty staff canteen, having breakfast. 'Mind if I join you?' Reece asked.

Moles looked up from his newspaper and nodded silently as he dipped the pointy bit of a fried slice into the yolk of a runny egg.

'Can I get you another coffee?' Reece asked, taking a seat. 'Or tea, if you'd prefer?' Moles would have been experienced enough to know the conversation was about to lead somewhere he probably didn't want to go. 'It won't take long,' Reece said, before calling to the lady behind the serving counter: 'Two refills over here please, Doris?'

'I'll be right over,' she said, wiping her hands on an apron tied around her waist. 'Anything to go with it? There's plenty of bacon. I can do you a nice breakfast roll, if you'd like?'

Reece declined. He put his elbows on the edge of the table and spoke to Moles. 'Have we ever worked together in the past?'

Moles folded his newspaper and put it to one side. 'Radyr. I served my apprenticeship with Idris Roberts. You'd only just started there about the time I was leaving. A few weeks' overlap was all it would have been.'

'Didn't we all start with Idris in those days?' Reece folded his arms and grinned at the memory.

'True. But only you went on to marry his daughter.'

Reece recognised a barb when he heard one. He leaned out of harm's way and thanked Doris when she brought one coffee, one tea. 'How come you're still a sergeant? You should be clinking teacups with the likes of Harris by now.'

Moles spooned sugar into his tea and stirred it noisily. 'Events got in the way.'

'Events?'

'The case that marks your card. You know how it is. Someone else fucks up and you get tarred with the same brush, just because you were there.'

Reece took a sip of his coffee. It wasn't nearly as good as the one he'd enjoyed in Donald Breslin's office. 'That sounds familiar.'

'You did all right for yourself,' Moles said. 'Made chief inspector of the murder squad.'

'I sure as hell won't be climbing any higher. Harris has already seen to that.'

Moles closed his cutlery on an empty plate. 'What's this about? Tea. Chit-chat. There's a reason you're here.'

Reece sat back. 'Does the name Archie Ives mean anything to you?'

'Should it?'

'You tell me.'

'Do you have a picture of him?'

Reece reached inside his suit jacket and produced a photocopy of a still image from the bus CCTV. He unfolded the sheet of paper and handed it across the table. 'That's Ives.'

Moles took a moment before handing it back. 'Can't say I've set eyes on him before now.'

'You attended a disturbance on Glenroy Street the other night. One door down from where Archie Ives lives.'

'I still don't know him.'

'There was a report of someone carrying a handgun in the area,' Reece said.

Moles shook his head. 'Turned out to be a waste of everyone's time.'

'A firearm reported not a hundred metres from the scene of a recent shooting?' Reece lowered his mug to the table. 'You didn't think to give me and my team a heads up?'

'The witness was pissed. He didn't know what he'd seen.' Moles leaned over his plate. 'There was nothing to tell.' As an afterthought, he added, 'Look, I got an armed response team over there. Just in case.'

'But you didn't think to check the car?'

'I left it to them.'

'And?'

'They declared the scene safe.'

'Who was the commanding officer?' Reece asked.

'Mike Brogan.'

It wasn't a common name in the area. 'What do you know of him?'

Moles pushed his plate to one side and dragged his cup and saucer into the empty space. 'Who – Brogan? Not a lot.'

'Okay,' Reece said. 'The AFOs are on scene. What did you do next?'

'Leave. There was nothing to be gained by CID sticking around. I'm assuming Brogan's lot downgraded it to uniform once they were satisfied it was bullshit.'

'And that was it?' Reece asked. 'That was the sum total of CID's involvement?'

'It was a broken window. An attempted car theft. What do you expect me to have done?'

'What would you say if I told you there was a fragment of bullet lodged in that car's dashboard?'

Moles's left eyelid shut partially. 'I had no idea.'

'Was it you who told the owner to get the car shifted and cleaned?'

'Not me.'

'You're a dead ringer for the description given.' The drunk named Geoff hadn't been able to provide much of one, but Reece gave it a shot, regardless.

'We spoke.' Moles said, sounding irritated. 'That's why he remembers me.'

'I'll ask one last time: was it you who told the owner to get the vehicle valeted?'

'And I'll answer in kind. It must have been one of Brogan's team.'

Reece was already reaching for his phone as he walked towards the canteen's exit. Inspector Mike Brogan had some explaining to do.

Chapter 54

ARCHIE HAD SPENT THE night in a narrow alleyway. Propped up in a sitting position against a battered garage door. He'd watched a couple of tomcats have a noisy scrap. At least one plump rat had given him a quick sniff before buggering off in fear of the cats' return.

The unidentified resident of the bush opposite kept it rustling most of the night. Archie thought it best not to venture over there to find out what it was. Needless to say, he'd managed little sleep after that, and now his head hurt.

To compound things, he had a bad case of bed hair. A humongous tuft that poked out from the side of his head at ninety degrees. Not that he had been anywhere near a mattress and pillow in days.

He licked his hand and wiped it across his head with no positive effect.

After a quick pee, he made his way along the alley, tugging at the hem of his T-shirt in a failed attempt to remove at least some of the creases. He looked a right mess, and that wasn't going to help him achieve what he had in mind.

The main university building was on Park Place, at the edge of the city centre. It was imposingly grand as a design, and not constructed using rectangular moulds of prefab concrete.

Archie waited next to the main road, a stride or two outside the official university boundary. He was attracting unwanted attention from some in the area, but as yet, didn't know why that was. He gave his T-shirt another tug. Maybe the stubborn creases were to blame for other people's interest in him.

He needed access to the internet and Google Drive. The former, to keep abreast of developments in the bus shooting case. The latter, for access to the photograph he'd earlier uploaded for safekeeping. The cheap phones he'd bought were useless for that. They were pretty much limited to making and receiving calls and texts only. Maybe it was time to give that number another ring and rattle some cages? The thought terrified him.

He made his move, leaving behind the prying eyes and loose tongues.

The car park had signs warning it was for the use of university staff only. Archie had no car of his own. He moved between the vehicles, using them where he could to shield himself from view. Ahead was a man in a yellow hi-viz jacket, checking permits stuck to windshields. Archie needn't have worried. The warden was soon waving his arms at a white van pulling in off the main road. Archie took his opportunity and jogged towards the front door of the building; a hand held to the side of his head in an attempt to hide most of his face. He knew he looked like shit served on a plate. His body and clothes were in need of a good wash. His teeth were furry and his breath stank like the morning after a good night out. Much like any other student, he decided.

He was in. So far, so good. But which corridor did he need to take? He stopped a couple of female students who looked like they might be Chinese. They were walking in the opposite direction. 'I can't find the library,' Archie said, turning in every direction. 'Any idea where it might be?'

With sketchy instructions received, he was off again, wandering down corridors that were mercifully cooler than the temperature outside. Who said it always rained in Wales?

The library was surprisingly modern-looking, with an anti-theft archway next to the exit. Archie wasn't there to snatch books. Students' laptops and phones wouldn't be barcoded.

Once he got his bearings, he knew exactly who to target. There was a small huddle of foreign students sitting at a circular table near the centre of the room. Not those. It would be far too difficult to preoccupy the entire group. Behind them were individual seating areas. All but one of them empty.

The girl occupying it had her back to the rest of the room. Her skin was milk-bottle white and punctuated with spotty acne. A mop of unruly ginger curls cascaded over her narrow shoulders.

Archie took the seat next to hers and said: 'Hello.' The student nodded in reply. He hadn't fully creeped her out. Not yet, anyway. 'You're working through the summer recess like me. Did you fall behind with the work?'

The student rubbed her abdomen. 'I took some time off during the term. Medical issues.'

'Oh, right. Sorry to hear that. Hope you're feeling better now?'

'I've got Crohn's. It's a bitch of a thing.'

Archie knew the condition had something to do with the bowels, but wasn't entirely sure what it entailed. 'I've heard,' was all he could think to say. He needed to get himself a book so that he didn't have to keep the conversation going. A pile of books. Blend in and not get kicked out for bothering people.

He went to a shelf and searched along it before selecting four choices at random. Once back at his seat, he dropped the books onto his desk and made an apologetic gesture when the pasty-faced student looked up again.

She was using a Windows laptop similar to his own at home. It was larger than a tablet, making it more difficult to pilfer and carry out of there without being seen. Beggars and choosers and all that.

He leaned towards the girl. 'What course are you doing?'

For a moment, she didn't reply. Then she said: 'Law. You?'

It was best to leave as few clues as he could. 'Media and Politics.'

She rolled her eyes. 'Rather you than me.'

'Tell me about it.' Archie shrugged. 'Too late to change now.'

The student smiled and looked away. Then caught Archie's eye again. She put a hand against her side and winced. 'Do you mind keeping an eye on this lot while I pop to the loo?'

Archie massaged the back of his neck. This was going to be far easier than he could ever have imagined. 'Go ahead. I'm here for a while yet.' He waited until the student was out of sight before pulling the laptop's power cord from the wall socket. He couldn't risk closing the lid. That would put the machine into hibernation mode and then he'd need a password to wake it up again.

It was only then he saw the iPhone poking from under the open pages of a textbook. The student had been using it only moments earlier and hadn't taken it with her. The device had not yet entered lock screen mode and displayed an image of a litter of kittens. Archie grabbed it, checking no one was looking. He fumbled through the settings—more used to an android device—and selected *Never* from the *Auto-Lock* choices. No need to worry about passcodes now.

He regretted what he was doing and took one of the student's pencils to write **SORRY - YOU'LL GET IT BACK** in full capitals on a page torn from her notepad.

He counted out one hundred and fifty-five pounds—most of what he had left of his savings—took a small amount for himself and left the rest under the notepad. Even as used items, the iPhone and its charger were worth a lot more than that. He'd make it up to the girl. When this was over, he'd return to present her with a brand new model paid for with the royalties of his worldwide exclusive.

As a thief, Archie felt conspicuous. It sickened him to know he'd stooped so low. But it was to make Cardiff a safer place. It was a public service he was performing; the theft therefore justified in his view. He stuffed the charging cord into his pocket, the bulky plug digging into his thigh as he made his escape.

The woman at the exit was busy fixing protective sleeves to a pile of books and didn't look up when he went past. Someone was even kind enough to hold the door open for him. He took the stairs to the ground floor. It would be quicker than waiting for the lift to arrive.

Exiting the stairwell, he found himself back in the corridor leading to the front of the building. He didn't have far to go. He quickened his pace and lengthened his stride. A student went past—not *the* student—his gaze alternating between Archie's face and the iPhone plug bulging in his pocket. It was probably nothing. The student couldn't possibly have known it was stolen. Archie didn't turn to see if the teenager was still watching him, but guessed that he probably was.

The glass doors to the outside were just ahead. No alarms had yet sounded. No echoes of footsteps racing behind him. No shouts of 'Stop. Thief!' Only the woman at reception to get past, and then he was safe.

When the doors to the outside opened, Archie was momentarily blinded by the sun. The heat hit him like a hairdryer set on high.

He scoured the car park for the man in the yellow jacket. He was nowhere to be seen.

This time Archie didn't shy away from the security camera. Instead, he turned to face it, gesturing with the knowledge that the rogue police officers would understand its deeper meaning.

There were sounds of shouting coming from the depths of the corridor. The woman behind the reception desk pointed towards the exit and used her other hand to raise a telephone to her ear.

Archie was running.

It was becoming a habit of his.

Chapter 55

Reece found Jenkins waiting in the incident room and could tell immediately that she was eager to speak to him. 'What is it?'

'They've found a body on the Taff Embankment. This side of the Grangetown Mosque.' It would have been a walkable distance from the police station under different circumstances. 'Male. Mid-twenties. A little over average height.'

'Please tell me it's not Archie Ives?'

'They haven't been able to ID him as yet.'

Reece grimaced. Water did horrible things to corpses. Fish and rodents took a feed wherever they could. That's before the hungry gulls got to them. 'How long has he been there?'

'The on-scene doctor says death occurred twelve to eighteen hours ago. That fits with what I was told about the tides. The victim would have gone in the water sometime overnight.'

'Drowning?'

Jenkins shrugged. 'That's all I know so far.'

'Let's get over there and see for ourselves,' Reece said. They took the stairs, much to Jenkins's loudly voiced protests. Reece took no notice as usual and used the front steps outside the main building to get round to the staff car park. It was well into the afternoon and the day showed no signs of cooling.

'Where is it?' Jenkins asked.

'Where's what?'

'The *new* car.' She exaggerated the word.

'We've been through this already,' Reece said. 'It needs an MOT before I collect it.'

'A pool car it is, then.' Jenkins stood looking at him. 'You did book one out?'

'No. What about you?'

'You know I didn't,' she said, retracing their footsteps. 'You could have told me while we were still inside.'

Reece watched her go. 'If you only listened in the first place.' He knew she'd said something in response, but a passing bin lorry prevented him from hearing what. It was several minutes before she returned, juggling the keys from one hand to the other as she approached. 'In your own time,' he shouted across the full length of the car park. 'It's not like we've got anything important to do.'

'I said I'm coming,' Jenkins shouted back. 'I'm knackered going up and down those steps.'

Reece held out his hand. 'Keys.'

'I thought *I* was driving?' Jenkins handed them over. 'I meant what I said about that pickup truck. You'll be driving that, not me.'

Reece got in and fastened his seat belt, starting the engine with the first turn of the key. 'Wait until you've seen it. You'll change your mind then.'

'Don't bank on it.'

'Did I tell you the house in Llandaff is going on the market today?' he said, abruptly changing the subject.

'Why so soon?'

'It's the right time. Moving to Brecon will be good for me.'

'It'll sell quickly,' Jenkins said, as they pulled onto the main road and turned left. 'It's close to the city centre. There's the beautiful cathedral, as well as private schools and acres of open parkland nearby. It'll sell in a flash. You mark my word.'

'I hope you're right.'

'Won't you miss living there?'

'Of course I will.' Reece lowered his head. 'I'm sorry. I didn't mean to snap. You don't think I'm doing the right thing?'

'It's what you and Anwen planned to do, wasn't it? Sell up and move out to the sticks.'

'We were going to use the cottage as a weekend retreat. Go there for Christmas, birthdays, and other special occasions. We'd both take early retirement and eventually live there full time. Anwen always wanted a kitchen garden, you see. That and chickens to fuss over.'

Jenkins turned sideways to look at him. 'This isn't your awkward way of telling me you're retiring soon?'

'Every day is a day closer,' Reece said.

'I'm being serious.'

'So am I.'

Their route took them along James Street. Across the river and onto Corporation Road. A right turn took them into Taff Terrace, and next left, onto the embankment. They arrived a little over three minutes after engine start.

Reece parked up and went round the back of the vehicle to check for wellies or walking boots. 'Great,' he said, slamming the hatchback shut. 'There's none in there.' He took a couple of elasticated overshoes from a uniform when he got closer to the embankment. 'Hold on to me before I go arse over tit into that lot.' The uniform did as told and held him upright while he covered his leather brogues.

The water level was low, revealing an expanse of mud-brown sand and silt. Reece trod carefully over to where the action was, looking like an astronaut negotiating the surface of the moon.

There was a duty Home Office forensic pathologist at the scene. Reece didn't know the man. The pathologist had obviously seen enough and was already packing up. 'Single stab wound under the sternum,' he said, taking his bag back to his car. He spoke over his shoulder and trudged unsteadily through the mud. 'I can't tell for sure yet, but it's a fair bet the blade penetrated the heart.'

'It's not Archie Ives,' Jenkins said, rising from a squatting position next to the corpse. The skin on the dead man's face was deathly white. His hands and fingers puckered – consistent with being submerged in water. His lips were purple. Cheeks scratched where he'd snagged on the branches of overhanging trees during his journey down the river. There was a hole in the front of his T-shirt; a deliberate puncture wound made with a sharp implement. 'That's something, I guess?'

'What did that Human Resources woman say about Ives having no next of kin?' Reece asked. 'Only a friend as his first point of contact?'

'This could be anybody,' Jenkins said. 'The chance of it being Ives's friend is . . .' She shook her head sceptically.

'I've got a feeling about this,' Reece insisted. 'They were the same age, weren't they?'

'Even so. It's a hell of a long shot.'

'Humour me. Check it out.'

Jenkins leafed through her pocketbook to remind herself of the name. 'I'll get a car sent over to Daniel Coombs's address. It shouldn't take long before we know for sure.'

Reece was left staring along the embankment, towards the bay. They'd been lucky the body had snagged and then settled on the mud at low tide. 'If there's no answer, I want his place searched. And get uniform onto the neighbours for a proper description of him.'

Reece's phone rang. 'Ffion, what's up?'

'There's been a possible sighting of Archie Ives at Cardiff University.'

'Get over there and see what you can find out,' Reece told her.

'I'm already on my way.'

Chapter 56

Archie chose the Queen Street McDonald's as his temporary operational hub. Not out of culinary choice. He'd already received an alert for exceeding data usage. The student had obviously reached the limit of her capped allowance. What Archie needed was quick and free access to functioning Wi-Fi.

He knew he couldn't risk keeping the handset indefinitely. There would be a *Find My iPhone* facility on it, exposing him to the possibility of being tracked again. There would be a way of turning the function off, he assumed, but he was now preoccupied with other things.

The smell of mass-produced burger and French fries made him salivate. He was beyond hungry and moved to one side of the queue once he'd made his order. By the time his food was ready and bagged, all seats were gone. Checking upstairs for another meant him being unable to see who came in through the doors. Police. The killer. He'd have no warning until it was too late.

Halfway along the nearest row of tables, a woman got up and collected her purse and phone. Archie made his move, competing with a number of others. He got there first. 'Are you leaving?' he asked.

The woman was folding a screaming toddler into a stroller that refused to keep still. She stamped on the front brakes and tried again, this time with a little more success. 'In a minute.'

'I'm not trying to rush you,' Archie said, wedging his order under his arm to grab hold of the stroller and steady it. 'Take all the time you need.'

The toddler was still trying to turn its lungs inside out. The woman had it pinned down and strapped in, despite its flailing arms and legs. She yanked the stroller sideways, knocking another table, spilling someone's drink. She'd had enough and was in tears.

Archie called after her. 'You've left this behind.' He held the cuddly toy aloft and almost dropped his food. The woman neither turned nor answered and was now stuck in the swing doors of the exit, trying to free several shopping bags that ballooned from the stroller's handles.

The screaming quietened. The woman and toddler were gone.

Archie sat and tore at the packaging of his meal. When he bit into the burger, his salivary glands contracted with an agonising force.

The bread stuck in his oesophagus with a heavy ache felt halfway down his chest. He arched his back and banged his front, shifting the obstruction only after he'd taken a drink.

He started on the fries with less haste. Pouring them out onto the brown bag he was using as a makeshift plate. He'd have paid a hundred quid for that meal. More, probably. It was amazing what the pangs of real hunger did to a person.

He took the code from his receipt and used it to log onto the free Wi-Fi service. Clicking through the adverts and *terms and conditions* of use, he went straight to the Wales Online site. Two thumbnails immediately caught his eye.

He clicked on the first of them. It was a full colour image of him looking into the camera on Doug's bus. They mentioned him by name and requested he hand himself in at a local police station. There was even a telephone number for him to call a Detective Chief Inspector Brân Reece. Archie scratched the side of his head. They'd kill him before he got anywhere near an interview room.

The other headline nagged for his attention. There wasn't much of a story as yet. Minor details only. **BREAKING NEWS — Body Found on Taff Embankment,** it read in bold print. The body of a white male had been found at low tide. The man was the victim of stab injuries. Police were working to identify him and were calling for potential witnesses.

The dead man was Coombsie. Archie knew. His anonymous phone call to Emergency Services had fallen on deaf ears. Or corrupt ones. Regardless of which, Coombsie's well-being hadn't been checked on. Surprise, surprise. The police had done nothing.

Chapter 57

Reece stepped out of the stairwell and came to a halt on the landing. He didn't recognise the number. 'Hello.'

'Is that Detective Chief Inspector Brân Reece?'

'Who is this?'

'You won't know me. Not properly.' The caller was quietly spoken and nervous sounding. 'Can I trust you?'

Reece sensed this wasn't a crank call. He hurried along the landing, clicking his fingers above his head as he entered the incident room, drawing attention to himself. He lowered his hand and put his phone on speaker for the others to hear. 'You have my word,' he promised.

'How do I know that means anything?'

'You wouldn't have called me if you were in any doubt.' Reece took a chance. 'Archie. It *is* Archie Ives, isn't it?' There was a click, followed by a monotonous dial tone. 'Shit. He's gone.'

Chapter 58

Reece pinched the bridge of his nose. He'd been too pushy and had scared Archie off.

'Ring him back,' Jenkins said. 'He might have moved and lost his signal.'

Reece tried. It rang. No answer. He tried a second time. Same result. Hanging up, he gave Ginge the number and told him to get onto the telecommunications companies. He wanted a location for the call and as quickly as the young detective constable could manage it. This was their chance to make some real progress with the case.

'What do you think?' Jenkins asked. 'Is Ives preparing to hand himself in?'

Reece didn't get to open his mouth in response. He pressed the *answer* prompt on his phone. 'I'm sorry, Archie. We got cut off there.' He waited, listening to the silence. This time, he'd let Ives speak at his own pace.

'I need to know I can trust you.'

'You bet you can.' Reece's response was sincere and had a reassuring warmth to it.

'How do I know for sure? You could be in this with the rest of them.'

Reece didn't push for the deeper meaning in that. He cleared a space on the edge of Ginge's desk and sat down. 'Look me up on the internet. There's been plenty written about me over the years. It's easy to see whose side I'm on.'

'I already have,' Archie said. 'It's the only reason I'm making this call. That and what I've heard Maggie Kavanagh say about you.'

Reece was sure that Kavanagh had said plenty. 'Where do we go from here?' he asked.

'Who's with you?'

'A few of my team.'

'Get rid of them. I'm only talking to you.'

Reece glanced around the room. 'I can vouch for the integrity of everyone here.'

'I'm saying nothing until they're gone,' Archie said. 'I'm only talking to you.'

'Give me a second.' Reece made an apologetic face and waited until he was alone. 'Okay, Archie, you've got my undivided attention.'

There was a short pause. 'If you're anything as good as Maggie and your record claims, then you'll already know what's going on here.'

Reece moved off the desk and lowered himself into Ginge's seat. 'I'll tell you where I'm at so far?'

'You'd best make it quick. I'm not staying on the line long enough for my whereabouts to be traced.'

'I think you recently saw or heard something you shouldn't have. Something involving Billy Creed and a serving police officer. How's that, for starters?'

'It wasn't only Billy. His sister is in on it too.'

Reece doubted that was the case. It wasn't how Marma normally operated. She'd want full control of anything she was involved in, rather than have her strings pulled by some shady puppet master. 'What makes you say that?'

'I saw all of them last night. In front of the castle.'

'*All?*' Reece arched his back. 'Who did you see?'

'Marma and a police officer, for starters.'

'Together?'

There was a brief pause. 'Not exactly. Me and Coombsie were supposed to be meeting there. They showed up. Coombsie never did.'

'Have you seen or heard from Daniel since?'

'He's not answering his phone. I saw the news about the body you pulled out of the river. That's him. I know it is.'

'We haven't formally identified him as yet,' Reece said.

'Check his knees. Then you'll know. He tattooed them himself when we were kids. His mum went nuts and wouldn't let him wear shorts ever again.'

'What do these tattoos look like?' Reece asked.

'Acid tab faces.' Archie managed a brief chuckle at the memory. 'Just eyes, nose, and a mouth. A smiley one on his left knee and miserable one on the other.'

'I can see why his mum wasn't impressed.'

'You'll get it checked though?'

'Definitely. It's a simple enough thing to do. We can't officially identify him using a tattoo—not anymore—but it'll give us something to be getting on with.'

'Did he suffer?' Archie asked. 'Was it over quickly?'

The vivid flashback hit Reece like a ten tonne truck. He pulled at his shirt collar and gasped for breath. He saw Anwen clutching her abdomen. She was bleeding. Crying. Calling his name. Reece ran towards her but sank into an ever-deepening volume of liquid sand. He went over to the office window and threw it open, inhaling greedy lungfuls of air.

Anwen had taken several minutes to die.

It wasn't quick.

Yes, she'd suffered.

He'd failed her.

Archie was repeating his name. 'I'm still here,' Reece said, swallowing hard and wiping his eyes. 'Go on.'

'I asked if my friend suffered when they killed him.'

Reece lowered his hand and brought his breathing under control. 'I think your friend was dead before he knew what was happening.'

Chapter 59

Reece called the team back into the room and had them sit at their desks.

'What did he say?' Jenkins asked as the first in.

Reece waited until they were all present and seated. He rubbed his hands together and looked excited. 'The chase is on.' He told his audience about Coombsie's knees and had Ginge ring the mortuary to find out if the corpse's were a match. It took a single phone call and a few minutes on hold to confirm that they were. Reece penned a name next to the photograph of the man pulled from the river. 'Ives and Daniel Coombs had arranged to meet last night. Outside the main gates of Cardiff Castle.'

'And that's all it took to get him killed?' Ginge asked.

Reece nodded. 'Ives was convinced there was someone else present during their phone call.'

'Listening on the line, or in person?' Ginge again.

'There in the room with Coombs,' Reece said.

'Setting a trap?'

'It looks like.'

Jenkins joined in: 'You're still not buying the bit about Marma Creed's involvement in this?'

'She wouldn't grease anyone's grubby palm,' Reece replied. 'If she is involved, then it's for other reasons.'

'So, who was the officer Ives saw in the crowd? Did he give you a name or description?'

'Nondescript, was what he said.'

Jenkins tutted. 'How did he know it was a serving police officer?'

'The man had the look, apparently.'

'The *look*. What's that supposed to mean?'

'I want Marma Creed brought in for questioning,' Reece said, steering the conversation on. 'I don't care where she is or what she's doing. Get her down here, pronto. Ginge – you get all the CCTV footage you can for that area.'

Jenkins looked puzzled. 'But I thought you said Marma wasn't involved?'

'I don't think I did.' Reece got up. 'She was at the castle last night. That was no coincidence.'

Chapter 60

When Reece had phoned Brogan following his discussion with Arthur Moles in the staff canteen, he hadn't expected the AFO to arrive with Cable and Harris in tow. He wondered why that was, but had no time to ask. Harris wanted an immediate update on developments.

'That's what he told me,' Reece said, once he'd recounted his conversation with Archie Ives. 'It makes sense.'

'Let's not be jumping to any conclusions here,' Harris replied in a fluster. 'Ives is of questionable character, after all.'

'You don't know him,' Reece said. 'Not a thing about him.'

'I know he left the scene of a murder. And today he's thieving from a university campus.' Harris guffawed. 'He's hardly the model citizen.'

'Ives is alone and trying to stay alive,' Reece argued. 'What else would you expect him to do?'

Harris patted his combover: a sure sign that Reece was getting under his skin. 'I want him to stop playing silly buggers and give himself up, for one.'

'Have you not been listening to a word I've said?' Reece asked. 'Ives doesn't trust us. Doesn't trust the police.'

Harris's combover got more attention. 'He has you wrapped round his little finger. For all you know, he could be a member of the hit team. There to send you off course.'

'Sir—'

Harris was in full flow and refused to be silenced. 'Peter Larson was the victim of this shooting. Ives and the hitman were the only two people to walk away from the scene. Have you not asked yourself why?'

Reece shook his head in silence.

'And now you have a known associate of Ives washed up dead on the embankment. He's cleaning up and playing you like a fiddle.'

Reece turned to Brogan. 'You attended a disturbance in Glenroy Street the other night.'

Brogan nodded. 'A fuss about nothing.'

'It was hardly that,' Reece said, arching his back.

'A car thief,' Brogan told Harris. 'A smashed window and a drunken witness.'

'*His* team attended because there were reports of a firearm present,' Reece quickly added for Harris's benefit.

'Made by a man who was two sheets to the wind,' Brogan insisted. 'There was nothing to substantiate his claim.'

'You went nowhere near the car. Never checked it over for yourself.'

'Because the owner told us the thief ran off as soon as he was challenged.'

Reece held Brogan in a steely stare. 'That part of his story you *do* believe? Give me strength.'

Brogan shuffled a few inches closer. 'What are you getting at?'

Harris went to say something, but this time Reece succeeded in silencing him. 'If you'd done your job properly instead of sodding off soon after you arrived, you might have found *this*.' He held up a photograph of the bullet fragment positioned next to a scale of length.

'We left the vehicle with CID and uniform,' Brogan said, as though that was enough.

'Someone screwed up,' Reece told Harris.

'You're not accusing Inspector Brogan or an officer from CID of being involved in this, are you?'

'Was it you who told the owner to get his car shifted and cleaned?' Reece asked.

'You'd better be asking CID the same thing?' Brogan said.

'I already have.'

'And what did they say?'

Reece pointed a finger. 'One of you let our killer get away. My question is, which of you was it and why?'

Chapter 61

Reece jerked his head to one side as ACC Harris's thumb and index finger shook only inches away from his face.

'This close,' Harris said, lowering his arm. '*This* bloody close to getting your marching orders.'

Reece thought about biting the finger off should it stray anywhere near enough again. That would get him the sack for sure. 'Are you ordering me to ignore these allegations?'

'Investigating claims of Force corruption is above your pay grade, as well you know.'

'Not when they're connected to a double-murder.'

Harris vented a hiss of air through his front teeth. 'See sense, man. Ives is your suspect.'

Reece was ready to do his boss some serious harm. 'You're wrong.'

Harris turned to Cable and looked like he was close to suffering a stroke. 'Have a word.'

Cable's face crumpled. She retreated behind the security of her office desk and sat down. 'Let's take a moment to reflect on what we know so far.'

Reece closed his eyes and took a deep breath. Terms such as *reflection* seldom failed to bring him out in a cold sweat. They were management speak for *let's do sod all*.

'I'll ask Mary to fix us some tea,' Cable said, getting up again.

Reece couldn't believe what he was hearing. Why not send out for buttered scones? Get the vicar round while she was at it. He poked a finger over her shoulder at the window beyond. 'I should be out there on the streets, hunting for our killer before he strikes again.'

'You'll do as you're told,' Harris said, turning a shade beyond purple. 'Sit down.'

Reece shoved his hands in his pockets. 'I'll stand, thank you.'

Harris wobbled on his feet. 'I'll have you Tasered and cuffed to that chair if I have to. *Sit!*'

Reece did, but took his time about it. 'I'm not drinking tea.'

Harris's fist came down hard on the desk. '*Fuck* the tea!'

Cable gave Reece a look of warning. He winked in response. She turned away.

'How dare you accuse Inspector Brogan of professional impropriety,' Harris said. 'And in front of the junior ranks, of all places.'

'It was a fair enough question to ask,' Reece insisted. 'A simple root around in that car and they'd have found what we did. They could have shut the area down and brought in a dog team, as well as get a helicopter up in the air. Instead, they did nothing.' Reece shook his head. 'That's shoddy at best.'

'I've known Brogan for years,' Harris said.

'That means nothing,' Reece countered. 'How long was Ken Ward with us?' He let that thought hang there.

'I've served with the man, for God's sake. On the same firm.'

Reece's eyes narrowed. 'Is that why you're protecting him?'

Harris snarled his response: 'I'm protecting no one.'

'Then let me do my job.'

When Harris next spoke, it was with a calmer voice. 'What do you want, Reece?'

'Same as always, sir.'

'Don't play games with me. Spit it out.'

Reece was on his feet, already turning the handle of the office door. 'I'm going to nail this killer,' he said, alternating his attention between Cable and the ACC. 'Even if that means tearing this station apart.'

Chapter 62

'Where were you last night? Between the hours of nine and midnight?' Reece asked.

Marma Creed was playing with her hair. Twirling a curl around her finger. She leaned towards her brief, taking advice, and with a smile answered: 'No comment.'

Reece shifted in his seat. 'We're acting on a call made by a member of the public, claiming you chased him most of the way down Queen Street.'

'No comment.'

'You're not going to play that game with me, are you? I was expecting something better.' Reece turned to Jenkins. 'Are you as disappointed as I am?'

'Absolutely gutted, boss.'

Marma stared at her. 'You should be more careful of what you wish for, girl.'

'Is that what Daniel Coombs wished for?' Reece asked.

'No comment.'

'He was found dead on the embankment this morning. Did you have anything to do with that?'

'No comment.'

'Do you know who did?'

'No comment.'

Reece folded his arms. 'Me and Billy had many a ding-dong across this very table. A proper tug of war. Or wills, I should say. When I bumped into you at the funeral, I thought things would be turning a bit tasty again.' He forced his head across the table. 'But you know what? I've changed my mind.'

'I'm an honest business woman.'

'Like hell you are. You're a Creed.'

Marma didn't reply.

'Do you know a Daniel Coombs?' Reece asked.

'No comment.'

'Have you had recent contact with Daniel Coombs?'

'No comment.'

'Did you have contact with him last night?'

'No comment.'

'Why would someone ring Emergency Services claiming you'd abducted Coombs?'

'No comment.'

'Did you abduct Daniel Coombs?'

'No comment.'

'Did you kill Daniel Coombs?'

Marma put a hand to her mouth and yawned. 'No comment.'

'Are you paying off officers working at this station?'

Marma laughed. 'No comment.'

For a while, Reece said nothing and sat staring across the table. 'Your car is being forensically examined as we speak. Torn apart in the search for DNA belonging to Daniel Coombs. If it's there, we'll find it.'

Marma leaned into her brief and whispered. The brief responded likewise. 'No comment.'

The brief spoke to Reece. 'Detective Chief Inspector, as you have nothing with which to charge Miss Creed, I suggest you put an end to this vindictive charade and let her get back to running her family's businesses.'

Reece stood and tidied several sheets of paper, putting them away in a thin card file. 'No can do,' he said with a smile that hid his teeth. 'Miss Creed will be staying the night.' He paused in the doorway and directed his attention fully on Marma. 'I'm getting close to blowing this thing apart.'

Marma watched him from where she was. 'Then Copper knows things are about to get messy.'

Chapter 63

ON THEIR RETURN TO the incident room, Reece and Jenkins found Morgan and Ginge deep in conversation at Ginge's desk. Reece helped himself to a cup of water from a dispenser fitted following several complaints about the recent hot weather. The machine made a glugging noise as several large air bubbles made their way to the surface of the tank. He went over to the evidence board, quenching his thirst. 'Anything we don't already know about your visit to the university library?'

'Ives left the student some money for the stolen phone,' Morgan said. 'And a note saying he'd replace it when he could.'

'That's good of him,' Jenkins said sarcastically.

'It gives us better insight into his character, don't you think? I mean, he seems to be an honest person. I've been showing Ginge the footage from the camera at the main entrance.'

Ginge loaded it again for the benefit of the others. 'Ives puts forked fingers to his eyes and then points them directly at the camera before leaving. A message he's watching whoever he expects to be viewing this.'

'Too bad for him it's only us watching it,' Jenkins said.

Morgan swivelled in her chair. Jenkins was obviously irritating her. 'He wasn't to know that at the time. The whole station might have viewed it, for all he knew.'

Reece had the makings of a banging headache and thought he might have a pack of paracetamol lurking in one of his desk drawers. He was searching through the third when his estate agent phoned. 'Already? That was quick.'

The agent told him that his Llandaff property had received an offer of purchase on the very first viewing. 'And for the full asking price.'

'I didn't see that coming,' Reece said. 'Yes, of course I'm pleased.' He stuck his head through the open doorway but could no longer see Morgan, who was like a walking pharmacy most days. 'What happens now?' he asked the agent.

The woman explained that the prospective buyers had recently sold a property in London and were in the fortunate position of being able to move in as quickly as he could move out. He thanked her for the update and hung up. 'There you are,' he said, finding

Morgan in the cramped kitchen. She was stirring a mug of coffee. She went over to the fridge, put the milk away, and then gave the counter a wipe with a damp cloth.

'Fancy one?' she asked, taking the milk out again.

'Do you have any paracetamol? My head feels like John Bonham's drumming inside it.'

A vacant stare. 'Who?'

It wasn't worth him trying, he decided. 'Paracetamol?'

'Follow me, boss.' Morgan led the way. 'I've got something for everything in that little bag of mine.'

'I thought you might.' Reece followed her with one eye shut.

When they got to Morgan's desk, she handed him a choice of several brands. Emptying a few more bits and pieces from her bag, she said: 'I'm sure I had something in here for migraines.'

'These are fine. Honestly.'

'Who was on the phone?' she asked. 'Not Archie Ives again?'

He told her about the house selling on its first viewing. 'I'll be out of there by the end of the month.'

'You don't have to accept,' she said, restocking her handbag. 'I'd get a bidding war going, if I were you. Make a mint out of it, you could.'

'That's not fair to people,' Reece said with a half-hearted attempt at a grin. 'They offered what I asked for. That's good enough for me.'

'You're too generous. That's *your* problem.'

He managed a brief chuckle. It hurt. 'Don't make that common knowledge.'

'I won't.' Morgan tapped her nose. 'Your secret is safe with me.'

'Is it me, or is Jenkins acting weird these past few days?' Reece asked, dry-crunching both tablets.

'Tetchy, definitely. She's bitten my head off a few times.'

Reece had no idea why. 'Right. Come on then,' he said. 'It's time we all went home for the night.'

Morgan began the shutdown process for her computer. 'Boss, now that Ginge is into post-mortems, can he be sent to the latest one instead of me?'

'One of the others is doing it,' Reece told her.

Morgan closed the laptop's lid. 'Fab. Forensics on Marma Creed's car should be back first thing in the morning. I got it fast-tracked like you asked.'

'Good. I'll see you then.' Reece helped himself to more water from the dispenser. 'We'll also have the footage from outside the castle to look at.'

'It's going to be a busy one,' Morgan said, disappearing onto the landing. 'Sleep tight.'

By the time Reece arrived home, the headache was a lot better than it had been at work. He made himself a sandwich but couldn't face food when it came to eating it. Keeping himself well hydrated was the answer to getting rid of the headache altogether. He'd not drank nearly enough during the day. A big mistake in a heatwave.

He lowered himself into an armchair, whinging like an old man as he got there. His fingers milked the plump upholstery, his eyes filling with tears as he surveyed the room.

He hadn't expected the sale of the house—their house—to happen anywhere near as quickly as it had. He shook his head. 'What do you think about that, Anwen? We're off to live in Brecon like we always wanted.' He broke down and cried. Full-blown sobbing that left no part of him untouched by violent tremors. He composed himself and reached for a towel. There was usually one close at hand.

He took a deep breath and whistled as he inhaled. 'I needed that,' he admitted. Crying helped. He hadn't realised in the beginning. In the early weeks and months following Anwen's murder, he'd wept tears of rage. Woe betide anyone who disagreed with him. Or sounded as though they were telling him what to do. Crying had embarrassed him. Made him feel less of a man.

More recently, crying had taken on a different purpose. It helped relieve much of the pent-up anger still trapped inside. It rebooted his circuit board and mostly had him behave somewhere closer to normal.

His elbow nudged the small plate he'd balanced on the arm of the chair, knocking it and a doorstop of a ham, tomato, and mustard sandwich to the floor. He was up in a flash. That was no longer his carpet. It belonged to someone else. 'Sorry, whoever you are,' he said, dropping to his knees with the towel in hand.

Chapter 64

It came to Archie in a dream. Not that he'd been enjoying much in the way of quality sleep these past few days. He was beyond tired and knew he couldn't continue as he was.

In the dream, he'd got his hands on Billy Creed's journal. Coming across it while putting empty pizza boxes in the recycling bin. He had no idea how, but it had been on his kitchen counter all along.

Its handwritten contents were far easier to decipher than the blurred photograph he'd saved on Google Drive. Knowing who was involved, he'd simply walked into Donald Breslin's office uninvited, shouting: 'There's your story right there. Let's run with it before Maggie gets wind and wants to take over.'

Breslin had shooed everyone out of the room and poured Archie a large brandy. He made a phone call and invited him to sit in his chair. 'You could be the next editor of this newspaper,' Breslin said. 'My successor.'

Archie put his feet up on the desk and puffed on a thick cigar that hadn't existed only moments earlier, leaving him wondering where it came from. That was the magic of dreams. Things happened and couldn't always be explained by the simple application of logic. 'How do you want to play this, Don? You don't mind me using your first name, do you?'

'Not at all,' Breslin said, fetching the decanter of spirits with him.

'This is good stuff,' Archie said, feeling all grown up. He held his glass to the light entering the room through the floor-to-ceiling window. 'Where do you get it?' Now on the verge of something big, he was planning on making an order for some himself.

'Same place I get the cigars,' Breslin said.

'And where's that – Don?'

'Billy makes sure I don't run out.'

Archie took the cigar from his mouth. His top lip twitched. 'Billy?'

Breslin crossed his fingers. 'Didn't you know? Billy and me are like *that*.'

Archie took his feet off the desk. He put the glass down, spilling brandy on the front of him as his boss went to answer a knock at the office door.

'Billy's a good friend of mine,' Breslin said, ushering two men inside. One of them was bald and heavily tattooed. The other's identity remained completely hidden behind a visored motorcycle helmet. 'You *must* know him?'

When Billy Creed helped himself to the journal, Archie made no attempt to stop him. 'You've been a naughty boy,' Creed said. 'Naughty, naughty, naughty.'

'I wasn't going to do anything with it,' Archie whimpered. 'Honestly.'

'Shut it.' Creed slapped Archie across the side of the head with a fistful of sovereign rings. 'Babs told me where I'd find it.'

Archie shrunk when the biker reached inside his leathers. He knew what was coming. There was no arsehole sitting in his seat. He should have listened to Coombsie and stayed away from the snooker hall in the first place. Archie Ives wasn't destined for big things. He was a nobody who'd earned himself a hole in the ground for being stupid.

Chapter 65

Reece paid his taxi fare and made his way inside the building. He didn't know how people managed it regularly. How they afforded it. Ginge had suggested he get a hire car for the week. It would certainly have worked out a lot cheaper.

There was no sign of George. The desk sergeant must have been on a day off. Either that or in the staff canteen, feeding his face as usual. Reece smiled at the thought. He liked George.

Something had been bothering Reece since day one of the shooting. How did the gunman know where to find Archie Ives among all the other passengers on that bus? It hadn't been a case of him scouring the vehicle until he found his target. Witnesses consistently stated that he'd gone directly to the correct seat—or the wrong seat on that particular day—and pulled his trigger three times. Reece promised himself an informal chat with the driver. Before that, though, he had Marma Creed to deal with.

'Sleep well?' Reece asked, entering the interview room with Jenkins following close behind. 'I know. No comment.' He settled into his seat and got things going once the usual preliminaries were out of the way. 'Our forensics people tell me you've had more than the weekly shop in the boot of that Lexus.'

'No shit?' Marma Creed scoffed.

Reece shook his head. 'None that we came across. But we did find blood.' Marma didn't take the bait. 'Why would Daniel Coombs's DNA be all over the boot carpet of your car?'

Marma grinned. 'I didn't get a name, but a very helpful young man changed a flat tyre for me the other night. The poor thing cut his hand for his troubles. That wheel hadn't been off in a long while.'

'Cut his hand, or bled from the hole you put in his belly?'

Marma's brief peered over the top of his half-rim spectacles. 'My client has provided you with an explanation for how Mister Coombs's DNA was transferred to the boot area of her vehicle. Unless you have proof to the contrary, I suggest this interview is brought to a swift end.'

'Do you really?' Reece said, nodding. 'Just as well no one's daft enough to put you in charge.'

The brief's face reddened in response to the putdown.

Reece knew he had nothing more than the DNA evidence from the boot of the Lexus. Ginge was still chasing the CCTV footage from outside the castle. There was no way the CPS would consider the blood found in the boot enough to proceed with charges. Especially given Marma Creed's explanation of how it got there. He tried another angle: 'Who do *you* think killed Billy?'

Marma's eyes narrowed. 'Copper's treading on thin ice.'

'You don't buy the Arvel Baines angle, do you? A parolee sent to do the dirty work of someone inside.'

Marma put a knuckle to her mouth and bit down on it.

Reece had her attention. He moved his chair closer to the table. 'Did Billy ever mention a ring of corrupt police officers to you?' Jenkins tapped her foot against his. He moved it out of the way. 'Officers who might have considered him surplus to requirements after his knee injury?'

Marma stared. 'Is Copper trying to tell me something?'

'Maybe.' Reece got up and pushed his chair under the table. 'I'm sure you'll work it out for yourself.' He left it at that and made his way out of the interview room. It wasn't long before Jenkins joined him in the corridor.

She stood with her hands pinned to her hips. 'What the hell are you up to?'

Reece didn't answer and walked away.

'What am I supposed to do with her?' Jenkins shouted after him.

He about-turned and shrugged. 'Let her go. See what happens next.'

Jenkins followed a few paces. 'This is serious. You've more or less told her we're to blame for her brother's death.'

'It wasn't one of us.'

'She could go on a killing spree, picking off uniformed officers in a random act of revenge.'

'She won't. She'll wait until she knows what's what.'

'How can you be so sure?'

Reece rounded the corner and opened the door to the stairwell. 'Trust me. I know what I'm doing.'

Chapter 66

Big Babs had Billy Creed's journal. Archie was convinced and couldn't believe he hadn't thought of it any earlier. He'd been so freaked out with everything going on in his world, he clearly wasn't thinking straight.

Babs must have helped herself once he'd left the snooker hall. Took it and blamed him. It was *her* they should be after.

But what was her motive for doing such a thing? For purposes of bribery, maybe? Or a show of allegiance to a person or group? It could be either. Or she could be playing both sides for her own personal gain? Babs was obviously a tricky and dangerous character to be dealing with.

And even if they—whoever *they* were—discovered where the journal was, Archie knew he'd still be a target. He was a loose end to be silenced because of what he'd already found out. That's why he had to get it back. Get it back and take a chance in passing it on to DCI Reece before anyone else lost their lives. The detective was the key to shutting this thing down.

But where did Babs live? Not that Archie could knock on her front door, demanding she give the journal to him. Besides, the woman looked perfectly capable of loosening a few of his teeth if she needed to. And if she was one of them, then she could just as easily stall him while summoning the gunman to carry out unfinished business.

He'd have to break in and take it. Not *him* exactly. He wouldn't have a clue how. But there was someone who might fit the bill. A man he'd met only twice previously, and although Coombsie had never admitted it, Archie had the distinct feeling the pair of them might have been cousins.

But where to find this man? Especially now Coombsie wasn't there to help. Archie took a chance and went to the last place he'd seen *Dodgy Bob*.

It took him a little more than an hour of searching to find the man he was looking for. Sprawled on a bench in Bute Park—next to the castle—two cans of unopened lager trailing from his outstretched hand.

'Wake up.' Archie tapped Bob's face with increasing amounts of effort before the man woke from his drunken stupor.

'Who are you?' Bob asked, dribbling saliva down his whiskered neck.

Archie recoiled from the heady mix of stale alcohol and body odour. 'It's Archie. Don't you remember me?' He leaned close enough to give the other man a fighting chance. 'I was with Daniel the last time we met.'

Bob drew the cans close to his chest and opened one eye. Only the left side of his face moved. He'd obviously suffered a facial palsy of some sort. 'Tops, man.' He closed the eye and smacked his lips, wetting them.

Archie gave him a heftier nudge. 'No. No. Wake up. This is important.'

'I'm on my lunch break,' Bob said, turning onto his other side with a loud fart. 'Speak to my secretary.'

Archie grabbed the cans and hid them behind his back. That got Bob's attention. He sat up and reached for them. 'Listen to what I've got to say,' Archie said, bringing the cans into view again.

Bob got to squeezing a blackhead on his chest. He yawned widely, looking disinterested. 'Get on with it, then. Beyoncé is sending a car for me in an hour.'

Archie couldn't tell if the man's attitude was down to the lager alone, or the consumption of something a lot more intoxicating. Either way, Bob didn't look like a man who'd be of much use to him. 'Daniel's dead.' It was best not to dress it up in unnecessary flannel. Archie waited long enough for the comment to spiral away inside Bob's skull. 'We got caught up in something we shouldn't. Me mostly.'

Bob was rolling a cigarette on his folded knee. He sprinkled tobacco onto the open paper and brought it to his mouth. He gave the paper a lick before folding it over. Then licked it again. 'Got any puff on you?'

'I don't smoke.' Archie bent at the waist. 'Did you hear what I said about Daniel?'

Bob struck a match on his dirty jeans and brought the fragile flame to the end of the cigarette. Archie wondered how it lit in such a way. 'Friction,' Bob said, reading his mind. 'Generate enough heat and it'll ignite without a spark.'

'*Hello!* Daniel.'

Bob swiped at the cans and missed. 'I heard you the first time.'

Archie handed them over. There wasn't much point in him not doing so. 'Don't you have anything else to say?'

Bob inhaled deeply, releasing copious amounts of smoke from his nostrils. Against the backdrop of the castle, he looked like a dragon from legends of old. 'Who did it?'

Archie scratched his head. 'I don't know exactly.' It wasn't a lie.

'You don't know?'

Archie spent the next few minutes telling Bob what little he'd so far pieced together.

'And you came to me because you thought I'd be able to sort this out for you?'

Archie lowered himself onto the bench and wedged his hands between his knees. 'I've screwed up. My friend is dead and I don't know who else to turn to. You and Daniel were cousins, right?'

Bob had a good scratch. 'Daniel was my nephew. My sister's boy.' He offered a can of lager. 'Take it. You look like you could do with a drink.'

Archie sat staring at the can. 'You know what? I think I will.' He picked at the ring pull and took a long gulp.

For a while, they spoke about Coombsie. Then they sat in silent contemplation, staring at the castle opposite, ignoring people who knew no better than to turn their noses up as they passed by. There was no shortage of their type. There never is.

Bob offered the cigarette. Archie declined. 'You still haven't told me what you want.'

Archie knew he was risking a third man's life. He also knew that there were few alternatives. 'I need you to steal something for me.'

Chapter 67

'You really thought I wouldn't warn him?' Reece said, shaking his head in disbelief.

Jenkins was walking with a half-trot to keep up. 'I've no idea what you're doing. Whatever it is, it's messing with my head.'

Cardiff Marina was on a bend in the wide river. Not too far from the police station. Opposite was a mix of greenery and new apartment blocks. A pair of cranes stood lifeless in the distance. Tall and red. Their long jibs reaching a good fifty metres or more out in front of them.

Reece stopped on the quayside, admiring the boats. It was sunny, with a cooling breeze that had all flags pointing in the same direction.

'You ever fancy doing something like this?' He took off his sunglasses to get a better look at their surroundings.

'When would I have enough money for one of these?' Jenkins paused alongside a cruiser, watching a couple who would have been in their sixties cook themselves an early lunch. She gave them a wide smile, but got no offer to board and take a share.

'You don't have to be a millionaire,' Reece said. 'Some of these smaller yachts are quite affordable.'

'For the likes of you, maybe.'

They walked further on. 'Did I tell you the house in Llandaff has sold already?'

'No.'

'It must have been Ffion. First day. First viewing, in fact.'

'Told you, didn't I?'

'And you weren't wrong.'

'I seldom am. Not that you ever notice.'

'There's a canal up in Brecon,' Reece said, steering the conversation back to boating. 'Runs for thirty-five miles through the National Park to Cwmbran. An absolutely stunning area.' He stared past the tottering masts and flapping sails, watching the gulls rise and fall on the swell of the water. 'Anwen and I did a day trip the summer she died. We hired a narrowboat at Goytre Wharf.'

'I'll mention it to Cara,' Jenkins said. 'She might want to have a go.'

'I could buy one of my own and take you both out for the day.' He paused to stare at his junior colleague. 'What's so funny? Why are you laughing at me?'

Jenkins composed herself. 'I'm trying to imagine you dressed up in Captain Birdseye clobber.' She put her hand to the side of her head and saluted him.

'Do you ever take anything seriously?'

'Come on. *You* with a pipe and flat cap? I'd pee myself laughing.'

Reece blushed. 'I don't know why I bother telling you any of this?'

'Hey, we're having a nice time by the sea, boss. You haven't mentioned a pleck or a child with a snapped neck once.'

After threatening to throw her into the sea if she didn't shut up, they walked the rest of the way in silence. The name of the boat they were looking for was *Aquaholic*.

'There it is.' Jenkins pointed. 'That one parked over there.'

'Moored,' Reece told her. 'Boats moor. They don't bloody park.'

Jenkins kept her distance, not wanting to get soaking wet. 'One day on the Brecon Canal and already he's Admiral of the Fleet.'

Reece chuckled, but didn't let it show.

Aquaholic was moored between a pair of tall-masted yachts and was something in the order of eighteen metres long. It was mostly white with a red and blue line running the full length of its hull. The blue matched a canvas canopy that provided welcome shade to the helm area of the deck.

Looking very comfortable in a cream leather chair next to a polished chrome wheel was Inspector Mike Brogan. He brought a hand to his forehead, squinting into the bright sun. 'You found me.' He stood and welcomed them aboard. 'Mind you don't slip,' he said, catching Jenkins by the waist. If Brogan was still annoyed at Reece's comments back at the station, he wasn't showing it. He offered a hand, which Reece didn't take. 'Can I get you both a drink?' Brogan asked.

It wasn't a social visit, but Reece was thirsty. 'Do you have any lemonade?'

'Do *I* have lemonade?' Brogan said theatrically. He swung open a fridge door and reached inside. 'My wife makes the best lemonade to be found anywhere in the world. *Ta-da*.' He handed the detectives a glass each and poured a generous measure for both of them.

'This wouldn't have been cheap,' Reece said, giving the yacht an appraising once over.

'A man has to spend his money on something.' Brogan returned the almost-empty jug of lemonade to the fridge and closed the door. 'What about you?' he asked. 'Don't tell me – golf?'

Reece winced. 'Wasn't it Mark Twain who said: "*golf is a good walk spoiled*"?'

Brogan shook his head slowly. 'If you say so.' He pulled two wooden chairs that were almost hidden beneath a table. 'Sit down. I'm guessing you've got something to ask about the bullet found in the car?'

Glad to have left his suit jacket in his office, Reece let his arm hang over the side-rail to catch some sun. For a moment, he shut his eyes and savoured the warmth on his face. He could certainly get used to this slower pace of life. He took a sip of lemonade. It was sour and not a patch on Anwen's. He put it to one side. 'I've been chatting to Marma Creed.'

'Billy's sister?'

'Is there another one you know of?'

'Thankfully not.'

'She has it in her head that Billy was taken out by a serving police officer and not Arvel Baines.' Marma had, of course, said nothing of the sort and would still be stewing on what he'd told her at the station.

Brogan turned a finger towards Reece, then himself. 'One of *us?*'

'I know *I* had nothing to do with it,' Reece said. 'What about you?'

Brogan lowered his glass. He stood and poured his lemonade over the side and into the water. 'You really are way off the mark with this.'

'Time will tell.' Reece stepped off the yacht and stretched an arm for Jenkins to grab hold of. 'We didn't have enough to detain Marma,' he said with a cursory wave goodbye. 'She's back on the streets and was looking pretty pissed off when we let her go.'

Chapter 68

'Did you get hold of the bus driver?' Reece asked.

Ginge looked up from what he was doing. 'He's downstairs, waiting.'

'You asked him to come here? There was no need for that.'

'He offered,' Ginge said. 'And I thought it would be easier than you going over to the depot.'

'Fair enough.' Reece tried to get a better view of the newbie's computer screen. 'Is that the footage from the castle?'

'We're still waiting for it. They've promised it'll be no later than tomorrow.'

'They *do* know this is a murder investigation? Get on to them again. Tell them I want it tonight.'

'Yes, boss.'

'What are you looking at there?'

Ginge turned the screen away from him. 'Uniform found what they think is the gunman's motorbike. Burnt out on the Ely Trail like we expected it would be.'

'That's good news, isn't it?' Reece said. 'You look like you're bothered by something?'

'That spot isn't far from the chandlery.'

'What's one of those?' Jenkins asked.

Reece answered: 'In this context, it's a retailer to the shipping industry.'

'Or the leisure market,' Ginge added. 'Cardiff Marina being only a stone's throw away.'

Reece glanced at Jenkins. 'And we all know who's got a boat *parked* there? Brogan could have carried out the shooting on the bus, made his getaway on the stolen bike, and got round to the marina using a dinghy he'd hidden next to the trail.'

'He'd know we'd be watching the roads,' Jenkins said. 'But not the rivers.'

'There's something else.' Ginge closed the laptop lid. 'I didn't think to mention it before. That day I went to Peter Larson's post-mortem. I saw Inspector Brogan and ACC Harris talking in the staff car park before I left.'

'We know,' Jenkins said. 'They came up here together, remember?'

'My point is, Inspector Brogan arrived on a motorbike. It looked powerful.'

'Did he indeed?' Reece made a fist. 'Brogan's a biker. Interesting.'

'Are you going to bring him in?' Jenkins asked.

Reece didn't answer. 'Ginge, get hold of past case files where Brogan and Billy Creed might have rubbed shoulders? Look for anything with ACC Harris's involvement.'

'How far back are we talking?' What Reece was asking of the young detective involved a tremendous amount of work, spanning decades of elapsed time. 'Are you able to narrow it down a bit?'

Reece came away. 'Give Maggie Kavanagh a call and tell her I'm asking. If there's any dirt from years ago, she'll have been aware of it.'

Chapter 69

'You're not under caution,' Reece said, resting his coffee mug on the table. 'But I do need to get a few things cleared up while you're here.'

Doug, the bus driver, was fidgety. He kept looking up at the clock on the far wall, checking it against the time kept by his wristwatch. 'Okay. Whatever you say.'

'Thanks for coming here to the station, by the way.'

'I clocked off at five and came straight over.'

'You saved me a trip. I'm grateful for that.'

'I've already told your people everything I know,' Doug said. 'I wasn't lying, if that's what you think?'

'No one's calling you a liar.'

'Right.'

'Can I get you more coffee?'

Doug tapped his paper cup. 'Any more than this and I'll be up all night needing to pee. You got that problem as well?' he asked.

'It's a badge that comes with age,' Reece said. 'I'm up twice a night as it is.' The reason for him going along with such bland and unrelated conversation was to have Doug trust him enough to drop his guard should he have anything to hide.

'Broken sleep does nobody any good,' the driver continued.

Reece wouldn't disagree. He studied Doug with a critical eye. The man looked an honest sort and reminded him a little of Albert Einstein in his later years. A heavier Einstein. Reece was fairly sure that all bus drivers underwent periodic medicals, though how Doug got through his, dumbfounded him. Reece imagined the man racing fifteen tonnes of metal across a busy junction, gripping his chest in mid-cardiac arrest. It was a frightening thought. 'I want to ask you about Archie Ives,' Reece said.

'What about him?'

'Do you know him well?'

'From the bus, mostly. Bumped into him a few times at the football. That's what got us talking in the first place.' Doug stopped picking at his nails to ask: 'You a Bluebirds fan?'

'I can't stand football,' Reece said without hesitation. 'Grown men rolling about the place like they've been machine-gunned down.' He pulled a face. 'Rugby's my game. That and boxing.'

'Fair enough.' Doug folded his arms and rested his elbows on the edge of the table. 'What do you want to know about me and Archie?'

'How long have you been driving that route?'

'The twenty-two? It's got to be more than a twelve-month. Nearer eighteen. Yeah. Eighteen months, definitely.'

'You'd get to recognise the habits of your regulars, I'd imagine?'

'I suppose.'

'If they have a favourite spot to sit?'

'Probably.'

'Did you ever notice which seat Archie usually sat in?'

'There's no *usually* about it. Always the same one where he was concerned. Halfway up on the right as you look at it from the front of the bus.'

'Except for the day of the shooting,' Reece said.

'I don't know what happened there.' Doug waved an arm like he was swatting an invisible fly. 'But I'd be doing the lottery if I was wearing that boy's shoes.'

'Did anyone ask you about Archie in the lead up to the shooting? Where he gets on? Where he sits?'

Doug shook his head. He started to say something. Then stopped and pulled a face.

'What?' Reece asked. 'This is important. If they did, then I need to know.'

'He said he'd nick me if I opened my mouth. Something about jeopardising an ongoing police investigation.'

'Who told you that?'

'Someone from the drugs squad. One of your lot.'

Reece scratched his head. 'Drugs?'

'He said Archie was under surveillance for couriering them in that bag he always carried over his shoulder.'

'And you believed him?'

'Like I told you, I only know Archie from talking football. He could have been up to anything, as far as I knew.'

'Did you ever mention it to Archie?'

'It was no business of mine. Besides, I'm retiring next year. A quiet life is what I'm after till then.'

'Did you get the officer's name?' Reece asked.

'I'm not sure he told me.'

'He would have done. He has to identify himself.'

Doug puffed his cheeks. 'I'm shit with names. Always have been.'

'Brogan?'

'That doesn't ring a bell.'

'What did he look like? Tall? Short?'

'Do you know how many passengers I see in a day?'

'But only one asked you about Archie.'

'Still.'

'Wait here. I'll be five minutes.' When Reece returned, he was slightly out of breath and was carrying two sheets of paper. He put the first in front of Doug. 'Is that him?'

Doug studied the photocopy of Brogan's face. 'Nope.'

'You're sure that's not the police officer who was asking questions?'

301

'Definitely.'

For completeness, Reece placed the other photocopy on the table. It was of Detective Sergeant Arthur Moles, CID. 'What about this one?'

Doug shook his head. 'Nah. Nothing like him.'

Reece slouched in his seat and collected the paperwork. 'There would be CCTV footage of the officer talking to you, wouldn't there?'

'The driver's cabin is always filmed,' Doug said. 'Do you know how many drivers were assaulted before they started doing that?'

The statistic was of no interest to Reece right now. 'I could request footage of the conversation?' he said, hopefully.

'Not anymore. Our company's equipment records for seven days before it's full.'

Reece did a quick count. He was out of luck. 'What happens to it after that?'

'It's wiped clean unless there's a reported incident that needs looking into.'

Reece stood. 'Would you do me one last favour before you go? If I get someone to sit in front of a computer with you, could you give a description of the officer you spoke to?'

'No problem at all,' Doug told him.

Jenkins left Ffion Morgan alone in the incident room, tidying up loose ends before leaving for the night. Ginge had worked hard getting Reece the files he'd wanted and had since left for home. The rest of the team had flitted out, one by one, until the place was near enough deserted. She'd told Morgan she'd see her the next morning and could have taken any one of several exit routes through the building. She had a habit of alternating them, with no real reason for doing so.

As she exited the lift and followed the corridor, she decided to call in on Reece—to remind him that the files he wanted were upstairs—and doubled back on herself, heading for the interview room. She knew which one he'd be using for the informal chat with the bus driver and entered the cramped observation room annexed to it. 'Whoa, sorry,' she said, thinking she'd gatecrashed the wrong interview. Looking through the one-way glass, she couldn't see Reece, but recognised the bus driver.

'No problem,' said Arthur Moles.

'What are you doing here?' Jenkins asked.

'I thought I'd listen in. Your boss was right to have a go at me over that car window. I jumped to conclusions and was wrong.'

'You don't know where he's gone, do you?'

'He popped out a couple of minutes ago,' Moles said, collecting his wallet and phone. 'Well, I think that's enough for me.'

'Me too,' Jenkins agreed. 'I'm supposed to be visiting my mum on the way home.'

'Why the sad face?'

Jenkins pulled on the door and waited for Moles to pass through. 'You know how it is when people grow old.'

Chapter 70

JENKINS LET HERSELF IN with a spare key she always kept about her person. 'Mam,' she called down the hallway. 'It's only me.'

'Hiya, Love,' her mother called back. 'I'm in here, watching Corrie.'

Jenkins entered the front room. It was tidy enough. She leaned over the back of the sofa and gave her mother a hug. 'Had your tea yet?'

'Yes.'

She poked her head through the door to the kitchen. There was no evidence of any meal preparation. 'What did you make?' she asked, re-entering the living room. 'Something nice?'

'Sausage and mash. I've put yours in the fridge. There's brown sauce in the cupboard next to the sink. I'll do you some bread and butter when you're ready.'

'I'll take it home with me,' Jenkins said, dropping onto the sofa. She cuddled up close and rested her head on her mother's shoulder.

'You're going out again?'

Jenkins worded her answer carefully. 'I live in Rhiwbina, don't I? With Cara.'

'I know that.'

'So I wouldn't be staying here every night.' She sat up. 'Unless you need me to?'

'I can look after myself.'

'I know you can. I was just saying, if you need me to stay, then—'

'I said I'm all right.'

Coronation Street went to the adverts. 'Fancy a cup of tea?' Jenkins asked.

'I've just had one, thank you.'

There was no teacup on the arm of Margaret's chair. Empty or otherwise. Jenkins plumped a cushion and held it against her. 'What have you been up to today?'

'Watching Coronation Street.'

'I meant earlier.'

'I went shopping.'

'I thought you did that yesterday?'

Margaret gave that a great deal of thought before answering. 'I went again today.' She nodded, reaffirming her answer.

'Where did you go?'

'Town.'

'Get anything nice?'

Margaret tore her gaze away from an advert selling car insurance. 'I know what you're doing,' she said accusingly. 'You're testing me again.'

'I'm doing no such thing.'

'You think I'm losing my marbles.'

'I'm making sure you're okay.'

'I can look after myself, thank you very much.'

'I didn't say you couldn't.'

'Then why are you always checking up on me?'

'I'm not. You weren't answering your phone earlier. What was I supposed to do?'

Margaret went back to watching the television. 'That's because I couldn't find it. Not because I've gone stupid overnight.'

'I'll go make us both a cup of tea, shall I?' Jenkins put the back of her hand against an electric jug kettle. It was cold but filled to the lid. She emptied some of the water into the sink, then set it to boil. She put two mugs on the counter and opened the fridge. 'Mam?' She started but didn't finish. There was no plate of sausage and mash to be seen anywhere. On the second shelf down was Margaret's house phone.

Jenkins hadn't travelled very far when she first thought someone might be following her. The long stretch of winding tarmac was mostly bordered by trees and fields, with little in the way of useful lighting.

Her mother had earlier laughed off the phone-in-the-fridge thing, putting it down to absentmindedness. "*I even put milk in my gravy granules last week, thinking it was coffee,*" she'd joked. "*I'm doing it all the time, lately.*"

Jenkins had noticed for herself. And for several months now. At first, she'd laughed with her mother; teasing her about her age. It was no longer funny. Things were definitely not right.

The lights from the car behind were blinding. So much so, she had no chance of reading the number plate. She pressed the anti-glare lever on the interior mirror, darkening its screen. That also improved her ability to get a proper view of the road ahead.

She pressed the accelerator, edging close to the maximum speed limit for the area. The gap between the two vehicles got no wider. The car behind was also speeding up.

She thought about ringing it in and asking if there was a patrol car nearby that could tail them for a while. 'Don't be daft,' she told herself. 'You've been watching way too much telly. Mam's playing on your mind.'

Jenkins lurched forward in her seat—her head almost impacting the steering wheel—when the car behind first nudged her back end. 'What the—' She sounded her horn and fought to avoid a collision with the kerb. Her right foot sank lower on the accelerator pedal, sending her way outside her comfort zone.

The car hit her a second time. She crossed the white centre lines of the road, lucky that nothing was travelling in the opposite direction. The oversteer to correct that made her Fiat 500 skid about its axis before toppling and tumbling down the banking, coming to a halt in a wheels-up position against the trunk of a tree.

Chapter 71

Reece nursed a generous measure of Penderyn Sherrywood whisky, while Blackberry Smoke played an acoustic session on vinyl in the corner of the room.

There was a handwritten note from Ginge, paper-clipped to the uppermost file in his lap. Reece would have described its style as something of a scrawl. It was barely legible. He thought it read: ***These are the ones Maggie says you'll be interested in.***

He leafed through the first file, noting the date. It was well before his time in plain clothes. Jack Stokes was the SIO on the case. Idris Roberts was Stokes's detective sergeant. Reece's stomach turned over. He wasn't expecting to come across his dead father-in-law's name. His mind was suddenly flooded with memories of Idris. And only moments later, the inevitable images of his deceased wife.

The case in question involved a gangland killing. Two rising wannabes fighting over ownership of a local nightclub. One of them was found in a cold and wet alleyway, bludgeoned to death with what had probably been a crowbar or other similar implement. What went around, came around, was Reece's view on the matter.

The survivor was a very young Billy Creed. He was climbing the ranks of the Cardiff underworld. Reece took a sip of whisky and continued his homework. Creed got an eighteen-month prison stretch for the crime. An act of self-defence being the successful mitigation offered by his legal counsel. The sentence was lenient by any standard.

The next file documented a crime committed a few years later. Again, gangland related. Again, involving Idris Roberts and no surprise – Billy Creed. This time, Idris was the SIO on the case. Reece thought Jack Stokes might have retired by then. Pensioned off under suspicion of taking backhanders and possibly worse.

The Force didn't need the negative publicity of hauling one of their own senior detectives over the coals. Besides, those were the days when all might be forgiven should an *unconventional* officer do the decent thing and leave without making a fuss.

Creed was arrested for the offences of discharging a firearm in public, and endangering the life of another man. The case never made it to trial. There were issues with the legality of the search conducted by Idris's team. There was incorrectly filed paperwork.

Lots of it. And cock up of all cock ups – the firearm went missing while being processed as evidence.

Reece closed the file and slapped it against the arm of his chair. 'Idris, for God's sake, man. What were you doing?'

There were two more files to go through. Reece was tired, but pushed on regardless. He put the unfinished whisky to one side. It wasn't helping his need for wakefulness and concentration.

The names hit him like a slap in the face. There they were in black on white. Roberts. Creed. And this time, Mike Brogan. Reece felt a sinking sense of foreboding. 'Not you, Idris. Not you.'

The case involved a shooting on a local council estate that Billy Creed needed for a monopoly of the area. According to witnesses at the scene, only one shot was fired during the entire confrontation, and that belonged to the victim himself. The rival drug dealer was dead. Creed crowned king at last.

But how did Ali Osman come to shoot himself? Reece rubbed his aching eyes and read on.

There had been a violent struggle as officers attempted to disarm the man; the sound of a gunshot ringing out across the estate. Osman had slumped to his knees, gripping his belly, and died in the back of an ambulance as it made its way to the city's main hospital.

The attached post-mortem report concluded that Osman had died of a massive haemorrhage caused by a lacerated liver and transected portal vein.

Rumours soon circulated on the estate. The police had turned a blind eye. Some said there was more to it than that. But none of the locals made their concerns official. Billy Creed and his boys made sure of that.

Reece felt sick to his stomach. Idris hadn't once mentioned a word of this. Not even when the two of them sat and drank whisky into the small hours. He felt betrayed. Sad. Angry. He repeated his earlier mantra of 'Not you, Idris. Not you.'

Reece made three separate telephone calls before going to bed. The first was to the retired Home Office forensic pathologist, Twm Pryce. The second to the journalist, Maggie Kavanagh. Armed with enough information to be getting on with, he made a third call. This one to the Governor of HM Prison, Cardiff.

Chapter 72

ARCHIE WAS WELL BEYOND anxious, waiting for news. Dodgy Bob would surely have been up to no good by now. He might already have helped himself to the journal and be making his way back to the underpass near City Hall and the museum.

Bob knew where Big Babs lived. He also knew that she spent Friday nights handing out cloakroom tickets in exchange for coats at Billy Creed's *Midnight Club.* Or should it now read *Marma Creed's Club?* Archie didn't know what to think anymore. His brain was just about frazzled.

He was beginning to wonder if meeting in the underpass was such a good idea. If his assailants came from both sides of the tunnel simultaneously, he'd be done for. He could also quite easily be mugged by a passing druggie.

No, the underpass was definitely not one of his better ideas. He had his back and the sole of his right foot pressed against the graffitied wall when the dark silhouette of a burly man appeared at the castle-end of the tunnel. He watched the man approach. It didn't look like Dodgy Bob. He checked in the other direction. It was clear. For now, at least. He'd run if he needed to. Not towards the clear end of the tunnel as they'd expect him to, but past the man coming towards him. That would probably be the safer of the two options. But only if he managed to get past.

The man slowed. Then stopped altogether. He turned round and made off without uttering a word. 'He thought *I* was waiting to mug *him*.' If he hadn't been so scared, Archie would have laughed at the absurdity of it.

The other absurdity was the trust he'd put in Bob to do as promised. The drunk might well be lying face down in the gutter, blotto. Or had forgotten about their meeting completely.

But what if he was floating down the river? Bleeding like his nephew had? Now that was a sickening thought.

Archie needed better quality air than the damp and urine-tinged variety on offer in the underpass. He made his way out. Went up the slope and sat on a concrete bollard next to the road.

Armed with little more than a crappy torch and one of the cheap burner phones, Bob entered Babs's house via the back door. The cloying smell struck him first. The woman wasn't emptying her food recycling bin anywhere often enough.

The kitchen was small. Tiny, in fact. He kept the puddle of light low and just ahead of his feet. Something hissed to his right. It sounded like a venomous snake poised to strike. He swung the torch in an arc-like motion, settling its beam on a cat that looked none too happy with him being there. He let it be and went searching through the cupboards, looking for something to drink. He came across a half-bottle of cheap gin and drank three fingers of it in one go. He pocketed the rest, apologising to Big Babs in her absence.

The glass door to the living room opened with a loud click of its catch. Bob gripped the handle and listened for footsteps on the floorboards upstairs. 'She's not here,' he told himself. 'She's still at work.' He reached into his pocket and helped himself to another couple of fingers of gin.

Something brushed against his ankle. He lost his footing in the disorientating shroud of darkness and fell against a television set that crashed to the floor with him and the spilled bottle. He rolled onto his back; his eyes closed as he took a deep breath to calm himself. When he opened them again, the wedge of torchlight illuminated the carpet in front of him. It was only when he got to his knees and pushed on the chair for added balance that he saw Big Babs staring lifelessly at the wall opposite.

Chapter 73

'Where's Redlar?' Reece peered into the crowded rear of the Land Rover Defender. 'I thought you were fetching him with you?' They were on their way to collect his Land Cruiser from the farm in Brecon. The old Peugeot had already been scrapped in exchange for a hundred quid. He'd donated the money from the sale of the car to the Air Ambulance Charity. They needed it more than he did. He'd then matched the amount with a separate donation to Cancer Research Wales. Nagging worries for Ffion Morgan's well-being, his motivation for doing so.

Life was so full of unfairness and questions left unanswered. Reece had many himself and knew he couldn't be the only one.

It was the end of an era.

A sad day indeed.

He'd courted Anwen in that car. Raced it across the undulating roads of the National Park. Windows wound all the way down with the pair of them singing *Bon Jovi's*, 'Living on a Prayer' at the top of their voices.

They'd picnicked next to reservoirs that sparkled with the jewelled light of the setting sun. Skinny-dipped in the cold, black water. Then huddled together under a blanket, camping out beneath the stars.

How he missed those days.

Missed Anwen.

Only memories now remained.

'Too much hassle,' Yanto said, keeping his eyes on the road. 'The dog's with Ceirios.'

Reece was disappointed. He missed the pup and needed to know it was okay. 'Oh,' was all he managed in response.

'Stop moping.'

'Who said I was?'

'I did. You've got a face like a smacked arse again.'

Reece didn't need an argument. His mind was still trying to comprehend what he'd found in the old case files the night before. 'The MOT must have gone well?' he said. They were travelling along the A470 dual carriageway towards Merthyr Tydfil. Rugged examples of rock face and forest on either side of the road.

Yanto changed down a gear as they began a gentle climb. 'One or two advisories was all it came up with. Easy enough to fix now we know about them.'

That didn't sound so good to Reece. 'Like what?'

'Needs a good run on an open road to sort out the emissions.'

'You sure there's nothing seriously wrong with it?'

Yanto gripped the steering wheel. 'Stop worrying all the time.'

'I'm just saying there's no point in me having it if it's still got problems.'

'And *I* told you, it needs a good run. Nothing more. It's been sitting in that barn for years, doing nothing. You can't expect it to be perfect straight out of the box.'

Reece put his head against the side glass, watching a Red Kite circle above the road. He wound the window down and craned his neck until the bird of prey was out of sight. 'I phoned Twm Pryce last night. Had a proper chat for the first time since he retired.'

'About what?'

Reece checked the sky in the hope of another sighting. The bird wasn't there. 'Things in general. Work. Idris came up a couple of times.'

'Idris?'

'Do you think we had him all wrong?' Reece asked.

'What do you mean?'

'Maybe I was too close to notice. Being married to his daughter.'

'What are you on about?' Yanto pointed over his shoulder. 'You lost me way back there.'

'I only wish I knew.'

They travelled in silence for a short while. 'Twm never got married, did he?' Yanto said, slowing to cross the roundabout.

'Divorced years ago.'

'Lucky sod. I'll have to ask him how he managed that.'

Reece grinned. 'You'd be lost without Ceirios.'

'I'd be far less busy.' Yanto took a sideways glance. 'She's a bit like you. Needy.'

'*Me?*'

'Look at all the work you've had me doing on that cottage of yours?'

'It's mostly cosmetic stuff from now on.'

'Bollocks, it is.' Yanto flashed his headlights to let a flatbed lorry pull in ahead of them. 'The bathroom and kitchen still need gutting. I can't see you doing that by yourself.'

'I'm getting someone in to do the bigger jobs while I crack on with the rest.'

Yanto's eyes narrowed until he'd developed a monobrow. 'Who?'

'Not you. Don't worry.'

'Who then?'

'Proper tradespeople.'

'I'll believe that when I see it.'

'I've got someone coming next week to measure up. Anyway,' Reece continued. 'Twm was wondering if you and me wanted to go fishing? Said he'd get us a reservoir day-licence.'

'When?'

'It might be a couple of weeks before I can make it. This latest case is going to drag on a bit. You two can always go without me for now.'

Yanto turned down a narrow lane. 'Maybe.'

The Toyota Land Cruiser was waiting outside the farmhouse when they got there. 'You've given it a wash,' Reece said, pinching Yanto's left knee. 'It looks fab.'

'I wasn't handing it over covered in hay and chicken shit.'

'Still. Thanks. How much do I owe you?'

'Only what it cost to get it back on the road.'

'What's the going rate for the truck itself?' Reece asked.

'You can have it.'

'I can't just have it. What's the total cost?'

'Shut up, Brân.'

'Yanto—'

'Call it a moving in present from me and the wife.' Yanto climbed out of the Defender. He arched his back and stretched his legs. Reece did the same. Like two old men.

Ceirios was waiting in the doorway of the farmhouse, Redlar fighting to break free of her arms. 'Happy if I let him go?' she called.

'Come on, boy,' Reece shouted. He was down on all fours on the gravel. 'Look at the size of you.' He let the pup lick his face and shrieked when it tucked into his neck. When it rolled onto its back, he tickled its belly. 'Has Uncle Yanto been good to you?'

Yanto stood over them, shaking his head. 'You bloody idiot.'

'I keep telling you, he's not a working dog,' Reece said. 'He's a pet.'

'I've been speaking to people in the pub.' Yanto was still watching him. 'Can't be sure yet, but we'd put a few quid on this one being a New Zealand Huntaway.'

Reece stopped tickling Redlar. 'Never heard of it.'

'*Working* dogs. And big buggers that don't need all that fuss you're giving it.'

'You don't have to work them?' Reece argued.

'It's bred into them. Their natural instinct will be to herd. And he's going to need heaps of exercise.'

'That's a good thing,' Reece said. 'I can take him out on a run with me.' He stared into the distance. Towards the summit of Pen y Fan. 'And whenever I pay Anwen a visit.'

'You going up there today?' Yanto asked.

'I have to get straight back to Cardiff.' Reece checked his watch. 'I've got a meeting with an ex-con this afternoon.'

'You're not staying for breakfast?' Ceirios looked disappointed.

'Sorry.' Reece gave Redlar a final round of rough and tumble. Ceirios got a peck on the cheek. He squeezed Yanto's shoulder. 'You're a top bloke and I'm lucky to have you as a friend.'

'Jesus Christ,' Yanto said, moving well out of reach. 'You'll be wanting to hug me next. Go on, sod off back to the soppy city.'

Reece laughed. 'See you both in a few days.' He squatted to pat Redlar on the way past. 'Yes, and you too.'

Chapter 74

Reece hadn't gone far. He pulled into a narrow lay-by at the side of the road and left the engine running, much to the interest of the nearby sheep. 'What's up, Ffion?' he said, lowering the window.

'Boss. We've got ourselves another body. This one's been shot through the head as well.'

Reece asked the obvious question: 'Is it Ives?'

'The bus driver.'

'You're kidding me?'

'On the Ely Trail. And not far from where the burned-out bike showed up.'

Reece felt sick to the stomach. 'Who found him?'

'A couple of dog walkers.'

'That must have ruined their day?'

'One of them was hysterical and had to be taken to hospital for sedation.'

'Did anyone get a statement from her first?'

'She was good for nothing,' Morgan said. 'I'll go over there later and see if she's calmed down a bit.'

'I'm a bit behind on time,' Reece said. 'Had to pick the car up from Brecon earlier. Can you and Jenkins get across to the scene and take a look? I'll meet you both over there.'

'I thought Elan might have been with you,' Morgan said. 'She's not come in yet this morning.'

'I'm assuming you've tried her phone?'

'Two or three times already. There's no answer.'

Reece scratched his chin. 'I told everybody I wanted them at work today. We're starting to make some real progress on this.'

'She knew, definitely. Even volunteered to buy the coffees on the way in.'

'Okay. Get yourself over to the crime scene anyway and keep me posted.' Reece almost hung up. 'Oh, Ffion. Take Ginge if you need to.'

'He's busy with something. I think he's trying to find a match for the photofit the dead driver gave yesterday.'

'Best leave him to it then,' Reece said. 'I'm on my way. Should be there within the hour.'

The Land Cruiser made short shrift of the loose gravel and undulating off-road terrain. A section of the Ely Trail was already cordoned off. Blue and white tape running from the lopsided fencing to a few sad-looking bushes.

There was a heavy presence of fly-tipping and firearms officers. Reece marched up to the nearest person with a carbine slung across his chest. 'Where's Brogan?'

'Stay behind that line,' the man said in an authoritative tone.

Reece produced his ID. 'I asked where Brogan was?'

The AFO nodded towards another wearing the same visored helmet and tactical gear. 'You'll have to ask our team leader.'

Reece went over and had his ID on show before the man could ask to see it. 'Are you in charge?'

Following a short standoff, the AFO briefed him fully. After that, he called his team in and left Reece and uniform to oversee the crime scene between them.

'Is that the deceased man's car?' Reece meant the scratched Skoda.

'The registered owner check correlates with the name found in his wallet,' the uniform said.

What was Doug doing there in the first place? Reece wondered. 'Any sign of a dog missing an owner?' He didn't like the thought that Doug hadn't been entirely truthful with him.

'No dog. No leash, sir.'

'This is starting to look more than a bit iffy,' Morgan said. 'He's got no business being anywhere near here.'

'Maybe *business* was the only reason,' Reece said with a defeated sigh.

'He doesn't look the type to be involved in this sort of thing.'

'Type? Is there one?'

Morgan tried Jenkins's number again. 'There's still no answer.' Something caught her eye on the other side of the crime scene tape. 'Boss. It's the ACC.'

'That's all we need.' Reece's phone rang in his pocket. He turned away as Harris got out of the black Jag and approached. 'Archie,' Reece said. 'I'm sort of caught up in something at the minute. Can I—'

Archie didn't wait for him to finish. 'Believe me, you'll want to hear this.'

Chapter 75

ACC HARRIS WAS TALKING to Ffion Morgan. Reece walked away and kept his back to them. 'Make it quick,' he told Archie. 'It's all kicking off over here.'

'Big Babs is dead,' Archie stammered. 'They killed her too.'

The name initially threw Reece. 'Who?'

'Babs,' Archie said. 'She worked for Billy Creed. At the snooker hall and his club in town. It's all starting to make sense now.'

'For you maybe.' Reece whistled through his fingers, trying to catch Morgan's attention. 'Just you!' he shouted. 'Jesus Christ,' he mumbled when Harris followed her. 'Hang on a minute, Archie.'

'Reece—' Harris began.

'Not now, sir.' He took Morgan by the elbow and walked her away.

Harris went after them. *'Detective Chief Inspector!'*

Reece lowered the handset. 'With all due respect, sir, will you please fuck off and let me deal with this in peace?'

Harris stormed away. Twice he turned and pointed.

Morgan's eyes widened. 'Now you've gone and done it.'

'Never mind him. Write this down.' To Archie, Reece said: 'Start again. From the beginning.'

'Babs,' Archie repeated. 'I don't know her full name. I only met her twice.'

'I know who she is,' Reece said, now that he had more information. 'Barbara Davies. Our paths have crossed a few times over the years.'

'She was at the snooker hall the night I was there with Coombsie. The night Billy Creed died. Only, I went back for my coat after we all got chucked out and there was this leather journal on the desk in the office and—'

'Slow down,' Reece said. 'You say you went back inside the snooker hall that night? Just you?'

'Yeah. When Billy Creed and everyone else had gone chasing after that Arvel Baines fella.' Archie described the argument about the missing girl and the subsequent scuffle in the doorway. Baines running off. Creed hunting for him in the growling BMW.

'And this journal?' Reece said once he had the gist of what it contained. 'Where is it now?'

'They think I've got it. That's why they came after me. That's what this is all about.'

'And do you have it?' Reece waited for the answer.

'No.'

Reece gritted his teeth. 'Shit.'

'Not all of it, anyway.'

'Throw me a line, Archie.'

'I did get a telephone number and a couple of dates before Babs caught me with it.'

'Did you see any names?'

'I didn't get time.'

'A firearms officer?' Reece offered. 'A Mike Brogan?'

'Like I said, I was rushing.'

'I want that number,' Reece told him. 'As soon as we're done here, you send it to me.'

Archie assured him he would. 'When I left the snooker hall, the journal was still on the table in the office. Babs must have gone in there and taken it. Maybe she threatened to blackmail them and that's why they killed her?'

Reece watched Harris's Jag speed away. He was in for another ear-bashing before the day was over. 'How do you know she's dead?'

There was a pause before Archie answered. He gave the address and a brief explanation of what he knew. 'You'd better get somebody over there.'

'I know you won't come to the police station,' Reece said. 'But can we meet? Somewhere of your choice. Anywhere.'

'No way. Not until this is over.'

'I can ask Maggie Kavanagh to join us. You trust her, don't you?'

'I'm not meeting anyone. Not yet.'

'Then how can I help you? You need to work with me to have any chance of staying alive.'

'At least two people are dead because of me,' Archie said in a voice that was only just audible. 'I'm going to sort this out myself.'

'Don't be foolish. Where would you even start?' Reece asked.

'With the name you just gave me. Mike Brogan, wasn't it?' The call ended without warning.

Chapter 76

'Where the hell is she?' Reece kept asking. 'This is not at all like Jenkins.'

No one knew. Not even Cara Frost. 'Elan called in on her mum last night,' the pathologist said. 'I've checked with Margaret, who says she wasn't there long.'

'And you're sure she didn't come home and then go out again while you were asleep?'

'Why would she?'

'Just thinking out loud,' Reece said. 'And there was no argument between the two of you?'

'Absolutely none at all.'

'What route would she have used?'

'Doctor Frost's already told me that,' Ginge piped up. 'I've got a patrol car onto it. There's nothing from them so far.' He swivelled in his seat. 'ACC Harris is upstairs with the chief super. George phoned to warn you.'

Reece closed his eyes. That's all he needed. Another telling off from Tweedledum and Tweedledee. 'You haven't seen me,' he said, collecting his suit jacket from his office.

'Where are you going?' Ginge asked.

'I'm not telling you. That way, you don't have to lie to a commanding officer.'

The young detective constable nodded. 'What can I do while you're out?'

'Find Brogan. Use whoever you need to help track him down. I want phone records. Bank records. Anything you can lay your hands on.'

'I'm not authorised to do that,' Ginge reminded him. 'It needs to be put to a senior officer.'

Reece knew that to be true. 'Okay. I'll sort the phone and bank stuff. You get him found and brought in for questioning.'

'What do I tell him?'

'That we're keeping him alive, for starters. God only knows what Archie Ives is planning to do.'

'And after that?'

Reece stopped at the doorway to the landing. 'I'm going to arrest him for the murders of Peter Larson and Douglas Finch.'

Chapter 77

Archie found the street outside Big Babs's house to be swarming with police activity and cordoned off in both directions. DCI Reece had taken him seriously and acted upon the information given. Logic was: if corrupt, Reece would have delayed investigating the crime scene for as long as he believed he could get away with it. The detective was proving himself to be trustworthy.

There was a solitary ambulance waiting against the kerb. Its rear doors open. A wheeled stretcher on the pavement. A silver van was parked further up the road. On its side was the emblem of the South Wales Police. Below the emblem, **CRIME SCENE INVESTIGATION** was written in bold print. Next to the silver van was a white version of it. **HEDDLU — POLICE —** on its side panels and back doors.

There were several cars. Plenty of uniformed police officers. As well as people in hooded coveralls coming in and out of Babs's house. Some of them carried cases. Others had lighting poles. One held a camera and was photographing just about everything in sight.

Archie stood among the crowd, watching. He remembered something he'd read about killers often returning to the scene of the crime to admire the chaos they'd caused. Was the killer only a few feet away? Were the two of them standing shoulder to shoulder? That sent a cold streak through him.

There hadn't been much to find of Mike Brogan online. Unsurprising, with him being a firearms officer. He and the Force wouldn't have wanted to draw attention to anyone on that team.

DCI Reece clearly thought Brogan was involved. Why else would he have let slip the name? It made sense. The killer had used a gun and was quite obviously a professional. Brogan fit the bill.

Archie found a single photograph of the man. Not a recent one. It was from a line-up of South Wales Police rugby players. He had to enlarge the image to see anything of it. The result was pixelated and not very good. He checked the crowd again and couldn't see anyone resembling the AFO, even allowing for the passage of time and blocky pixels.

'Archie *bloody* Ives.' The voice came from behind him. Someone pinched his elbow. He pulled free. Rooted to the spot, he didn't know what to say or do. 'You involved in this as well?' Maggie Kavanagh asked, nodding towards the activity across the road.

Archie pushed through the crowd with Kavanagh following. 'Go away. It's safer you have nothing to do with me.'

Kavanagh wasn't listening. 'Maybe I can help,' she said.

'Only one person I know can end this.'

Kavanagh couldn't keep up. She'd have died trying. 'Who?' she managed, bent over in fits of coughing.

'I'm gonna tell Marma Creed everything I know, and leave it to her.'

Chapter 78

When Reece's phone kept ringing, he could no longer ignore it. He pulled off the road and parked up. There was a short list of missed calls. Some had left voicemail. He'd ask Yanto if it was possible to install some sort of hands-free setup the next time the pair met. Chief Superintendent Cable had left two messages. Both of which he chose not to play. 'You can wait,' he said. 'It'll be nothing useful if Harris has anything to do with it.'

He called Morgan first. 'It's Reece. I'm returning your call.'

'Boss. Thank God. They've found Elan. She's in hospital.'

Reece stiffened, his stomach turning over. 'Is she okay?' He held his breath.

'A few bruises and a mild concussion. They've scanned her head to make sure it's nothing worse.'

'My God. When and where did they find her?'

'Less than an hour ago.' Morgan was tearful. 'Trapped upside down in her car for most of the night. She couldn't get to her phone and the passing traffic wouldn't have seen her from the road. She's lucky to be alive.'

'Did she fall asleep at the wheel?' Reece asked. He'd been working his team hard and couldn't bear the thought that he might have been complicit in the accident.

'No. Some bastard ran her off the road. That's the only bit she can remember. There's a smudge of blue paint and a dent on her back bumper where the other vehicle hit her.'

Reece gripped the steering wheel and worked his fingers open and closed. 'Get that paint analysed. It'll give us the make and model of whatever hit her.'

'Hang on a second. Ginge wants to talk to you.'

'You go over to the hospital,' Reece said before Morgan swapped the handset with her colleague. 'I want to know all the details as she recollects them.'

'Will do. Here's Ginge.'

'Boss. Hi. I thought you should know: Brogan's boat isn't at the marina. It left overnight and hasn't been seen since.'

'Did he tell anyone he was going on a fishing trip?' Reece asked. 'Did you check with his wife?'

'There isn't one. He's never been married. He lied to you.'

Reece removed his seat belt and made himself more comfortable. A passing van hooted its horn. He was too preoccupied to react to it. 'And not just about being married.'

'Looks that way.'

'Has Cable been on the prowl?'

'ACC Harris has got her looking for you.'

'What did you tell her?'

'That I hadn't seen you since we were all here with Doctor Frost.'

'She knows what happened to Jenkins?'

'She does now. Even sent a couple of uniforms to stay at the hospital.'

That made Reece nervous. 'Are they people we know?'

'They're sound, boss. They're on our side.'

'I'll give Cable a ring,' Reece said. 'That way you're in her good books for passing the message on. Look, we need to keep everything we have between the four of us for the time being. Assume no one else can be trusted.'

'What about the chief super?' Ginge asked.

'Just the four of us until I tell you otherwise. Have you finished with the footage from the castle yet?'

'I will have done by the time you're back. I got waylaid arranging for the labs to look at the paint on Jenks's car.'

'Finish that first and then get back to the CCTV.'

'Will do.'

'Ginge, before you go. I've sent you a phone number. I doubt you'll get anywhere with it, but give it a go, just in case.' He hung up and checked the other missed calls. One was from Maggie Kavanagh. He assumed she'd somehow got wind of them looking for Brogan's boat. She'd be wanting an angle, at the very least. An exclusive, probably. Reece closed his phone without calling her back.

Chapter 79

IN FOR A PENNY, Archie decided. This had to be brought to a close before anyone else died because of him. He was loitering on the pavement opposite the snooker hall. Standing in roughly the same spot he'd been on the night his world went shit-shape.

He'd seldom felt so frightened. Except for that afternoon when he'd stood beside his mother's breathing machine, waiting for the doctor to switch it off. At the same time, he'd never been so determined to see something through to its end.

He crossed the road and tried the front entrance door. It was locked. He raised his head to the camera above it and couldn't tell if it was working or not. He hammered on the door. Waved at the camera and waited.

Nothing and nobody.

He walked a few steps away, scanning the full height of the old building. There were a few windows to be seen from where he was, but as far as he could tell, there was no activity behind any of them.

He went round the side. To the same concrete pad Billy Creed's BMW had screamed away from. It had since been replaced by a Lexus SUV that waited there with its engine ticking as it cooled after recent use.

Was that Marma's car? If so, why wasn't she answering?

Archie was still pondering that question when the side door opened to reveal the woman herself. She was much taller than she'd appeared in the photographs. More frightening, too.

Maybe this wasn't such a good idea. Meeting DCI Reece would be the safer way to go. When Archie turned to flee, he walked straight into a fast-moving fist.

He came to and found himself sitting upright on a plastic chair in Billy Creed's office. There was a table next to him. The journal wasn't there. He scanned the room but still couldn't see it.

Marma Creed lowered her head to the same level as his. 'The thief came back for more. Needs his hands chopping off.'

'I'm not here to steal anything,' Archie said, massaging an ache in his chin. He rocked his jaw from side-to-side and wondered if the bigger man had fractured it with the punch. 'I'm here to ask for your help.'

Marma rose to her full height and laughed loudly. 'You've got a fucking nerve.' She bent and forced her forehead against his. 'What happened to my Billy?'

He'd been a fool to think the gangster's sister would listen to anything he had to say. 'It's all in the journal.' He was shaking with fear. 'But I don't know where that is.'

Marma slapped his face; her fingers catching his earlobe. It stung and burned. 'I beg to differ.'

Archie ducked when she aimed a second blow. 'I swear to you, I didn't take it. They must have it.'

Kahn switched on a wall-mounted TV monitor and fast-forwarded to the relevant part of the *show*.

'There,' Marma said when the moment came. 'Now tell me I'm wrong to think you're a thief.'

Archie watched the recording in black and white. The picture wasn't of great quality. It was grainy, like an old VHS video tape. Even so, the on-screen star was undeniably him. He took the journal off the desk and checked behind him. Seconds later, the screen went blank. 'That's not it,' he pleaded, rocking in his chair. 'There's plenty more to see after that. Look at the time in the top right corner. Why would it have stopped recording just after ten o'clock?' He saw Marma check for herself. Maybe he did have a chance to sort this out. 'It wouldn't have done. It would have carried on until it was set to record over. That tape's been messed with.'

Marma drew her eyes from the screen. 'Who else was here?' she demanded to know.

Archie wasn't sure where to start. From the beginning was probably best. With Arvel Baines and everything that happened after that. When he'd finished, Marma was staring at him. Squinting, almost.

'That's some story you've got there,' she said.

'It's true,' Archie insisted. 'Why else would I come back here? The police killed your brother. They killed Coombsie and Babs. They've tried to kill me twice. And next they'll come for you.'

Marma glanced at Husam Kahn, who nodded in response. 'Brogan is the main man, you say?'

'He's a firearms cop. It makes sense.'

'Get up,' Marma told him.'

Archie's legs were unsteady. He wobbled and almost fell. 'Are you going to help me?'

'You'd better be telling the truth,' Marma said, marching him out of there. 'Or I'll hang you by the ankles and empty you of all blood.'

Chapter 80

Reece found ex-Detective Constable John Venn propping up the bar of the Royal Oak in Whitchurch, Cardiff. 'Can I get you a refill?' Reece asked, squeezing between two tall stools.

Venn looked up from his newspaper. He was unshaven and reeked of alcohol. Releasing a pen from his nicotine-stained fingers, he cleared his throat and declined the offer.

Reece caught the barman's eye. 'Two pints of whatever he's drinking.'

Venn put up no real argument and didn't leave when Reece helped himself to one of the stools. 'What do you want?' he asked in a gruff voice.

Reece introduced himself without producing ID and chose not to extend a hand in greeting.

'I know who you are.' Venn finished what was left of the first pint and took a fair gulp from the full one. 'And I can guess why you're here.' He turned the newspaper over to expose the main headline. Doug, the bus driver, had made the front page. A second fatal shooting in a week would.

Reece left his drink where it was and rested an elbow on the bar. 'It's getting out of control.'

Venn watched him over the top of his glass. When he took another drink, it left him with a moustache of froth. He wiped it away with the back of his hand. 'Do you have any idea what you're up against here?'

In all honesty, Reece had no clue how deep the rot went. Regardless, it wouldn't put him off. Concerned the barman might be listening to their conversation, he asked if they could go and sit against the far wall. Given the compact size of the pub, that meant an increase in distance of only a few feet.

Venn left his newspaper where it was and took his pint with him. Reece followed close behind. There were a couple of old men sat at a circular table playing dominoes. A younger man wearing orange railway gear fed coins into a games machine in the corner of the room. None of them were paying any attention.

Venn lowered himself onto a wooden seat with a well-practised groan. His pint was almost finished. He sat staring at it until Reece called for another. 'If you've come here expecting me to give you a list of names . . .' Venn said, once the fresh pint arrived.

'I want to start by making sense of what happened the night Ali Osman died all those years back,' Reece said.

'What's the big deal to you?'

'That's when I think it all started for Creed and this crooked lot. You were there. You must know something?'

'I kept my eyes and mouth shut.'

'Why?' Reece asked, sounding incredulous. 'A man died that night.'

'If he'd been an innocent bystander, I'd have acted differently. But Osman was a killer. If he hadn't died, there's no doubt he'd have killed again.'

'But you requested an immediate transfer to Dyfed and Powys.'

'Let's say my face didn't fit after that night.'

Reece needed to know. 'Was Idris Roberts involved in corruption?'

Venn waved an arm dismissively. 'It started well before Idris's time in charge. Backhanders. Drugs. Anything you wanted. Including women and kids. Stokes was heavily involved, of course. *Shadows,* was how we referred to his gang. Nobody really knew who they were. Not for sure. Everyone was under suspicion, including Harris.'

Reece's head came up quickly. 'The ACC?'

Venn rested his empty pint pot on the table and this time spoke without the need for liquid bribery. 'Harris was only the station superintendent in those days. He had his favourites for sure. Idris wasn't one of them.'

'But Harris was a no-show at Stokes's funeral a few months back?' Reece said, remembering that there had been no representation from Headquarters in fact.

'Because he's moved on and distanced himself from them.'

'But he did go to Billy Creed's funeral,' Reece whispered, as though talking to himself.

'I've heard he's been making things difficult for you? The legacy of being Idris's son-in-law, I guess.'

'Maybe. Sometimes I think it's more than that.' Harris being obstructive didn't necessarily make him corrupt. Besides, he was too stupid to have carried it off for so long. Or was he clever to have made it look that way?

'What's that saying about rats?' Venn scratched his head. 'Isn't it something like, you're never any more than six feet away from one?'

Reece knew that to be a popular exaggeration, but understood the other man's point. 'Idris,' he said again. 'Where was he that night?'

'Hospital.'

'For what reason?'

'He had his gall bladder removed sometime around then. Got a clot on his lung to go with it. Touch-and-go at one point, if my memory serves me correctly.'

It was news to Reece. His father-in-law had never mentioned a word of it. 'Hang on. How come his name is on the case file if he wasn't there?'

Venn's laughter drew the attention of the pair playing dominoes. The man on the games machine was too busy losing his weekly pay packet to notice. The barman had since disappeared from sight. 'Do you really need to ask?'

Reece knew the management of paperwork was very different in Idris's day. Lacking in the sophisticated computer software that currently enabled authenticity checks on everything they did. There were dusty boxes in makeshift storerooms. Files shedding paper on shelves. Humans dealt with it then. Clerks and other civilians who were as susceptible to a bung as the next man.

'Go fetch us another couple of pints,' Venn said. 'We're both going to need them.'

Chapter 81

Reece had five more missed calls and the makings of a plan by the time he left the Royal Oak. He also had more questions than answers.

He flicked through the missed calls as he walked back to his car. Cable was unrelenting in her quest to get hold of him. As was Maggie Kavanagh.

He had a few things of his own to check with the journalist. Venn might easily have been feeding him a diet of bullshit. If nothing else, he prayed the stuff about Idris was true. Leaning against the imposing front wing of the Land Cruiser, he dialled.

'Maggie, what's up?'

'Where the hell have you been?' she demanded to know. 'Ives is trying to get himself killed again.'

'Wait. Slow down.'

'The stupid sod thinks he can end this by going to see Marma Creed.'

'That's my fault,' Reece said. 'Harris was on-scene and hassling me.'

Kavanagh took a while to recover from a bout of raucous coughing. By the time she did, Reece had already hung up.

Reece stomped through the incident room, his head buzzing with activity. Cable was waiting for him. 'Just the person,' he said, ignoring the fierce look on her face. 'We've got ourselves a situation.'

The chief super's eyes took on the appearance of someone suffering with advanced thyrotoxicosis. 'You bet we do. My office. *Now!*' She turned to lead the way.

'It'll have to wait,' Reece said, taking a seat beside Ginge. 'Get that CCTV footage from the castle up on your screen.'

Ginge didn't know which one of them to land his gaze on. 'Boss? Ma'am?'

'The crowd,' Reece said. 'I want to see them.'

'And I want to speak to you,' Cable repeated, this time leaning over his shoulder.

'There he is.' Reece poked a finger at the screen. 'I've been focusing my attention on the wrong man all along. Venn was right. It's not Brogan we should be after.'

'Reece, Goddammit. I'm talking to you.' Cable was red-faced and highly animated. 'ACC Harris has instructed me to—'

'*Look*,' Reece said, banging the back of his hand against the screen. 'Moles is our man. Never mind Marma and her sidekick. That's Arthur Moles, right there. *He* killed Daniel Coombs. This is when he chases Archie Ives. See – there he goes running towards Queen Street.'

'Reece.'

'Let me explain. Marma must have had Coombs in her car at some point. That's how we came across his DNA in the boot. What she was intending on doing with him in the long run, I don't know. What I *do* know is, he was alive for a short time after that.'

'Reece.'

'Ives had a telephone conversation with Coombs the day he died. Said he had a feeling his friend wasn't alone at the time. That someone was pushing him to arrange a meeting that evening.'

Cable hadn't given up. 'Reece, this is all well and good, but—'

'I think it was Marma Creed with Coombs. That's how she and her goon knew where to go. She had questions of her own—about her brother's death—and wasn't there to kill Ives. There was nothing to be gained from that. Whereas Moles had been working everybody – Coombs included. That's how he knew about the meeting at the castle.'

Cable put a hand to her head. 'Reece, ACC Harris has ordered me to—'

'We don't tell him a word about this,' Reece said. 'Harris was station superintendent at the time this started. We have to go right to the top. To the chief constable himself.'

Cable's jaw fell open. 'You're off the case. Aren't you listening to me?'

Reece got out of his chair. 'That's exactly what I expected would happen. If you don't phone the chief constable, then I will.' He turned to his team. 'ACC Harris isn't to set foot in this room while the investigation is ongoing.'

Chapter 82

The weather forecasters had been late to pick up on the presence of the approaching thunderstorm. But on its way, it was, regardless.

'Thanks for backing me up,' Reece said, ringing the doorbell. 'I wasn't sure you would.'

'You left me with little choice,' Cable answered. 'You should come with a warning sticker. That, or indemnity insurance.'

Reece grinned and rang the bell for a second time.

Cable slapped his hand and spoke through gritted teeth: 'Will you *please* behave.'

He was about to poke the button for a third time when the door opened to reveal a thin man in a neatly ironed shirt and chinos. Chief

Constable Lowe peered at them over the metal rims of his spectacles. 'Alyson, how lovely to see you.' He turned his attention to Reece. 'You'd better come in, Detective Chief Inspector.'

Lowe took them to a study furnished with wood panelling and leather seating. There was a captain's desk and matching chair just off the centre point of the room.

Reece lifted a silver greyhound ornament off the desk, turned it over in his hand, and checked the hallmark. He nodded his approval. Lowe told him to put it down. Cable visibly shrunk.

'Sit,' Lowe said, repositioning the ornament well out of reach.

Reece was there to win the man over and saw no reason to antagonise him with the mind games he so often played with ACC Harris. He lowered himself onto the sofa, next to Cable, leaving only a few inches of space between them. 'Thank you for seeing me, sir. This had to go right to the top, obviously.'

Lowe stood and poured three equal measures of whisky from a cut glass decanter. He handed two out and tasted his own. 'You can't possibly believe that ACC Harris is in any way involved in this?'

It was a good whisky. 'I can't be absolutely sure of that,' Reece admitted. 'But there's enough circumstantial evidence to suggest it might compromise the ongoing investigation should he have any further jurisdiction over it. Harris wants me off the case,' Reece added. He turned to Cable for confirmation.

'That's *ACC* Harris,' Lowe reminded him.

'Sorry, sir. ACC Harris.' Reece spent the next five or ten minutes repeating what Venn could remember of the shooting on the council estate. And how he'd been forced to request a transfer out. 'The names of most of those under suspicion can be found in these case files.' Reece handed them over and waited patiently while the chief constable read parts of them himself.

Lowe raised his head. 'I assume you know that Idris Roberts is in here?'

Reece swallowed. 'I do, sir.' He knew Anwen would never have forgiven him for doubting her father's professional integrity. 'It's my belief that the contents of some of these files have been altered. Others removed completely and replaced with fictional versions of events and fake signatures. Not at the time the cases were being worked, obviously, but several years later. Idris was clean. You can check for yourself – he was on sick leave at the time.'

Lowe closed the last of the files. If he'd made up his mind, Reece couldn't read him. 'Fast forward to what's going on now. How are the two things related?'

Reece collected his thoughts. They were jumbled, with several gaps left unfilled. 'Venn referred to the corrupt ring as *Shadows*. That's what others knew them as at the time. They recently got wind of a journal Billy Creed was keeping.'

'Yes, yes. You've already said. But how?'

'Barbara Davies.' Reece saw the blank expression on Lowe's face. 'She cleaned and did a bit of management stuff for Creed. I think she was a plant. Put there to keep an eye on him and report anything of potential compromise to the group.'

'But they killed her anyway?'

'Not *they,* as such. I think Moles has gone rogue on the group. He's shutting the whole thing down in an act of self-preservation.'

'But you had your eye on Inspector Brogan. Or am I incorrectly briefed?'

'I did, sir,' Reece admitted. 'And probably still would, had I not spoken to John Venn.'

'Are you on board with this?' Lowe asked Cable.

She nodded, even though she'd heard most of it for the first time herself only an hour previously. 'I do, sir.'

'Brogan's boat is missing from the Marina,' Reece said. 'We've checked his home and favourite haunts. Nothing. Nobody's seen or heard a word from him.'

'Do you think Moles has him captive? A bargaining chip, perhaps?'

'It's possible, sir. And the description given by the bus driver fits, even if it's not the best likeness of him.'

'So the driver was killed before he could say something he shouldn't?' Lowe said.

Reece nodded. 'And there'll be more targets out there. Moles knows he's working on borrowed time.'

'Is Inspector Brogan alive, do you think?'

Reece didn't know. 'Moles moved Brogan's boat to draw more suspicion on him. To make it look like he was the one on the run.'

'You've notified the coastguard?' Lowe asked.

'I have, sir.'

'Nothing so far?'

Reece shook his head. 'Not that I've been told.'

Chapter 83

THE RAIN WAS COMING down hard by the time they'd left the chief constable on the phone to a local magistrate. Reece had told him nothing about Archie Ives giving Brogan's name to Marma Creed. There was no need. Not now Arthur Moles had him. And if Marma was out and about in search of the missing firearms officer, she'd be wasting her time on a hunt for what was likely to be a corpse.

The *Big Red Key* put Moles's front door through on the first strike. Wood and a small panel of glass submitting with little resistance. The uniform wielding it stepped aside to let a pair of firearms officers in first. Reece and the team were waiting a safe distance away. The radio came alive with a sudden burst of static, informing them that it was safe to approach.

'Any sign of him?' Reece asked, crossing the threshold of the house with Ffion Morgan following.

'He's long gone,' one of the AFOs said. The bottom half of the man's face was hidden behind a black snood scarf.

'Sir. *Sir!*' someone shouted. It took Reece a moment to register they meant him and not one of their own. 'There's a car in the garage.'

'I bet it's blue,' Morgan said. 'And a match for the damage on Jenks's back bumper.'

'Let's hope the engine isn't still running,' Reece said, making his way round there.

Morgan walked alongside. 'He doesn't have the guts to kill himself.'

The car fit easily in the garage. At the opposite end to the up-and-over door was a small workbench and a rusted vise. Lying next to the vise was an old rasp and a few brass filings. A small tin of gun oil and a box of hollow-point bullets sat on a shelf above it. 'I think we've found our weapons factory,' Reece said, taking a Biro from his pocket. 'Get someone over here to photograph this lot.'

Morgan was circling the car with her phone held to her ear, already speaking to someone from Sioned Williams's team.

Reece pushed the pen into the front catch of a bright red toolbox. He lifted the lid and peered inside. 'Take a look at this.'

One of the AFOs came over and retrieved five individual parts of a disassembled handgun from the bottom of the box. He reached inside again and produced a noise suppressor. 'That's an Osprey.'

'Meaning?' Reece asked.

'The short version is, this thing reduces the decibel level of a discharge by around twenty-five percent.'

'Still has some noise to it then?'

'It's definitely not silent,' the AFO confirmed.

'There we go. Told you, didn't I?' Morgan was squatting at the front end of the car. She wiped her finger along the bumper. 'Red paint that'll match Jenks's Fiat.'

'How is she, by the way?' the AFO asked.

'She should be home by now,' Morgan said. 'The boss has given her a couple of days off to recover.'

'Tell her we were all asking about her.'

'I think we've seen enough,' Reece said, stepping through an internal doorway between the garage and kitchen. 'Let's get out of here. There's a killer to find.' They were only halfway along the garden path when Ginge phoned to report a sighting of Brogan's boat washed up on the rocks at Ogmore-by-Sea.

Chapter 84

THE TEAM WAS JUST about running on empty. Professionalism and the determination to bring a killer to justice, driving them on. Brogan's boat had been found by a couple of amateur fishermen braving the storm.

Reece parked up in front of the coastguard building. He slammed the car door shut and ducked instinctively as a fork of lightning struck only a mile or two inland. He ducked again when a clap of thunder followed it. His shirt and trousers were already getting soaked. He swept a handful of wet hair from his line of sight and made his way down the concrete path to the sand.

The view of the rugged coastline would have been breathtaking had there been any remaining daylight. As it was, the lights of

Minehead were little more than a blur across the water. Those of Porthcawl were hidden off to the right of where he was.

There were more lights behind him. Several of them belonging to the press. Their vans making their way down the narrow hill to the car park.

Reece could see *Aquaholic* listing on the rocks. Harshly illuminated beneath a battery of halogen bulbs fuelled by a red diesel generator. The turn of the tide was little more than an hour away. 'Have you been inside yet?' he shouted over the roar of the wind.

'Yes, sir.' The young constable was fighting to stay in one place. 'He's definitely dead.'

That came as no surprise to Reece. Moles had killed pretty much everyone else. 'Can I get aboard?'

'Coastguard says it's stable for the time being, only because of how it's wedged on the rocks. Once the tide comes back in . . .'

'I'll be off it by then,' Reece told him.

'He ain't pretty, sir.'

When was a corpse ever a pleasure to behold? Reece donned full PPE over his soaking clothes and walked the same deck on which he and Jenkins had sipped sour lemonade. It was more difficult this time, given that the yacht had a thirty-degree left-to-right tilt. He went below and stopped at the bottom of the steps, shocked and unable to believe what confronted him.

The dead man wasn't Mike Brogan. Archie Ives, neither. The corpse belonged to Arthur Moles. Even the fire damage to his upper chest, neck, and one side of his face couldn't hide his identity.

'I'm guessing the killer used that.' Cara Frost pointed to a flare gun lying on the lowermost point of the hull. Shot on deck and made his way down here. Presumably looking for a fire-extinguisher in his panic.'

'Why didn't he just throw himself into the sea?' Reece asked.

'In this storm? He'd never have got out again.'

'A decision that cost him his life.'

'There's plenty of evidence he put up a good fight before he died,' Frost said. 'He sustained offensive, as well as defensive injuries in the process.'

Reece cast an eye over the mess. Not all of it could be attributed to the storm and subsequent beaching. Only one man had walked away from this alive. Brogan was still at large. Reece reprimanded himself for taking his eye off the ball and shifting his focus from Brogan to Moles. Yes, he'd been well and truly played.

There was shouting from somewhere outside. Reece went back up on deck, steadying himself using the chrome handrail. 'What is it?' he asked, jumping down onto the sand with a slight stumble.

'They've found Brogan.'

'Where?'

'Near the estuary inlet.'

'Do we have dogs yet?' Reece asked.

'Still on their way.'

He flicked off his overshoes and ran towards the wide estuary, fighting against a competing wind. It was bread and butter for the likes of him. The shouting was louder the nearer he got.

There was breaking surf off to his left, and people shining torches at the water's edge. Like wartime search lights illuminating enemy bombers. But this wasn't an aircraft they were following. This was a ruthless killer wading against the relentless flow of water.

Reece was closing on his prey. Not entering the mouth of the estuary until he had to. He swung a punch and took Brogan down, swallowing a mouthful of salty seawater. He struck out again. Brogan put up no fight. It was over as easily as that. Reece rolled onto his back, feeling the water push him towards the sea as he read the killer his rights. 'Get a paramedic over here,' he called when finished. 'This man's not to die. Not before I've finished questioning him.'

The walk back to the car park was flooded with mixed emotions. Reece had his man, but too many people had lost their lives in the meantime. The fact serving police officers were to blame was impossible to reconcile.

There was a Lexus SUV parked near the Land Cruiser. Two of its windows lowered simultaneously. Marma Creed was sitting up front. Archie Ives in the back. Archie's door opened, and he got out. He looked nothing like the pictures taken by the camera on the bus. He was a lot thinner and sported a week's worth of beard. 'How did you know where to come?' Reece asked.

'We've been monitoring the coastguard channel,' Archie said nervously. 'Just as soon as we knew Brogan's yacht was missing from the Marina.'

Marma hung an arm from the window and patted the door panel. 'Thanks for getting my wheels back to me so soon.'

Reece nodded. 'We had no further use for them.'

When Archie turned to say something, the front window of the SUV was already on its way up. He raised a hand and waved instead. It was impossible to tell if he got a response. The Lexus reversed and then pulled away. Reece let it leave unchallenged.

'Get out of the rain,' a gravelly voice shouted across the car park. Maggie Kavanagh wagged a finger at Reece. 'It's time for my exclusive.'

'Maybe Archie should get this one?' Reece teased. 'I'd say he deserves it.'

Archie gave his head a firm shake. 'I don't think the crime desk is my cup of tea, to be honest.' He came over to Reece and held out a hand. 'You're one of the few good ones,' he said.

Reece smiled. 'You've got us all wrong. *They* were the few bad ones.'

Chapter 85

IT WAS A FULL day before they were allowed to interview Brogan. On medical grounds. Reece sat across the table from him in Interview Room Three. Detective Constable Ffion Morgan was at her boss's side.

'You're waiving your right to legal representation,' Reece said. 'Are you sure that's a good idea?'

'Look at the money I'm saving the taxpayer.' Brogan sniffed when no one else in the room reacted to his attempt at humour. 'What good would it do me, anyway?'

'None at all,' Reece said without looking up from the file he was leafing through. 'I'm just making sure you don't wriggle out of this on some minor technicality.'

'Aren't you the thorough one. Idris *would* be proud.'

Reece could play this game, if that's what the other man wanted. He lowered the file onto the surface of the table and let the silence hang there for a long while. Brogan would be keen to get the interview over and done with. Reece, on the other hand, intended to draw it out and get the answers he wanted. 'Why?' he asked.

'Why did I kill them?'

'Before that. Why hitch up with Creed in the first place?'

Brogan drew a couple of bruised knuckles across his mouth. 'His hourly rates were better than Her Majesty's. Plus, there were other perks we don't normally get our hands on.'

'Prostitutes?'

'Who said I ever paid?'

'Simple as that?' Reece said. 'Money and sex were the main driving forces behind it all?'

'Aren't they always?' Brogan ran his eyes over Ffion Morgan's designer blouse and jacket. 'You'd know where I'm coming from.'

'I'm a million miles from anywhere you've been,' she replied.

'That night on the council estate,' Reece said. 'What really happened to Ali Osman?'

Brogan slumped in his chair with his gaze fixed on the wall opposite. 'I suppose it doesn't matter much now.' He pushed himself upright again and rested his chin on a pair of handcuffed fists. 'I'll give you the bare bones. Don't expect me to be trawling through every little detail. Billy Creed was establishing a name for himself back then. He was a real piece of work and most on the patch knew better than to stand in his way.'

'But Osman was slow to catch on,' Reece said.

'Just a bit.'

'So you put a bullet in him and claimed it happened in a struggle with Creed.'

'Correct. Billy was acting in self defence. It was him or Osman and we were there to witness it.'

'Lucky him. And that's how the alliance was formed?'

'Creed had made indirect approaches to me even before then. A few quid offered for this and that. I'd always turned him down.'

'So what changed?'

'Venn trying to impress Idris Roberts and land himself the next DS job. That meant him hounding Creed and making it difficult for me to ever jump ship. Making sure that Creed got away with things made working at the station far more interesting.'

'And he, in turn, greased your sweaty palm. But Jack Stokes leaving under a cloud must have made things more difficult for you?'

Brogan was slow to respond. 'That was unfortunate.'

'Idris suspected you were up to no good, didn't he? That's why you messed with his paperwork and forged his signatures. To sully his name if anyone ever went looking through those case files and pointed a finger at you.'

'It was Idris who suggested I apply for firearms training. I think he just wanted me off his team. That suited me. It took the heat off for a while. That's what it was like back then – keep the problem moving. Out of sight, out of mind.'

Reece had been there and knew that to be true. 'The alterations to the paperwork. How did—?'

'That was all Arthur Moles's doing. I was gone by then, remember? With Venn out of the way, and Idris in hospital for months, Arthur could pretty much do as he wanted. There was no one properly overseeing him. Harris didn't know his arse from his elbow. Still doesn't, from what I've seen.'

'That's when the pair of you established the so-called *Shadows?*' Reece said.

'Other people called us that. We didn't. I always thought it was cringeworthy. Made us sound like a group of four-eyed guitarists.'

Chapter 86

'Let's move on to more recent events,' Reece said, taking a sip from a mug of lukewarm coffee. 'Billy Creed's death. Did that have anything to do with you and Arthur Moles?'

'Billy wasn't the same once his knee got shot up. It made him vulnerable and messed with his head – that and the drugs. He was paranoid. More than usual. Convinced we were gunning for him.'

'And were you?'

'Someone had to shut him up before he drew attention to us. Everything was in place. He'd have been dead before the week was out.'

'But when Arvel Baines took him over that cliff, you backed off. End of problem. Job done.'

Brogan scratched his head with both hands. 'Until that wannabe reporter came along and stirred it all up again. Can you believe he had the stupidity to ring and threaten me with what he knew?'

'How did you find out who he was?'

'Like I said, he's stupid. He gave his name to Babs when she asked – just like that. Even told her who he'd gone to the snooker hall with.'

'Daniel Coombs?'

'That's how we knew who to keep an eye on.'

'Was it Coombs who told you about the seating habit on the bus?'

'The hit on Ives had to be as public as possible. A warning to people like Venn that we'd hunt them down and kill them wherever they were.'

'Moles told the driver Ives was under surveillance for possession and supply of drugs,' Reece said.

Brogan chuckled. 'I gave him a few quid to make out it was Arthur asking the questions. I bet he gave you a fair enough description?' Brogan grinned at Ffion Morgan. 'Brilliant, don't you think?'

'Hardly,' she said, dismissively. 'The way I see it, you're stuck on the wrong side of this desk, banged to rights. That's anything but brilliant.'

The grin faded. 'Touché.'

Reece took off his jacket and hung it on the back of his chair. He stifled a yawn and faced the front again. 'Ives got away twice. Very careless of you.'

'I'd have got to him in the end. It was only a matter of time.'

'Who drove our colleague off the road?' Morgan wanted to know. 'Was it Moles? You?'

Brogan raised his arms. His wrists still cuffed. 'Guilty as charged.'

'You could have killed her.'

'Call it collateral damage.'

'You're a disgrace to the uniform,' Morgan said.

'Ouch.'

'What did you and Moles fall out over in the end?' Reece asked.

'Arthur thought we should leg it to Spain on my yacht. I don't know what he was thinking. Those days are long gone.'

'You had a fight?'

'He started it.'

'You finished it,' Reece said.

'Arthur came at me with a knife. I slipped on the deck when a swell knocked us sideways. The flare gun went off, and I went over the rail and into the sea.'

'You were lucky to be washed up on the beach.'

'Given a choice, I'd have rather died.' Brogan stood. 'As cosy as this has been, I'm done talking.'

'Where's the journal?' Reece asked.

'I'm not going there.'

'The judge might look favourably on your gesture to help us.'

'I'm dead, no matter what. Marma Creed will see to that.'

'Not necessarily. There are things we can put in place if you cooperate fully with our investigation.'

'This conversation's over,' Brogan said. 'Get me out of here.'

Reece could hear chatter from his position on the landing. The voices were familiar. Some he welcomed. Others, not so much. When he entered the incident room, ACC Harris was the first to approach him.

'I was wrong.' Harris said, offering a conciliatory hand. 'I hope we can put our differences behind us?'

Chief Constable Lowe made his move before Reece was able to respond. 'Of course we can. Isn't that right, Detective Chief Inspector?'

Reece glanced at Cable. She raised two sets of crossed fingers and closed her eyes. 'I suppose so.' Reece took Harris's hand and squeezed more firmly than was necessary. 'Excuse me a minute,' he said, making his way over to Jenkins. He gave her a gentle hug and then looked her up and down. 'How are you doing?'

'I'm good, thanks. A few aches and bruises here and there.' She put a hand to her head. 'At least the lump's gone down a bit.'

'You should be resting. I'll take you home.'

'Like hell you will. I wouldn't miss this for the world.'

'They've made a couple more arrests,' Reece said. 'We've opened up something big here.'

'That can only make it a safer place for everyone.'

Reece clapped his hands, loudly drawing attention to himself. 'Right, you lot. Time for the pub. Knock yourselves out. ACC Harris says he's putting a generous float behind the bar.'

Chapter 87

THE FOLLOWING WEEK

THE QATAR AIRWAYS FLIGHT to Doha had climbed from the tarmac of Cardiff Airport almost an hour earlier. The seat belt signs were off. Cabin crew handing out drinks and complimentary snacks.

It hadn't been a bad trip home. Marma now knew the truth behind her brother's death. She'd left Husam Kahn behind to deal with a few loose ends. And the South Wales Police were about to be systematically torn apart in an external review.

She couldn't help but admire Reece. His integrity hadn't wavered in his pursuit of the truth. He'd outed several of his own and that would have made him new enemies. She guessed the detective didn't care what others thought of him. 'Good for you,' she whispered.

And Brogan: he'd be a marked man as an inmate. His fate was already sealed. Napalm and shanking. He'd die in prison for sure. But first he'd suffer a few months as someone's bitch.

Marma accepted a second glass of Champagne and watched the sun set on the horizon from thirty-nine thousand feet.

Archie Ives was at the cemetery, talking to his mother's headstone. 'Have I got a story to tell you.' Careful not to stand on the grave itself, he stretched to clear weeds and tossed them onto the path for the time being. He caught himself checking over his shoulder and guessed it might take a while for him to stop doing that.

'I didn't know what else to do in the end,' he said. 'Billy Creed's sister was the only hope I had, as absurd as that sounds.'

He found a place to sit. 'At least I know the name of one good detective now. And I've made a decision. Investigative journalism isn't for me. I can't be putting myself through this every week. I've had a word with the editor of the newspaper. He says if I keep my nose clean for the next couple of months, there's a place for me on the sports desk. Can you imagine that? Being paid to go and watch Cardiff City play?'

He wiped a tear from the corner of his eye. 'Daniel's funeral won't be for a while. Brogan claims the other man was responsible for what happened to him. They need to do more tests and stuff to see if he's lying.'

Archie got to his feet. 'I forgot to say. I bought that girl a new phone, like I promised. You don't want to know what she said when I tried to give it to her. Shocking, it was.' He leaned and planted a kiss on the horizontal section of the headstone. 'Time for me to go now. I promise not to leave it so long next time. Night, night, Mam.'

Chapter 88

Reece brought the Land Cruiser to a halt on a patch of gravel at the side of the cottage in Brecon. He turned the engine off and opened the driver's door. 'Come on, boy,' he said, patting his thigh as he got out.

Redlar barked a response and leaped from one seat to another with his tail wagging madly.

'Whoa. You're not big enough to jump down on your own yet. It'll ruin your joints.' Reece took hold of the wriggling puppy and lifted him safely to the floor, where he promptly went chasing after a flock of starlings. 'Redlar. Redlar!'

The animal couldn't hear him. Or was acting as though it couldn't. It had found a large stick and was struggling to drag it somewhere safe to chew on. The starlings were already forgotten. Reece followed him behind the dry-stone wall, calling his name repeatedly. 'Recall is definitely something we'll be working on.' He tried an alternative tactic. 'Suit yourself. I'm going in for my lunch.' He went to the rear door of the Land Cruiser and swung a twelve-kilogram sack of kibble over his shoulder. It ached. A reminder of the shooting at the Midnight Club the previous year. 'Stay out here on your own. It's no skin off my nose.'

The stick was immediately abandoned. Redlar cocked his leg on the wall and then went racing towards the cottage. 'Down,' Reece said, losing his balance and almost falling over. 'Get out of the bloody way!'

Getting through the front door of the cottage was no easier. Redlar went in. Came out. Ran in circles and jumped up on him again. Reece put the sack down and stared at the pup. 'Lunch – then you and me are going to have ourselves a proper father to son chat.'

A good forty-five minutes later, Reece took his empty plate and mug to the sink and put them in a bowl of hot, soapy water. He went over to Redlar's corner—an area of the room that housed a dog bed, food, and water bowls—and squatted to deal with the mess.

'Have you got a hole in your chin?' he asked, scooping up spilled pellets of kibble. It was just about everywhere. 'We'll be needing chickens to clean up after you.' He took a mop to the patches of water the dog had dripped on the kitchen floor. 'Are all Huntaways this untidy?'

Redlar sat and cocked his head to one side, listening. He barked. Louder than expected from an animal of its size.

'And you can cut that out when you like,' Reece said, swilling his hands under the tap. He covered a loaf of homemade bread with a clean cloth and put the butter dish away in the cool pantry. The table was cleared apart for a few wayward crumbs and a faded receipt. Reece took the receipt to the window and read the telephone number under better lighting. He thumb-dialled, lowering the other hand to his side while he waited.

'Hello, my name is Brân Reece. We ordered an upright piano with you some time back and left a deposit.' He repeated the date of purchase when asked. 'Yes, it *was* a long time ago. Sorry about that. Is it still available? You haven't let it go to someone else?'

The salesperson said they needed to check with the owner and put Reece on hold. It was like waiting for test results to be reported on by a hospital doctor. Reece ground his teeth, anxious until he got an answer.

After what seemed like an eternity, the line clicked to life. 'Mr Gardner,' he said, worried it was going to be bad news. 'Nice talking to you again. Yes, it's been a long, long time.'

Reece came away from the window, listening to what the other man had to say. 'Really? That would be brilliant if you could.' Making a celebratory fist, he gave his thanks and hung up. He went over to the mantelpiece and put his phone next to a pile of unopened mail. Then turned to a space he'd cleared against one wall. He trembled with emotion, his voice faltering as he spoke. 'What about here, Anwen? Is this where you'd like your new piano?'